Savor

A Fredrickson Winery Novel

Barbara Ellen Brink

Visit Barbara Ellen Brink at
www.barbaraellenbrink.com

Cover design by Katharine A. Brink

Author photo by Barbara E Brink

Edited by Nancy Hudson

This novel is a work of fiction. Names, characters,
businesses, places, events and incidents are either the
products of the author's imagination or used in a
fictitious manner. Any resemblance to actual persons,
living or dead, or actual events is purely coincidental.

ISBN-10:1492365254
ISBN-13:978-1492365259

This book is dedicated in memory of
my friend Cory Krueger
who savored family and friendship
and made this world a better place for us all.

Other novels by this author

The Fredrickson Winery Novels:
Entangled
Crushed

Second Chances Series:
Running Home
Alias Raven Black

Amish Bloodsuckers Trilogy:
Chosen
Shunned
Reckoning

Split Sense

SAVOR

CHAPTER ONE

"You surely can't expect the bank to give us another loan based on this." Billie shook the copy of the financial statement her brother had printed out for her. "Didn't you even try to make us look good? I mean, really – the government puts out statements all the time that don't divulge the entire truth. They just skim the surface. Can't you do that for Fredrickson's, or are you too busy playing musician every night?"

*Any man of mine, better walk the line, better show me a teasing, squeezing, pleasing kind of time…*Shania's twang burst from Billie's cell phone sitting on the desk across the room, but she was too caught up in her argument with Adam to pick up. Handel would understand she was busy and leave a text like he always did.

Adam slammed open the file cabinet. He'd been growing a scruffy beard for some reason and looked more like a deer hunter than an accountant, but apparently it was what all the happening musicians were sporting these days. "Don't come down on me because your numbers are in the tank. You're the one who thought you could go from being a little known lawyer to running a little known winery without any little known expertise."

"Whoa!" Sally stepped between them, eyebrows and hands raised in self-defense. "Let me exit gracefully before you come to blows, please. I don't want to be a witness in the trial to whatever is about to happen." She pulled open the door and escaped down the hall.

"Thanks a lot!" Adam huffed. "Now you've scared Sally away from her desk and I'll have to answer the damn phone."

"As if! When's the last time it rang?" She threw the papers down on Sally's desk and crossed her arms, blowing an angry breath through her nostrils. "We are sinking here, Adam, and this is not going to help."

He ran a hand through his hair and shook his head. "I can't change the numbers. You know that. Either the bank gives us another loan based on our forecast or they refuse based on our past. There's no magical number crunching I can do to change their policies. We just have to hope they see a future for Fredrickson's."

She was silent, staring at a coffee stain in the carpet at her feet. All the anger had drained away in her tirade, but her shoulders drooped at the weight of responsibility she felt for the winery's employees and their futures. Sally. Margaret. Even Loren and Ernesto had become good friends and were like family to her now.

"Billie," Adam reached out and put a hand on her shoulder, squeezing gently. "It's going to be all right. If the bank won't give you the loan, I'm sure

Handel would love to invest in Fredrickson's. He even – " He broke off at the look on her face.

"You didn't tell him that we needed the money, did you?" she demanded.

"Are you delusional? I don't need to tell him anything. He already knows we need the money. Just because you refuse to speak with him about it, doesn't make the problem disappear. You're married now, Billie. Try acting like it." He turned to open the door, but she jumped in the way.

"How dare you tell me how to act! You don't know anything about my relationship with Handel. Fredrickson's has nothing to do with our marriage and I intend to keep it that way." She glared at him, arms crossed.

He just looked at her for a long moment, his face softening despite her attitude. "You might believe that, Sis, but I'm pretty sure Handel sees it differently. If you can't even share the ups and downs of your life with the man you married, then what's the point? Fredrickson's is a big part of you now and it's still a big part of who Handel is, whether he's monetarily invested in it or not. He wants to be a part of your life, not just the man who shares your bed. If you can't see that, then you need a heart transplant."

He reached around her for the handle of the door and she automatically stepped away. A tight ball of fear and guilt twisted her insides, but she fought to tamp it down. Adam didn't understand. He didn't know how hard it was to stay in control, to keep the different aspects of her life separate. She didn't want to worry Handel with her business woes. He had enough of his own problems, with a client he was trying to save from a murder conviction. Besides, he didn't need her input on his court case anymore than she needed his on the winery.

And yet... Handel did share his work with her. He often asked her opinion and discussed aspects of his cases in a general sort of way without infringing on his attorney/client confidentiality clause. He cared what she thought.

Why couldn't she do the same? Sometimes she had whole conversations with him in her head, but then face-to-face she struggled for words and many times things went unsaid. As if not saying something took away its power to hurt them.

Just this morning he'd called to talk before he went into court. He chatted about the weather, his client's terrible new haircut, and randomly announced that when or if they had children, he knew they would be extraordinary. She'd gone all quiet, unable to get past the glibness of the comment to what lay beneath. Knowing how much he loved Davy and spending time with the boy, she was confident he would make a wonderful father, but... she wasn't so sure about being a parent herself. She barely passed as an adult, much less an example to small clones.

She drew a deep breath and slowly expelled, loosening the knot around her chest. They really needed to talk when he got home. She missed him when he was gone overnight. This case had been taking him away far too many nights already. It would be a relief when it was over. She never slept as well when he was gone. Wrapped secure in Handel's arms, her nightmares no longer stood a chance.

Sally pushed the door open. "All clear?"

"Everything's fine. Don't worry about it," Billie said, retrieving the papers she'd thrown on the desk.

"Look," Sally said, taking her arm and gently turning her around. "Everyone around here knows that things aren't fine. The economy sucks. Why should Fredrickson's have it easy?" She sighed. "You should give your brother a break."

"I know," she said, "and I'm sorry you were forced to witness another one of my meltdowns."

"Meltdown? That was nothing." She waved a hand as though shooing away a fly. "You should see the fights my family get into at Christmas. Since there's no snow to pelt each other with, we just run the hose in the backyard and mud wrestle."

Billie shook her head, grinning. "Someday I've got to meet your family. For some reason I keep imagining you as a foundling left on the doorstep of the winery."

"Not far from the truth," she said, slipping back into the chair behind her desk. "I've been here nearly that long."

"And?" Billie asked, knowing there was always more to Sally's stories.

"Adam's right. Handel's already invested in Fredrickson's because he's invested in you. He married you, didn't he? So talk to him. Let him help, even if only as a listening ear for you to vent. He needs you to trust him, to confide in him."

"Why? Did he say something?" Billie asked, suddenly afraid her perfect world was about to crumble.

"No. He doesn't have to. Billie, he's your husband!" Sally dropped her head on the desk and bumped it repeatedly against the surface, auburn curls flopping.

"I suppose that's your way of saying I'm really

dense."

She straightened, a small smile of satisfaction on her lips. "Now don't go putting words in my mouth."

"Right." Billie pulled open the door but glanced back. "Thanks, Sally. If anybody needs me, I'll be down in the cellar."

••••

Handel pulled into traffic and sped up, eager to be home and spend what was left of the evening with Billie. The jury had been selected, the date had been set to begin, and Judge Matthews had reminded them all that this was a high profile case and she better not hear of anyone discussing any part of the trial or she would rethink her position on sequestering. Handel wasn't due back in court until Monday. He had the whole weekend to remind his new wife just whom she was married to. The past couple of weeks they had slept apart more than together, him spending lonely nights in the city working. He would be happy when it was over. Maybe they could get away to Maui for a few days or take a few weeks and visit all the islands – if Billie would trust her staff at the winery and leave it all behind.

Traffic slowed to a crawl on the freeway and he flipped the radio on as a distraction from the boredom of his commute. Smooth jazz played softly over the speakers, soothing the edginess he always felt sitting in bumper-to-bumper traffic. Thunderclouds rolled in from the bay, but there was little chance of rain this time of year. All the hovering clouds managed to do was keep the stench of pollution at ground level. He wrinkled his nose and turned on the air-conditioner. It had climbed to eighty degrees in the heart of the city, but once he got out into the country the temp would drop into the low seventies. This time of year in the valley was usually pleasant, with gentle breezes and clear cerulean skies.

Cars began to move forward in the lane beside him and soon his lane inched forward as well. He changed the station on the radio to the evening news and listened to the drone of the newscaster with only half his attention. A familiar voice interrupted his wandering thoughts. The Deputy District Attorney usually spoke in a blustery sort of way that put his listeners on the defensive. But today Alec Melendez sounded calm and sure of himself when he'd answered the reporter's questions outside the courtroom earlier.

"Mr. Kawasaki has maintained his innocence and pleaded not guilty," the reporter said, "He was even quoted as saying he had nothing to hide and would testify in his own defense. Do you think that will be enough to sway members of the jury to his side?"

Melendez gave a short laugh. "Mr. Kawasaki's attorney, Handel Parker, is a well-seasoned litigator, so I doubt he will allow his client to testify. No matter the smoke screen they throw up, I will prove to the jury without a shadow of a doubt that Sloane Kawasaki is not only guilty of illegal business practices and money laundering, but he was also an abusive husband who planned the murder of his own wife, and then proceeded to personally follow through with that murder even after a failed first attempt by a hired thug. Jimena Alvarez-Kawasaki deserves justice and I plan to see that she gets it."

From the sound of it, the deputy DA was

getting a head start on his opening statement – or running for office. He was definitely not stating proven facts, but rather innuendo from an unreliable source. Sloane's secretary had admitted that she was jealous after he married Jimena and made up stories to anyone who would listen that her boss was connected with gangs. The so-called first failed murder attempt had been a hit and run. Someone side-swiped Jimena when she stepped out of her car on a busy downtown street. She was battered and bruised but nothing had been broken and the hit and run driver had never been found.

Other reporters yelling out further questions faded into the background as the newscaster tied up the story. "That was Deputy District Attorney Melendez outside the courtroom this afternoon after the jury selection ended and the trial date was set to begin next Wednesday."

His cell phone buzzed over the speakers and he pushed the Bluetooth answer button. "Handel Parker here." There was silence for a moment and he thought maybe he'd been disconnected. "Hello?"

"I have information for joo about joor murder case." The man's voice was deep and raspy, with a strong Mexican accent.

"Who is this?" he countered, eyes narrowed as he glanced in the rearview and changed lanes. "If you know something about Jimena Kawasaki's murder, I am obligated to tell you to take it to the police."

"Dat's not going to happen. I don't talk to no police. Only to joo."

Handel's mind raced. "Fine. Talk to me. What do you know?" He didn't want to scare off a potential witness. If the man wouldn't go to the police then he

should at least hear him out. He was probably a
crackpot. They'd certainly attracted plenty of them
during the discovery phase.

"I don't want to say over the phone. Can joo
meet me by the dock…"

Handel cut him off. "No. That's not going to
happen," he said, repeating the man's words back at
him. "Tell me what you know and I'll decide whether
it's worth my time."

All four lanes of cars came to a dead stop and
Handel slammed on the brakes. He breathed a sigh of
relief when the cars behind him managed to stop in
time as well. Just what he didn't need was to be in a
freeway pileup.

The man sniffed. "Look, I need money. I'll tell
joo everything for two grand."

Handel laughed. "I'm hanging up now."

"No! Please. Listen. I'm telling the truth. I
know who killed Jimena."

The way the man said her name… it was
personal. Intimate. Like he'd actually known her.
Maybe he wasn't a crackpot. "All right. I'm listening.
But I need something from you before we can go any
further. I'm not going to meet you or give you two-
thousand dollars without a compelling reason."

He heard traffic noise and a car horn over the
speakers. "I loved her," he said, his voice so quiet
Handel had a hard time hearing. "Jimena was going to
leave Kawasaki and go to Mexico with me. But her
brother told her I was a heroin addict."

"Manny?"

"Sí." The small affirmative was filled with raw
anger. "He didn't want her to go. Said she had to stay
married to that *chapete*," he spit the word like a curse,

"because she had made a vow."

Handel suddenly had a heroin addict thrown into the mix of his trial. Not exactly someone above reproach, but that wouldn't stop the prosecution from using him to prove Kawasaki had motive for killing his wife. Why hadn't Manny mentioned this person before? Especially if the man was seeing his sister romantically and he knew about it. He rubbed a hand over his stubbly five o'clock shadow, thinking. "So you want me to believe that Jimena, a beautiful woman married to a rich man, would leave all that for you, a drug addict?"

"I quit eight months ago! I promised Jimena I was done with the life."

"And what were you doing at the Kawasaki residence the night of the murder?"

"We were leaving for Mexico. She finally decided it was time. I went to pick her up but he..."

A guy on a Harley flew by his door, riding between lanes, and passing everyone with devil-may-care nonchalance in a leather vest and red bandanna. The loud thumping of the exhaust pipes drowned out the man's words.

"... and when I woke up she was dead," he finished.

Red taillights flared on the pickup in front of him as it suddenly came to a complete stop. Handel slammed on the brakes. His dream of a getaway with Billie evaporated with a glance in the rearview mirror. A truck was bearing down and there was no way it could stop in time to avoid rolling right over him. He twisted the wheel hard to the right and pulled into the next lane without knowing for sure if there was enough space between vehicles. The screech of metal on metal as he slid past the edge of the pickup's bumper drowned out the last of the man's words. Handel was flung forward against the steering wheel when the truck slammed from behind. An explosive sound reverberated in his head and glass exploded around him.

"Mr. Parker? Mr. Parker?" He thought he heard a voice calling and then it faded away.

••••

"You've been here for hours. I've got a few minutes now. Why don't you come and have a cup of coffee with me?"

Handel didn't recognize the male voice tinged with a slight accent. Southeastern? Virginia, maybe? He fought to open his eyes but his lids were as heavy as bricks. There was a shuffling sound beside him and his hand suddenly felt cold as though someone had released it. He stretched his fingers, hoping to attract attention and let them know he was awake, but instead fog filled his mind again.

••••

The hospital cafeteria had the worst coffee Billie had ever tasted. Or maybe she was just so burned out on coffee that it all tasted like sludge. What she wouldn't give for a bottle of Margaret's wine right about now. Anything to help her get through another night. She automatically poured creamer and sugar into the murky blackness and stirred, watching the swirl of white slowly disappear.

Dr. Teledaga was the surgeon who'd performed emergency surgery when Handel was first brought in, repairing broken ribs and a collapsed lung. Afterwards, he'd come by ICU to check on his patient and they'd chatted for a few minutes. A couple days later she ran into him in a corridor of the hospital when she was looking for a snack machine and they'd had a light-hearted conversation about boating and his love of deep-sea fishing. He wasn't at all what she'd imagined a surgeon to be like.

He gently put a hand on her arm now and led her toward a table in a quiet corner, then pulled out her chair with a smile. "How's this?"

"Fine, thanks." She sat down and tried to stifle a yawn as the doctor took the chair across from her. Lacing her fingers around the cup, she sighed. "I don't think I would have survived the past week without your supervision, Doctor."

"I'm sure you would have done fine, once you found your way out of the custodian's storage closet," he said, in a teasing tone. He lifted his cup and blew softly at rising steam before taking a tentative sip. "I'm just glad I was there at the opportune moment to guide you back to your husband's bedside. It's not often I have the pleasure of meeting a fellow mid-westerner."

"I don't think West Virginia is really considered mid-west," she said with a slight quirk of her brows.

"No? Why is it in the name then?"

"You're crazy. How did you end up way out here in San Francisco anyway? You're a long way from your mountain mama."

"Like a bad country song, I left home right after high school. Hitchhiked for a year or so, seeing the country, working odd jobs. When I got to California I realized I couldn't walk on water so I enrolled at the university and decided to become a doctor. Of course, now that I *can* walk on water I no longer have a desire to travel further west," he brushed a hand over close-cropped hair, more silver than black and his lips thinned thoughtfully. "I liked the bay area, so I decided to stay."

"You don't miss your home? Your family?" she asked, leaning one elbow on the table to prop her chin on her hand. Exhaustion seeped all the way to her toes. She could fall asleep where she sat if she didn't keep talking.

He took another gulp of coffee and shook his head. "Not much family to speak of. None that I want to acknowledge anyway."

"That bad, huh?"

"I didn't invite you to coffee to depress you." He tipped his head to the side and his eyes narrowed. "I thought you might need a break from this unrealistic, self-imposed vigil you've set yourself on."

There it was. Out in the open. The elephant in the room.

He'd already told her she should go home and rest. Handel's neurologist, Doctor Chao, had said the same. There was no reason to believe her husband would wake up anytime soon. He was still in a coma and there had been no improvement since his last surgery. They said he was lucid when they first brought him in after the accident but he'd suffered brain trauma along with all his other injuries and the ER nurse said he lost consciousness soon after.

Billie hated that she wasn't here in time to tell Handel she loved him, to hold his hand, to reassure him that... She rubbed her nose and sniffed. "There's nothing unrealistic about staying by Handel's side until he wakes up. He needs me." She argued half-heartedly, cringing inside at the unthinkable – that he might never need her again. The lovemaking they'd so recently enjoyed, sharing things with one another that they'd never share with another soul, planning their future together... could all be over. The thought was intolerable. She couldn't bear losing him.

She'd taken to falling asleep in the chair beside his bed. The nurses had brought her a cot but she seldom slept on it because whenever she lay down she tended to dream. And dreaming never ended well. She'd dream Handel back to health, and then she'd wake up.

Dr. Teledaga reached across the table and brushed her arm with the tips of his fingers. She jerked away as though he'd prodded her with a red-hot poker. It suddenly felt traitorous to be sitting here enjoying coffee with a handsome doctor while Handel lay unresponsive in ICU. She had no business talking and laughing as though life could go on as usual.

"I'm sorry. I didn't mean to upset you." He slowly pulled back and stuffed his hands in the pockets of his white coat. "I know you want to believe and I'm all for holding out hope as long as humanly possible, but at some point you're going to have to take a step back and reassess your options."

She shook her head, anger surging up from under the surface. Unaware until now that it was building, she had thought she was taking this whole thing fairly well. How dare he? He had no right. The chair made a loud racket, scraping against hard tile as she scooted back and jumped up. "Handel is going to wake up and I'm going to be there beside him when he does. Thanks for your input but you're a cold, insensitive bastard and I don't think you understand what normal people go through after you cut their loved ones up and sew them back together. We don't just go on with our lives while the person we love lies there…" she choked on the words and turned away.

Dashing at her eyes with the long sleeve of her t-shirt, she blindly dodged tables in her rush to leave the cafeteria. After a near collision with an elderly woman holding a full tray, she was through the doors and into the hall, sucking in a deep breath to prevent sobs from pushing their way out. She ran into the nearest women's bathroom, slammed into a stall and locked the door. Tears coursing down her cheeks, she leaned against the stall partition and sobbed.

After a couple of minutes, the outside door opened with a soft squeak as someone entered. Billie held her breath and rubbed tears from her cheeks with the pads of her fingers.

"Are you all right, Mrs. Parker?" a hesitant voice asked. "Dr. Teledaga asked me to check on you."

She opened the door and stepped out to face a young blonde nurse in cotton candy pink scrubs. Her nametag said, Annie. Billie didn't know what had come over her. Tears and drama were so *not* her thing. She smiled at the young nurse, hoping she looked calm and collected now that the storm was past. "I'm fine, thanks," she said and began washing her hands at the sink.

The girl continued to stand behind her, watching. "I just wanted to let you know that we do have grief counselors available if you'd like to speak with someone. Religious or non-religious."

Billie looked up from drying her hands and met the other woman's eyes in the mirror. "My husband isn't dead."

"Oh, I didn't mean to imply…"

"Please leave unless you're here to pee. I don't need a keeper." She threw the wadded paper towel into the trash. "And by the way," she said when the girl opened the door to leave, "you can tell Dr. Teledaga that if I need a Doctor's advice, I already have plenty of them on call."

The door swung shut and Billie blew out an angry breath. The gall of some people! Insinuating themselves into her life as though they knew her. She pulled her cell phone from her pocket and turned it on to check for messages. They didn't like her to use her phone in ICU so she'd taken to shutting it off while she was in the room.

Sally had left a couple of texts relating to one of their regular customers who wanted to double their order for the year. They owned a high-end restaurant in Billings, Montana and apparently Fredrickson's Wine was a big hit in cowboy country.

She replied to the winery messages and then flipped back to read the last message Handel sent her right before he got onto the freeway that afternoon. Her eyes filled with tears and she bit her lip to keep from crying.

Be home soon, babe. I got big plans for tonight. Gonna memorize your curves till morning light. Don't start without me.

She couldn't bear to delete it. After seven days, she'd probably read it a hundred times. Handel was always sending her funny texts. Whenever he'd get a break during the trial or late at night in his hotel room, he'd type her a note. Silly, romantic, sexy…

If only she could rewind to the moment it came in and pick up the phone, instead of ignoring it because she was busy yelling at Adam about the financial statement for the bank. She pressed *reply* as she had every day since then and typed another message for him to read when he woke up.

You've been sleeping for seven days, Handy. Please wake up so I can feel whole again. Don't leave me without you.

••••

Margaret and Davy stood outside Handel's room when Billie returned. In a hot pink sundress and flip flops, and her long blonde hair pulled up off her neck with a silver comb, her sister-in-law looked much too young and beautiful to be the mother of a ten-year-old boy. Every male that passed by turned to stare but Margaret managed to appear oblivious to the attention.

Billie glanced at her watch. Eight o'clock. Her days and nights were beginning to blend together. She'd actually started thinking it was morning when it was obviously evening. Margaret had promised Davy she'd bring him in on Friday after work. And here they were. Visiting hours were until 9:00 p.m. but the nurses usually let Margaret stay longer knowing she had such a long way to drive.

Davy hadn't been to the hospital since Sunday, two days after the accident. Another five days had passed since then and although the swelling around Handel's face and head had been greatly reduced, he still looked pretty awful. Billie hoped his nephew wouldn't be frightened at the sight.

She forced a smile and gave him a hug. "Good to see you kiddo. How was school today?" she asked, hoping to avoid the kind of piercing questions that only a kid would dare ask. But Davy was more than a kid. Some days he was a wise old man in a child's body. Not always, but he had his moments. Maybe because of what he'd lived through just a few months ago; kidnapped by his own grandfather, drugged, and left alone in a dark shed. That sort of experience would either turn you into a pile of mush or strengthen you for the long haul. Like they said, *what doesn't kill you...*

He shrugged. "School's out for summer, Billie. Remember?"

"That's right," she said, flicking a glance toward Margaret. "I forgot."

"That's okay. You have a lot on your mind."

Margaret put a hand on his shoulder and glanced toward the door of the room. "How's he doing today?" she asked.

"About the same. Doctor Chao was here a couple of hours ago to check on him. He said there was no change. Handel should be waking up by now, but for some reason his brain is refusing. He said there are some drugs they can try but he wants to give Handel a couple more days to see if he wakes on his own." She forced another too-bright smile. "Why don't you go on in and talk to him a minute? I think he's sick of hearing my voice."

Margaret and Davy obediently trooped in and stood at Handel's bedside. Billie saw tears shimmer in his sister's eyes before she reached for his hand and held it gently.

"Hello, big brother. Davy and I drove all the way here to talk to you and you're still sleeping. You promised to help coach Davy's little league team this summer. We know you hate baseball but isn't this a little over the top just to get out of it?"

There were a few moments of awkward silence. Billie waited, knowing it took a while to feel comfortable having a one-sided conversation with a man.

"Hey, Uncle Handel," Davy finally said, his voice boyishly gruff. "I helped at the winery today. Mostly I just ran errands for Sally, but it was fun. Hey, Adam got a gig at some place called The Screech Owl. He said they were gonna pay him and everything."

The fingers of Handel's left hand twitched. Billie was sure of it. For long seconds she stared, wishing for a miracle that never seemed to come. She stepped to the other side of the bed and nodded, urging Davy to keep talking.

He kept up a constant patter of one-sided conversation seemingly oblivious to the turmoil her heart was in. She finally pulled the chair close to the bed and sat down, stroking her palm lightly over Handel's whisker rough cheek and across his forehead pushing the hair off his temple. He had some cuts and scratches on his face from flying glass, but nothing that would leave a permanent scar. She was careful not to put pressure on the bruise over his left eyebrow.

Margaret sat in the chair on the other side and listened as Davy told Handel about all the boxes he'd carried and stacked behind the winery and how he'd even gone with Levi to pick up supplies in town. "Levi said while he was gone on vacation for the next two weeks, that I could be in charge of the goats and moving them around the vineyard to keep the weeds down." His gaze shifted upward from Handel's closed and bruised eyelids. "Is that all right with you, Billie?"

"Of course. I trust Levi's opinion. If he left you in charge, then I'm sure you'll do a fine job." Levi was a twenty-year-old farm boy from Wisconsin who showed up at the winery a year ago looking for work. He was a natural with animals, so the care of Jack and Jill, their weed eating goat couple, was in his capable hands. She'd forgotten that he was flying out to visit his family this week.

Davy's face lit up for a second at the simple acknowledgment, and then he seemed to remember why he was there. He leaned closer to Handel, his fingers curled around the metal bar of the guardrail, and lowered his voice. "Don't worry if you can't coach this time, Uncle Handel. Really. Just get better. Okay?"

Handel lay as quiet as before. They watched him, hoping for a response. Any response. Billie was sure he would react to his nephew's presence. They were always so close. He would do anything for the boy. Without a word, Margaret stood and wrapped her arms around her young son from behind and together they listened to the steady beep of the monitor fill the quiet of the room.

Finally, Billie couldn't take anymore. "I need to make a call," she said, and barely escaped before tears fell. What was wrong with her? She was falling apart. She was always the strong one in her family, the one who forged ahead and made the best of a situation. But there was no best in this situation. Handel was the buoy in her life now, the lifeline. Without him she felt lost at sea.

She dashed at the tears on her cheeks and started walking down the hall without a clear destination in mind. A breath of fresh air would be nice. Maybe she could think straight without all the recycled oxygen clouding her brain and turning her emotions inside out.

"Ms. Parker?" A short muscular Hispanic man in dark brown slacks and a black t-shirt stood near the elevators as though unsure where to go from there. He raised a hand in greeting. One corner of his mouth lifted in a tight smile, stretching a pale scar that ran from his left cheek to just under his chin.

Billie hesitated, unsure what the man wanted. She didn't recognize him, but he seemed to know her. She was pretty sure she'd remember him if they met at the winery. He had a sleeve tattoo covering his left arm from the wrist up, another tattoo on the side of his neck and the familiar barbed wire tattoo around the bicep of his right arm. This guy was a walking ink well.

He reached in his pocket and pulled out a wallet, flipped it open. "You don't know me. I work for your husband. I'm a private investigator," he said, showing her his business card and photo I.D. "Better?"

"What?" she asked, flustered by his directness.

"You seemed wary. I want to set your mind at rest about speaking with me."

"I was on my way out. Are you here to visit Handel?" she glanced back at the nurse's station. "They're not allowing anyone but family in ICU at this time. Sorry."

"I didn't think they would. How is he doing?"

"His prognosis hasn't changed. He's still comatose."

"I'm sorry to hear that. Your husband is a good man. I'll light a candle for him Sunday at mass," he said.

"Thank you, Mr. Alvarez." She wasn't sure what else to say. If a lit candle meant more prayer for

Handel, then she was all for it. He could use all the prayers and good thoughts available. She'd done plenty of praying herself this past week, especially in the middle of the night when sleep wouldn't come and hopelessness tried to squirm its way into her heart and soul. "Thank you for stopping by," she added.

"Actually," he said putting a hand on her arm when she began to turn away, "I wanted to speak with you."

"Me? About what?"

"Handel had me working on something before his accident. We were looking into a spate of rival gang activity during the week before Mr. Kawasaki's wife was murdered. He believed it was somehow connected."

"I'm sorry. I don't really know much about the case other than what's been on the news. Handel was very careful about client confidentiality. We rarely discussed our work." She stared at the flashing floor number above the elevator doors, avoiding his eyes. She had shied away from discussing Handel's case for purely selfish reasons. Not because she was worried about client confidentiality, but because she was worried Handel would expect her to reciprocate and share her work with him. So rather than feel guilty, she shut him down time after time. Now when she had the opportunity to help him… she couldn't.

"I understand. But you must have his notes. The police gave you his briefcase they recovered at the accident, didn't they? Maybe there's a lead in there for me to follow while he's incapacitated. That way when he wakes up everything will be ready for him to jump right back into court without asking for another continuance."

Billie pressed her lips together and tried to clamp down her feelings. Would Handel ever be able to jump right back into court? Even if he did wake up soon, he had a long way to go to full recovery. They had no way of knowing how much damage was done until he...

"Are you all right?"

She cleared her throat and glanced back at the room where Margaret and Davy still sat with Handel, their eyes full of hope. "Honestly, no. Mind if we take a walk outside while we talk?"

"Not at all."

They took the elevator to ground level and made their way out to the street. The hospital had a quiet park area nearby and Billie headed that way wanting to avoid as much street noise as possible. A young man on a bicycle zipped in front of them without glancing their way and Mr. Alvarez pulled her back just in time to avoid a collision.

"Damn cyclists," he muttered, before releasing her arm.

She grimaced. "Don't care for them myself. I think I've had about a dozen near collisions since I've been here. They're whipping around all over the place."

"Pedestrians need helmets in San Francisco." He chuckled.

They found an empty bench by a fountain where a giant concrete fish spewed a continuous arc of water from his mouth. Two little boys bent over the pool on the other side of the fountain, splashing in the water and giggling while their father watched from a nearby bench, a stroller at his side.

Billie sat down, wondering at the source of the children's laughter. They wouldn't be here unless someone they loved was sick or injured. She imagined their mother, like Handel, lying unresponsive in a cold, sterile room, behind stonewalls. How did children continue to find joy in the bleakest of times? Did God give them an innate sense of hope in their naiveté? She longed for some of that.

The fading sun streaked pink above distant buildings. It reminded her of evenings at home with Handel when he'd take her hand after dinner and lead her toward the vineyard. They'd walk between rows of vines; closed off from the clamoring outside world, and watch the last rays of the sun paint the horizon ahead of them. The vineyard was their sanctuary; common ground where they were able to relax away from family and responsibilities.

Mr. Alvarez dug in the pocket of his slacks and pulled out a penny. He closed his eyes and flipped it into the pond. "For luck," he said, taking a seat beside her.

"I thought you were a praying man," she teased. "Where does luck come in?"

He shrugged. "God works in mysterious ways, or so my priest tells me."

"I wish he'd work a little less mysteriously," she said, pushing hair behind her ear. "I could use a blatant miracle right about now."

He was quiet for a moment.

Billie lifted her hair off her neck, feeling a trickle of sweat slip between her shoulder blades. "It's warmer out here than I thought."

"Si," he said. Sliding an arm along the back of the bench he turned to face her better. "Handel said you're from Minnesota. Is the temperature cooler there this time of year?"

"Not really. I've gotten kind of spoiled by the weather in the valley though. The city is always hotter."

She began to wonder if the man just wanted to make small talk, when he finally took out his wallet and produced a small photograph. "This is Jimena Kawasaki, taken about a year ago."

Billie took the photo and looked closely at the face of the woman whom the media and prosecuting attorneys said had been murdered by her own husband. She looked about thirty, with model perfect skin, long, silky black hair, and a dazzling smile. She seemed happy. Content. Billie wondered what happened to turn this stunning beauty into a victim. "She was Latino?"

"You didn't know?" Mr. Alvarez slipped the photo back into his wallet. A rather personal place to carry the photo of a murder victim. "That's the reason Handel had me investigating gang activity. Jimena's brother is a former member of MS-13, the *Maras*. They have a heavy presence in the Bay area. They're into smuggling people over the border, white slavery, drugs… the list goes on. Since Kawasaki has been accused of having connections to Las Boyz, we can't rule anything out."

"Las Boyz? I don't think I've heard of that one."

"They're fairly new to this area, but have already sunk their claws into a good chunk of illegal activity, especially down at the wharf. The Maras have drawn a line in the sand, so to speak, and will not tolerate any more Las Boyz' infringing on their turf."

"You think her brother had something to do with killing her?"

"Of course not," he said, shaking his head. His eyes sparked with anger before he turned away. When he spoke again his voice was quiet but laced with steel. "You have to understand, leaving that way of life is extremely dangerous. Old gang members harbor animosity for a long time. Revenge is a given. If Kawasaki truly has ties to Las Boyz, then the Maras may have used this opportunity to beat their opponents back further. And killing Jim would be a bonus for them."

The nickname for the murder victim was not lost on Billie. She studied the man's profile. His jaw clamped tight, his eyes riveted on the pond. Why was he lying to her? "Are you Jimena's brother?" she asked.

He blew an angry breath through his nose. "Sí! And I'll do anything to find her killer."

"Does Handel know how strongly you feel about revenge?"

"He knows what he wants to know – that I have ties to the Maras and could get information. Lawyers tend to turn a blind eye to things that have potential to harm their case."

Billie bristled at that. She knew Handel. He would never do anything to intentionally hide the truth. He believed Mr. Kawasaki to be innocent or he wouldn't be defending him. She knew it with her whole heart.

"Look," he slapped his palms down on the legs of his slacks. "I know Handel used you as a sounding board. He told me you're a lawyer too..."

"Yes," she said, "but I'm not a criminal

attorney. I specialize in family law."

He gave a short, mirthless laugh. "The most criminal type of lawyer."

"Excuse me?"

"Sorry." He put up a hand. "Ancient history. Lawyers and I don't really see eye to eye. Until I met your husband, I swore I'd never trust one again, and I definitely wouldn't have taken a job from one. Handel managed to change my mind. About him. About a lot of things."

"That's all well and good, but I still don't know what you want from me."

"Just think back. Maybe Handel told you something important and you don't even realize it. Something that could..."

"I told you, we don't talk about work that much."

"Something worth getting him killed to delay the trial."

"What are you saying? That it wasn't an accident?" She was finding it hard to breathe all of a sudden. Her chest contracted with dread. The excited squeals of the children splashing faded into the background as her heartbeat filled her ears.

He leaned closer and lowered his voice still more. "Anything is possible when it comes to a turf war. And living in yuppyville wine country doesn't make you exempt from danger."

"I don't like your tone, Mr. Alvarez." Billie stood up and faced him. "The police never said anything about the crash being more than... an *accident*. So I have to wonder what it is you think you know, and why you sound as though you're threatening me."

He ran a hand over his close-cropped hair. "I'm not threatening you. I'm trying to warn you."

"About what?"

"If the Maras think you know something, whether you do or not —" He broke off and shook his head. "Just be careful. Handel's my friend. I wouldn't want anything to happen to his wife on my watch."

"Don't worry. I'm not your responsibility."

He got up and held out his business card. "Take this. If you think of anything or Handel wakes up, give me a call."

When she didn't respond, he leaned down and placed it on the bench. "Nice to meet you, Mrs. Parker."

She watched him walk away, head up, muscular arms swinging slow and relaxed at his sides; the slow saunter of a confident man. Manny Alvarez was an enigma. Did he really want to help Handel or was he only seeking revenge for his sister's murder? And why did she feel there was a whole lot more he wasn't saying?

Billie snatched up the card and hurried back inside the hospital. Margaret and Davy would be wondering where she'd disappeared. She couldn't get what Alvarez said out of her head. Was Handel's accident actually something more sinister? Did it make any difference? He was still in a coma and she was still locked in this surreal world where she could see and touch him, but not actually be with him.

The nurse at the station outside Handel's room waved her over when she stepped out of the elevator. "Billie, your visitors went downstairs to get a bite to eat. They said to join them if you got back soon."

"Thanks, Chris." She had been here long

enough to be on a first name basis with most of the nurses. She forced a smile. "Hope you warned them off the green Jell-O salad. Those little grated carrots can get stuck in your throat."

"Especially when you're having a laughing fit." Chris shook her head, giggling as she remembered the conversation at lunch the day before. "When you told me what your mother said, I almost blew some pieces through my nose."

"I'm glad it didn't come to that," Billie said, smiling. "How long ago did they leave for lunch?"

Chris slipped one hand in the pocket of her blue scrubs and leaned on the desk with her other hand. "Oh, about fifteen minutes ago," she said.

"Thanks." Billie moved past the desk and opened the door to Handel's room. His face was pale under the hospital lights. She wondered how he could possibly sleep with the continual glare against his eyelids. He preferred total darkness when he slept. He would even cover the little red glowing light on the flat screen television because it kept him awake.

She stepped inside and closed the door, flipped off the light and moved beside him. It didn't make the room completely dark, but at least it wasn't glaring. She watched him breathe, his chest moving slightly up and down as his lungs expanded and deflated. They'd taken him off the ventilator tube on Wednesday. She'd nearly panicked, worried that without the oxygen he would stop breathing. Dr. Teledaga assured her that his lungs were strong and he was ready to breathe on his own.

Cupping Handel's whisker rough cheeks with her hands, she bent and kissed his lips. "Handy, I need you," she whispered close to his mouth. "I don't know what to do."

He made no movement at her ministrations, but the darkness felt intimate, and she could imagine he was listening. "Your private investigator friend came by. He doesn't seem to believe your crash was an accident. He thinks it has something to do with gangs." She brushed his hair back, letting her fingers linger along his ear. "I told him I didn't know anything. And I'm sorry, Handy. I'm so sorry." A tear dripped off her nose. "We're partners in this marriage, but I don't act like it. I don't mean to shut you out, but I do. What's wrong with me? I thought I was past the trust issue thing."

There was a soft knock on the door and Billie dashed the tears from her face. She straightened as Margaret opened the door.

"Can I come in?" she asked hesitantly.

"Of course. Where's Davy?"

"He stopped off to wash his hands. He had a jelly donut and the jelly attacked him."

Billie smiled. "I love that kid."

Margaret let the door swing shut behind her. She stood quietly, waiting.

"Thanks," Billie said.

"For what?"

"For not asking what's wrong."

She shrugged. "I know what's wrong. Handel has always been there for me too and now the tables are turned and there's nothing I can do. Except wait."

Davy pushed through the door, managing to smack Margaret before she could move out of the way. "Sorry, Mom."

"Slow down. This is a hospital, you know."

"Okay, I just wanted to tell you guys what I saw

in the…" his voice trailed off and his eyes widened as he stared past Billie.

Hope caught in her throat. She turned and met the cloudy gaze of the love of her life. "Handy," she barely breathed the word, afraid she'd wake and it would be another dream.

"Why's the lights off?" Davy asked, and flipped the switch up.

Handel's eyelids fluttered closed, and he groaned softly.

"Get the nurse!" Billie ordered.

Davy threw open the door and yelled, "911! My uncle's awake!"

Margaret didn't even bother to reprimand him, she was so busy looking at her brother and sobbing.

Billie didn't cry. He was awake. It was time to rejoice. She raised his hand to her cheek and said the words she'd not had the chance to say before his surgery. "I'm here, Handy. I'll always be here. I love you."

CHAPTER TWO

Handel managed to talk the doctors into signing his release on Monday. He was still moving gingerly about, but the surgical procedure that Doctor Teledaga performed when he was brought in, inserting titanium plates to stabilize his broken ribs, made it much easier to breathe and move about without excessive pain. He actually thought he'd be ready to return to court in another week. Billie had her doubts about that.

She shook her head as she watched him dress in his street clothes. He winced as he bent to pull up his slacks, but when his eyes met hers, he smiled. She took the newly pressed, blue, oxford dress shirt off the hanger she'd brought and helped him into it, then slowly buttoned it for him while he stood submissively still. His grin was contagious and she smiled back, thrilled he was coming home to her even though she was leery of him leaving the hospital so soon.

"What are you so happy about?" she teased.

"With your broken ribs, this is as close to making love as you're going to get for about four months."

"Say it isn't so," he bent his head and nuzzled the side of her neck, sending a tingle down her spine. "A couple broken ribs can't stop the love lawyer."

She breathed out a laugh and pushed his head back, holding his face between her hands. His blue eyes twinkled, but she grew serious. "Don't ever scare me like that again. Promise me."

"Okay," he said, his voice light and carefree as he moved in to kiss her.

"No. I mean it," she said, dropping her hands and stepping away for clarity. She knew it was insane to ask for something so intangible, but she couldn't help it.

He reached out and drew her close again, slid his hands slowly up her arms as though his touch was a promise. "Do you want that notarized?" he asked, his voice gentle with understanding.

"Yes," she whispered.

His lips moved over hers and she kissed him back as passionately as a woman could with three inches of space between them to spare his broken ribs. She felt a tear drop on her nose and slide off. She pulled back. "What?" she asked, alarmed by his show of emotion. Was he in pain?

"I thought I lost you," he murmured. "I dreamed you left me and went back to Minnesota. That you didn't love me or California anymore." His brows drew together in a frown of confusion. "That sounded really girly, didn't it?"

"The doctor did say your pain meds might make you act a little loopy." She grinned. "At least that's your story and we're sticking to it."

"Got it."

He picked up his overnight bag, but she took it from him. "No lifting. Save your strength for tonight."

"That sounds promising."

"Don't get your hopes up. I was talking about all the people who will drop by to welcome you home."

"After sleeping for a week, I'm sure I can handle a little conversation."

"If you say so. I'm betting you'll be in bed by seven o'clock."

"Only if you're there with me."

There was a rap at the door and Chris stuck her head in. "Ready to check out of here?" she asked, holding the door open to push a wheelchair through.

Handel frowned. "I'm fine. Really. I don't need that."

"That's what they all say." Chris flipped the metal feet pedals down and motioned toward the chair like Vanna White presenting a fabulous new car. "But we don't take chances," she quirked her eyebrows, "especially with lawyers."

"That is so unfair." He shook his head. "Lawyers get such a bad rap. We're verbally abused on a regular basis. Ninety percent of the things we're accused of are totally bogus."

Chris rolled her eyes. "Ten percent should get you put in jail," she said.

Billie stifled a grin and waited for Handel to sit down. Then she set the bag on his lap and picked up her purse. "We're out of here."

"Good riddance, I say," Handel stage whispered back at her. "This place is a real snoozer."

••••

Billie wasn't surprised when they pulled up outside the house and saw Sally and Loren over by the winery sitting at one of the picnic tables. It was past closing time but they were obviously waiting around to welcome Handel home from the hospital. They waved and started toward them.

Handel had the door of the car open before Billie had shut off the ignition. He struggled to climb out, wincing a bit when he twisted to stand. She knew he was stiff and sore from sitting for so long, but he wore his usual good-natured grin. "Hey, you two! Come on over and celebrate!" he called. "I'm pretty sure we have a bottle of wine around here somewhere."

Billie wanted to hurry around and help him inside but he was having none of it. He shook Loren's hand and let Sally give him a kiss on the cheek in lieu of a hug, then gestured them toward the house. "Join the party."

Billie grabbed the bags and hurried to open the front door. She hadn't been home for two weeks and couldn't remember what state she'd left the house in. Not that it was ever very messy with just the two of them. But she was her mother's daughter and it was drilled into her at a young age that you didn't invite people over if you hadn't cleaned from top to bottom. She unlocked the door and flipped the hall light on. So far so good.

"I at least expected Margaret and Davy to show up," Handel was saying behind her. "Where is that little rugrat? He's usually hanging around so much we can't get rid of him."

"I think Margaret was going to watch Adam

play tonight at some club downtown," Billie said, holding the door open. "I'm sure she would be here if she hadn't already promised."

"Loren and I are heading over there later tonight too," Sally added. "Your brother needs some friendly faces in the crowd. Thought we'd boost his ego by pretending to be fans."

Loren shook his head. "Be nice."

"It was a joke," Sally said. "Karok Indians don't have much of a sense of humor, do they?" she teased, slipping an arm around him as they came through the door.

Billie waved a hand toward the living room. "You guys go on in and sit down. I'll get the wine."

They didn't get two steps further before "Surprise!" rang out and people popped up from behind furniture like a team of synchronized Jack-in-the-boxes. Margaret, Davy, Adam – even Carl was there. That's when Billie noticed the banner hanging across the fireplace. In bright red and blue crayon colored letters it said, **Welcome Home, Uncle Handel!**

Davy was the first to rush over. Margaret must have already warned him to be careful of Handel's injuries because he didn't throw himself at him like he usually did, expecting to wrestle on the floor or play kickboxing. Instead, he handed him a neatly wrapped present and waited expectantly. His grin was wide and toothy, showing an early overlapping problem he'd soon need braces for. "Open it!" he urged, with a ten-year-old's impatience. "Mom and me found it at an antique store on the way home the other day. She said it would be perfect for your collection."

Margaret gave Handel a careful side hug and

kissed his cheek. "Welcome home, big brother," she said. They exchanged a look that bespoke their strong connection as siblings; those who had gone through hard times together and come out the other side.

He wrapped an arm around her and pressed his cheek to hers. "Thanks, Meg."

Billie already knew that Margaret had found a beautiful old fountain pen, trimmed in gold and onyx. It was even engraved with Handel's initials, although later, when the shopkeeper packed it in the storage box, she learned those letters stood for Henrietta Peterson. The original owner's full name was carved into the lid in a feminine font. But that didn't dampen Margaret's excitement. It was a one-of-a-kind find and she knew her brother would go crazy for it.

They waited to see his expression and it was priceless. Eyes wide with excitement, he stared at the pen in the box, looking much like Davy did on Christmas morning. Billie looked over his shoulder at the bulbous black and gold pen lying on a bed of red satin. It looked expensive.

"Wow! I don't believe it. This is a 1912 Pregnant Parker!" He glanced at his sister and back to the pen. "Where did you find it? And how can you afford it?"

"Pregnant Parker?" Sally looked at Billie and started laughing.

"Because of the shape," he explained, not detracted from his perusal of the writing object. He lifted the pen out and handed Davy the box. "They started making these eyedropper filled fountain pens back in the early 1900s. This is an amazing find! I love it!" He grinned, elated.

Margaret made an exaggerated expression of

relief, pretending to wipe sweat from her brow. "Whew! That's good. Cause you may have to help me pay for it. My credit card is maxed out."

"Fine with me," he said, as though she'd just asked him to pay a parking ticket. "The gift is in finding it. This is a rare and beautiful work of art. A perfect addition to my collection."

Billie loved the look of happiness in her husband's eyes. "Awesome. Another box to gather dust," she teased. "While you all practice your penmanship, I'll get the wine."

She hurried to the kitchen, a secret smile curving her lips.

Carl joined her a couple minutes later and opened the wine while she set glasses out on a tray. He showed her the containers of pasta he'd brought and put in the refrigerator for her and Handel. "Louis Linguini and Ziti Alla Nicolina. Handel's favorites," he said with a shrug. "Pasta is good for getting strength back."

"Thank you, Carl. That was very sweet of you."

He didn't seem in any hurry to return to the party. Leaning against the counter with arms crossed, he shook his head slowly, dark eyes glinting in the overhead light. "I thought for a bit there that we'd lost him," he admitted. "We grew up together you know. Like brothers. Almost family. Thank God he made it. I don't know what I would have done."

If anybody needed a hug, it was Carl. She put her arms around him and he hugged her warmly back. "You're not almost family, Carl. You *are* family."

"I see you don't need my help in here," Handel spoke from the doorway.

Carl released her like she was a hot potato. She

turned around to find her husband grinning at them like an idiot on painkillers. He laughed at Carl's discomfiture. "Don't mind me. I'm just the invalid husband."

"If you saw what he brought us for dinner, you wouldn't be giving him such a hard time. What do you think I was hugging him for? Not for his handsome Italian looks, that's for sure."

"Ziti Alla Nicolina?" Handel asked expectantly using his best Italian accent.

Carl laughed and lifted the wine bottle. He poured a glass for Handel. "Maybe."

"Don't get him all excited, Carl. He'll start drooling like a puppy. He hasn't had anything to eat but soup and Jell-O since he woke up."

"Mama Mia! How horrible for you. A man without food and wine is an empty vessel." He grinned and handed Billie a glass of wine as well.

"So true." Handel carefully swirled the wine in his glass and breathed in the bouquet. "I have a feeling this would pair magnificently well with a plate of Ziti," he said wistfully."

"A toast first." Carl raised his glass. "To second chances and living life to the fullest."

"Second chances!" Handel and Billie echoed.

"I wondered where you guys disappeared to. You're back here swilling all the wine. Figures," Sally said, her voice droll. She pushed a stray lock of red hair behind her ear, grinning. The others were right behind her. "See," she said, waving a hand toward the three of them, "I told you they'd started without us."

Crowding into the kitchen, everyone grabbed a glass and Carl poured the wine. He opened another bottle and they each made a toast, getting sillier and sillier until they were all laughing so hard Handel clutched his chest and begged them to stop.

Davy had his glass filled with apple juice and when it was his turn, lifted it high. "To Uncle Handel," he said. "I hope I'm as tough as you someday. You totaled your Porsche and didn't even cry."

Everybody laughed except Handel. He glanced at Billie, hoping for denial but getting confirmation. "My Porsche? Totaled?"

She shrugged. "Sorry, hon. I thought you knew. I mean... what did you think happened to it?"

Everybody grew silent, watching him as though he'd lost it.

The doctors hadn't found any signs of long-term brain damage, but they said he might experience short-term memory loss until he'd had time to heal. She didn't remember discussing the accident with him after he woke. The doctors kept him so busy with tests and therapy for the past two days that when they managed to have time alone, they didn't want to talk about why he was there. Instead they made plans to go away together for a vacation as soon as the trial was over. They talked about fixing up the house, maybe getting a dog, although Handel was still on the fence about that. Plans for the future.

"I don't know. I guess I didn't really think about it at all." He set his glass down on the table and ran his fingers through his hair, pushing it back. "No Porsche, huh?"

Billie met his eyes and smiled. "It's not all bad. You have a new pen."

••••

When everyone had gone, Handel let Billie talk him into getting in bed while she cleaned up. She could tell that even though it hadn't lasted long, the party had exhausted him. The lines around his mouth were etched a little deeper and she wondered if they were from the pain of his broken ribs or what his near death experience had wrought.

The house was quiet when she flipped off the lights. She stopped to look out the kitchen window at the tall oak and eucalyptus trees. Moonlight shimmered off leaves and spilled through the branches to the familiar tire swing swaying gently in the night breeze. She smiled, remembering the first time she kissed Handel there. On a night like tonight, with only the moon watching, she'd fallen in love all over again with her childhood friend. Handy. She closed her eyes and said a little prayer of thanks that God had seen fit to give them more time together. Life without him was unimaginable now.

Her cell phone, left on the kitchen counter, started playing Beethoven's Fifth Symphony. She hurried to pick up. "Hello, Mother."

She heard engine noise in the background and wondered what her mother was up to this time. She seemed to be on a mission lately to do all the things common sense had once talked her out of doing. After a short-lived long-distance romance with Carl's older brother, Antonio, she'd sworn off men and decided to quit worrying about love and start thinking about having some fun. Her exact words. Billie didn't know if she was fulfilling some crazy bucket list or she'd gone completely insane.

"Billie? Are you there? I can't hear you," her mother shouted into the phone.

Billie moved the cell away from her ear. "I'm here. What are you doing? Skydiving?"

Last week her mother had called to say she had signed up to go bungee jumping off a bridge up along the border of Canada. It seemed more than a little ludicrous that her conservative mother, who once told her not to jump off a bridge just cause everyone else did, would suddenly have a need for speed and a desire to take death-defying leaps of faith. Billie didn't know if her mother had lost her mind, but from the distance of California there was nothing she could do about it.

"No, of course not, honey. Stella and I are out at the races. Stock cars, you know? It's pretty loud but I wanted to see how everything went today. I suppose Handel's already tucked into bed. I was…" Revving engines and a voice over a loudspeaker drowned out the rest of her words.

Billie waited for the noise to die down before responding. "What made you choose stock car races tonight, anyway?" she asked, walking down the hall to check that the front door was locked. "You've always hated loud noise. When I was a teenager, you wouldn't let me turn my music up loud enough to hear the words."

"Oh, don't exaggerate. Your childhood was just as rebellious and wild as the rest of the population. Don't think I didn't know you listened to Hell on Wheels or whatever that group was, when I wasn't around. Anyway, I better let you go. I'm supposed to be getting popcorn for Stella. She's probably wondering if I got lost. I had to step into the women's bathroom to be able to hear."

"I'll let Handel know you called. He'll be sorry

he missed you, but he was exhausted, so I sent him to bed. We had a little welcome home party when we got here. Davy even colored a banner." Billie looked up at the paper strip still decorating the fireplace mantle and smiled before shutting off the lights in the living room.

"I wish I could have been there," her mother said, a touch of sadness filling her words in spite of the background noise. "I'm so happy he's all right. He is all right, isn't he?"

Billy expelled a laugh. "Yes, Mother, he's very all right. We both are now."

"Goodnight, honey."

"Night, Mom."

She shut off the phone, closed her eyes and drew a deep cleansing breath.

But for some strange reason she was still hearing the sound of an engine revving. She went to the front window and pulled back the drapes enough to look out. Headlights cut a swath across her face as a vehicle spun in the gravel. The driver gunned the engine and tore out again, then spun another circle, throwing rocks and dust into the air. The winery's security lights popped on across the yard as the SUV headed in that direction. They drove past the parking area, over the curb onto the sidewalk, slammed on the brakes and spun again, tearing up the flowerbeds she'd recently planted out front of the entrance.

Angry now, she ran to the front door and threw it open. She didn't know what she was going to do, but when the porch light came on and lit her up, the truck suddenly slid to a stop. The driver revved the motor. Vroom, vroom. It was obviously an intimidation ploy, and it was working. She took a step back, just inside the door and quickly punched 911 into her cellphone.

The driver backed up slowly, then turned the vehicle toward the house and hit the gas. Were they crazy? She slammed the door and locked it. But that wouldn't stop a truck. She turned to run toward the back of the house, when she heard them skid to a stop outside and the driver laid on the horn. They were definitely trying to get her attention.

"911, what's your emergency?" The voice asked from far away.

Billie lifted the phone to her ear. "This is Billie Parker at The Fredrickson Winery. There's someone outside driving their vehicle all over the place and damaging our property. Could you send out a patrol car?"

She moved back to the window and peered through the drapes. The vehicle's tinted windows reflected the porch light back at her, but made it impossible to see who was driving. While she watched, the driver side window of the SUV rolled down and the barrel of a gun stuck out. She dove for the floor, dropping the phone and hitting the end table with her head. There was a loud pop and the window cracked. Before she could find where she'd dropped the phone, she heard the truck speed away.

"Billie?" Handel called from down the hall. She heard the slap of his bare feet against wood floors before the light in the living room flashed on. "Oh my God! Are you all right?" He dropped to his knees beside her. "You're bleeding!"

She reached up and gently probed her forehead. Her fingers came away red. "I see that." She tried to stand up and he grabbed her forearms to keep her

from falling. "Sorry. I'm a little dizzy," she
apologized.

"What happened? Something woke me up, and
I heard you scream."

"They shot at me," she said, pointing at the
window, still shocked by that fact. It was the second
time someone had tried to kill her since she'd moved
to California and she didn't like it any better than she
had the first.

"They who?" he asked, eyes wide. He moved to
the window and pulled the drapes aside revealing a
bullet hole the size of a quarter. The tempered glass
splintered around the smooth hole like the rays of the
sun.

A siren wailed in the distance and Billie put a
hand on his bare back. "I think you better go put on
some clothes, babe. The police will be here soon."

He glanced down and seemed to just realize he
was standing there in the buff. "You already called
them?" He looked groggy and confused, glancing
around the room as though trying to fill in the blanks.

Billie pointed at her phone lying under the edge
of the recliner. She must have tossed it when she fell.
Handel reached down and picked it up. She took it
and held it to her ear. The dispatcher was still on the
line. "Go. Get dressed," she said, and waved him
away. "I've got this."

The police car turned into the winery entrance,
lights flashing. "They're here now," she told the
emergency operator. "Thank you."

She pressed a tissue to her forehead to stop the
bleeding. Slipping the phone into her back jeans
pocket, she opened the door. Handel caught up to her
before she stepped out onto the porch. He was fully

dressed now in khaki shorts and a green t-shirt.

"That was fast. The drugs must be wearing off," she said, remembering that he moved a little slower when he was on his meds.

"Tell me about it." He grimaced.

Two officers got out and came to the door. "Are you Billie Parker?" the older one asked.

"Yes. I called."

They were staring at Handel oddly and she realized they thought he was drunk. He was weaving where he stood. She grabbed his arm. "I think you better sit down. This is too much stress for you after just getting out of the hospital."

"I'm fine," he mumbled, but she could tell he was not.

"Are you sure you're okay, sir?" the officer asked, hands on his belt. He stepped forward, a look of concern drawing his brows together.

"My wife is the one who got hurt. Someone shot at her," he said, anger tingeing his words. He wasn't fully aware of the facts, but his protective side was out full force.

Billie invited the officers inside as she relayed everything that had taken place since talking with her mother. They took down the report and the younger officer asked, "How did you hurt your head, ma'am?"

"When I saw the gun, I dove to the floor," she said, pointing, "and managed to hit my head on the table over there."

The officer inspected the damaged window. The bullet hole was right at his chin level. Exactly where Billie's face had been when they took aim. She swallowed hard, thinking how quickly things could change. Handel had survived a near fatal car crash and before they had time to truly appreciate the reprieve, death came knocking again. Well she certainly wasn't ready to let him in.

The senior officer, who'd introduced himself as Officer Torn, dug the slug out of the far wall and put it in an evidence bag while his partner went outside and took a few pictures of the window and tire tracks. Billie had a feeling it was all a waste of time.

"Did you see the license plate or anything that could be used to identify this vehicle? Or recognize the face of the driver or shooter?"

She shook her head. "It was too dark and the windows were tinted. It was a mid-size SUV. Maybe an older Chevy?" She sighed. "I wish I remembered more, but to tell you the truth, being shot at really clears your mind. Literally."

"If you think of anything else, give us a call." He handed her his card. "Without a license or accurate description of the vehicle, there's not much we can do. I'm sorry."

"What about the ballistics report?" Handel asked, getting up from the couch and following them to the door. "Someone can just shoot at my wife and get away with it? Like it's some kind of prank?"

Billie could see the pain was starting to get to him. He was edgier than usual and not thinking clearly. She put her arm around his waist. "They're doing their job, Handel. It was dark and I was more worried about them tearing up the flowerbeds than trying to read their license plate. I'm sorry. If I'd known they were crazy enough to shoot at me..."

"You did the right thing, ma'am. Confronting them would have just given them a bigger target." He gave a curt nod toward Handel. "We'll definitely file a ballistics report but unless the gun is used in another crime and we catch the owner red-handed, there's not much chance of knowing who came here tonight and fired that shot. You understand that, don't you, counselor?"

The officer had obviously recognized Handel at some point. He'd probably watched the news about the trial and seen the report on Handel's accident and the trial's postponement.

Handel sighed heavily. "I'm sorry, Officer Torn," he said. "I don't want to come across as a pain in the ass but after what we've just been through, and now this…"

"I understand. We'll do all we can and I'll have a patrol car come by a couple more times tonight just in case it wasn't a random act of violence."

"Thank you."

Officer Torn touched his finger to the brim of his hat and nodded. "Goodnight, folks. Make sure your doors are locked and your porch light stays on the rest of the night. A patrol will check things out again in a couple hours, but chances are you'll never see or hear from these guys again."

"Let's hope not," Billie said. She watched the officers get in their car, then closed and locked the front door.

Handel was at the window again, inspecting the bullet hole. He slowly shook his head. "I can't believe this."

She came up behind him and gently eased her arms around his waist, trying not to put any pressure on his ribs. "I know. That window will probably cost a couple thousand bucks to replace. I hope insurance covers drive-by's."

He turned and cupped her face with his hands, one side of his mouth curving up. "I wasn't talking about the window."

"No?" she asked, wide-eyed and innocent.

"No. I was thinking that my chances of winning the lottery might be higher than I once thought."

"Excuse me?"

"Well, think about it. What are the chances of a criminal attorney marrying a woman so many people want to kill? Probably only one in a million, right? So, with those odds conquered, what's stopping me from beating even bigger odds?"

Billie scoffed and pulled back. "Now you're just being mean. Here I was trying to be all calm and matter-of-fact about the situation to keep your stress level low, and you come right out and accuse *me* of being the problem."

He laughed and pulled her close again. "I never said you were the problem exactly."

"Oh really? Cause that's what I heard."

"Maybe you should get your hearing checked," he whispered, and began leaving a trail of kisses down her neck and along her collarbone.

"I don't think this is a very good idea," she said, suddenly breathless. She closed her eyes under the fresh onslaught, and moaned when his mouth found hers. It had been so long.

Handel deepened the kiss, his hands exploring her body as though he needed a reminder of what he'd forgotten while he was asleep.

"We can't," she gasped, pulling away. "I don't want to hurt you."

"Then be gentle with me," he teased. He took

her hand and led her down the hall toward the bedroom.

CHAPTER THREE

When Billie woke up early the next morning, Handel was already missing from his side of the bed. She lay there drowsy, listening to the sound of birds calling outside the window. Not far away she could hear the tap tap tap of a woodpecker searching for bugs in the bark of an old tree. And from somewhere – probably in the woodworker's shed she had allowed Ernesto for personal use on weekends – a radio played Mexican pop music.

She reached out and pulled Handel's pillow against her chest, breathing in the familiar scent of him. After they'd made love the night before, he'd fallen almost immediately into an exhausted sleep. Still wide awake, she'd stared at his profile in the dark, one hand lightly resting on his chest, and felt the reassuring rise and fall of his lungs sending oxygen to his brain. And she finally told herself he would be all right.

It wasn't hard to imagine losing him. In fact, it was all too easy. Imagining that he would still be here ten years from now, that their lives would be happy and carefree, and that their love would survive whatever life threw at them, was much more difficult.

She'd had her innocence ripped from her at the age of eight, lost her father at the age of fifteen. She knew about loss. What she wanted to experience was joy. The kind of joy that didn't depend on circumstance, because circumstances change. People leave. Hearts are broken.

Joy? She'd thought about it a lot in the past week. Joy must be an internal position, completely unaffected by the external. An inner sanctum where car crashes and cancer and divorce and failing businesses and broken dreams, can't penetrate to destroy.

She threw her legs over the side of the bed and sat up. The smell of fresh-brewed coffee wafted into the room and she knew exactly where her husband had disappeared to so early. She pulled on a t-shirt and panties and padded down the hall.

Handel had turned the smaller of the guest bedrooms into an office for himself soon after they were married. He'd furnished it with an oak desk and hutch, an easy chair and a tall reading lamp. A carpenter had been hired to install bookshelves along one wall, leaving room for a 32-inch flat screen television in the center. Most of his reference books were at his law office downtown, so there was room for Billie's books as well, with shelf room to spare for framed photos and memorabilia.

She paused in the open doorway and watched Handel rifling through papers on his desk. He was so intent on what he was looking for that he didn't hear her come in. She cleared her throat to get his attention. "Is this what you call rest and recuperation? I don't think Doctor Chao would have signed that release form yesterday if he thought you'd go right back to it."

He let his eyes slide over her curves, a boyish grin on his face. "Good morning, sexy," he said. He picked up his coffee cup and took a sip, watching her over the rim. His hair stuck up at the back and his eyes still looked sleepy, but in faded jeans and an old t-shirt that said, *My book club reads between the wines*, he looked like a cool glass of sangria.

She went and stood in front of him, hands on her hips. "You could have at least stayed in bed past seven," she reprimanded. "I woke up all alone."

He set the cup down and reached out for her. She went willingly, curled into his lap and let him tell her good morning the old fashioned way – with slow, thorough kisses that deepened until she felt hollow and needy all over again.

Just when they were getting to the point of no return, Handel's cell phone rang. He pulled away with a ragged breath. "Sorry, babe."

She stood up licking her lips. "It's all right. I need some coffee anyway."

He answered the phone and she picked up his cup and went to sit comfortably in his easy chair to finish it. His gaze narrowed at her thievery, but his attention was quickly diverted by whatever the caller was telling him. "What did the judge say?" he asked.

Billie cradled the mug in her hands and sipped, listening to the one-sided conversation.

"That's fine. We'll make it work. I'll be in the city on Monday. We can talk then." He ended the call and set the phone down, his gaze riveted on the dark flat screen behind her head. He looked a million miles away.

"Is everything all right?" she asked. It went against all of her separation of work and home beliefs to ask the question, but she didn't want this wall between them anymore. She was beginning to think that Adam was right. Marriage meant sharing everything and their work was a big part of who they each were.

He blinked and met her gaze. "Just some loose ends with the case."

The way he said it made her worry antenna come up. What wasn't he saying? Maybe it was time to talk about his accident and what Alvarez suspected. She wanted him to heal and not worry about the case, but realistically that was not going to happen. He refused to even discuss letting another attorney take over. He was lead and he had no intention of letting that position go to another. This was a big case with lots of publicity, which meant if he won a not guilty verdict, high profile cases would come flooding in. He could pick and choose.

"Handel, before you came out of your coma," she began, "someone came to see me. He said he was working for you. A private investigator by the name of…"

"Manny Alvarez," he supplied, and lifted an eyebrow. "Why didn't you say anything?"

She shrugged. "There wasn't really a chance until now. The last couple days have been sort of busy." She ticked them off on her fingers. "You woke up. The doctors took over. We came home. There was a party. I was shot at. We made love. Now I'm telling you."

"Right. Well, what did he want to talk to you about?" he asked, eyes narrowed.

"He wanted to know if you had any leads for him to investigate." She got up, holding his now empty mug. "I told him we don't usually discuss business, but…" She sat on the edge of his desk and took his hand in hers. "I want to change all that. I want you to be a part of everything in my life, and that includes Fredrickson's. I don't want to keep my life all compartmentalized anymore. At least not from you." She smiled. "From now on, our lives will be one big, old, messy, junk drawer. How's that sound?"

He laughed and squeezed her fingers. "The messier the better, I say. But what brought this on?" he asked.

She bit her lip. "Alvarez told me that your accident might have been deliberate."

"I see."

"So he's talked to you about it already?"

"That's what got me out of bed so early. He called as soon as he heard I was released from the hospital. Said he wanted to warn me."

"That's what he told me too, but there was something not right…" She shook her head. "I don't know. How did you happen to hire the brother of the victim to investigate for the defense? Are you sure you can trust him?"

"Kawasaki thinks I can. He trusts him." He opened the desk drawer and pulled out his day planner. He still kept a record of his appointments there as well as in his phone. Old habits died hard. He flipped it open and ran his finger down the page.

"Did you know he was once a member of the notorious MS-13's?"

"Of course." He looked up. "What are you getting at?"

Billie walked to the window and pulled the blinds open, using the moments to get her thoughts together. "He suggested we might be in danger out here. That members of the gang put a hit out on you because they think you know something."

"I believe Kawasaki is innocent, but I don't know who really murdered his wife. All I need to do is prove reasonable doubt. I have no intention of pulling a Matlock and pointing out the real killer in court." He blew out a laugh. "I'll let the police take care of all that."

"So, you don't think maybe our drive-by shooting was more than a coincidence?"

He pushed a hand through his hair and sighed. "I hope not. It's one thing to target me, but they shot at you last night. Why would they do that?"

"Intimidation?"

He stared across the room, rubbing thoughtfully at his chin.

"So, how long did the judge give you to recuperate and get your case together before the trial begins?" she asked.

"Two weeks."

She took his hand and pulled him toward the door. "Come on. You can't think clearly on an empty stomach. I'll scramble some eggs."

••••

The outdoor bandstand and vine-covered arbor area were fairly new to Fredrickson's. So new that the vines weren't much of a cover yet, but in another year or two would make great shade for those who wanted to get out of the sun. Live entertainment had been one of Margaret's ideas and so far was attracting busy weekend crowds. They had to tear down a couple of old dilapidated sheds, build the bandstand, plant sod, and add some fun sculptures to the mix, but this investment seemed to be well worth it.

The weekend had sort of snuck up on Billie since she'd been spending so much time with Handel the last few days. But when cars began rolling in late Saturday morning, he pushed her out the door and told her to go and supervise the winery so he could have a break. He said it with a smile but she knew she was getting on his nerves.

People were already spreading blankets on the grass and settling down to listen to jazz with a bottle of Fredrickson's in hand when Billie skirted the parking lot. Seeing a familiar neighbor she'd rather avoid, she made a detour of the front entrance of the winery and snuck through the trees to a side door that opened onto the pressing floor.

Digging in the pocket of her khaki shorts for the keys, she glanced back and saw the same neighbor following. Obviously, she'd been spotted. She released a sigh and pasted on a bright smile. "Good morning, Hazel. What can I do for you?" she asked, knowing she'd regret the question but feeling compelled to make it.

Hazel Thompson had lived next door to Fredrickson's since the 1960s. She and her husband owned eighteen acres of land, planted with Cabernet Sauvignon. These grapes made some of the finest red Bordeaux in the area. Last year they'd decided to retire from winemaking and sell their grapes to the highest bidder. In spite of Billie's best offer, their crop went to some retired Hollywood director turned entrepreneur. He'd bought a small Napa winery and was pouring millions into turning it into the next Disneyland – only with wine instead of rides. More competition for Fredrickson's.

The woman wore bright pink capris and a lacy, cream-colored tank top. Her long hair, dyed to the shade of a raven's wing, was twisted into a chignon at the back of her head. She was a thin woman, to the point of emaciation, obviously believing the fable, *you can never be too rich or too thin*. Reading glasses hung from a chain around her neck and swung back and forth against unnaturally perky aged breasts as she hurried along.

"For starters, you can tell me what is going on around here!" She planted her stiletto heals in the soft ground, long-nailed claws on bony hips. "This was a gun free zone before you showed up and took over for Jack, but Monday night was the second time I've heard gunfire coming from your place. The first time resulted in death. What pray tell was the result this time?"

Billie tried to keep from smiling, but she had to look away when she noticed the brand new hummingbird tattoo on the old lady's ankle. She pretended to be interested in a stack of crates beside the door. "I'm sorry if it worried you, Hazel, but thankfully no one was killed," she said, straightening the stack. She wondered what took the woman so long to come and complain.

"When I saw police lights flashing across the vineyard I said to Herbie, 'I wonder if she's been shot? That husband of hers is the son of that horrible Sean Peterson after all.' He didn't try to kill you, did he?" she asked, with just a touch of gleeful hope in her eyes.

"No, Hazel. You do know my husband just got out of the hospital Monday. He was in a coma for a week. I don't think he's quite up to murder yet. Maybe after he's recuperated a bit." She turned and put the key in the lock.

Hazel wasn't going away. She followed her through the door, heels clicking on the concrete floor. "Who was shooting then? That sort of thing might be perfectly normal out there in the Midwest where they hunt and kill innocent animals, but here in the valley it's just not done."

Billie turned and blocked the way, arms crossed. "They might kill innocent animals in Minnesota, but in California they shoot people."

The woman gasped and put a hand to her throat.

Billie decided to take pity on her. "It might interest you to know that we had a bullet go through our front window. The police think it was vandals, so you might want to keep your outside lights on at night."

"My word! What is the valley coming to?" Hazel shook her head.

"Hell in a hand basket," Billie muttered and slowly eased the woman out the door, closing it soundly.

••••

Billie hurried through the distillery, and into the barrel room. She glanced down a row of oak barrels and saw Margaret busy taking samples of the Cabernet Franc. She tasted the wine then took notes in her little wine journal.

She turned around and saw Billie watching.

"Hey. Another week or so these barrels should be ready for bottling."

"That's good news. It's been our best seller recently and we're running low."

Margaret dropped her tools in a bucket to be cleaned and sanitized. "How's my brother doing? Driving you crazy yet?"

"Always," she said with a smile, absently running a hand over the side of an oak barrel.

Despite his recent weeklong coma and the last few days of home rest she'd tried to enforce, his eyes still had dark circles under them. He refused to admit he was tired. The murder case had him tied up in knots. The trial would begin in a little over a week and he planned to be ready.

"He was tired of me nagging him to rest," Billie said, "so he insisted I come over here and check things out while he goes through all his evidence and witness reports again."

"Sounds more fun than watching him *not* rest," Margaret teased. "He never has been able to sleep more than four or five hours a night when he's working a case. But I guess you know that by now."

"Yep, I learned the hard way." Billie pushed a loose strand of hair behind her ear. "He tries not to wake me up, but the quieter he dresses and moves about the room, the more alert I am to his every movement."

Margaret stifled a yawn. "I didn't get much sleep last night myself."

"Oh, why's that?"

Margaret looked at her strangely. "Did you forget Adam was playing the club again? I wanted to stay awake for his show and I drank too much caffeine. I didn't get home until after one and I still couldn't sleep. He did fantastic, by the way."

Billie shook her head. "I completely forgot about Adam's gig at The Screech Owl. I wish we could have been there."

"Don't worry. He'll be playing there a lot. I think they're signing him as a regular."

"That's great." She knew he wanted to be a musician and that he did the accounting for Fredrickson's more or less as a favor to her, but if he quit completely she would really miss him being around.

"Did I hear you talking to Hazel out there?" she asked and made a face. "That woman stopped by here Tuesday morning and wanted to speak with you. I told her you weren't in. She was complaining about hearing gunfire over here." She shook her head. "She's as batty as a..." she stopped, seeing the look on Billie's face. "What?"

"Actually, we did have some uninvited guests drop by Monday night."

"Are you talking about the same person who ran over the flowerbeds?"

"Sorry, I didn't tell you, but Handel and I thought we should keep that part quiet for now. The winery has gotten enough bad press and with Sally's ability to spread the news, it would be all over Napa Valley within minutes." She told Margaret all the gory details, not even leaving out the part where Handel came running—completely naked—to save her.

"So the police think they were just vandals?"

"That's the way it looks."

"But?"

Billie shrugged. "It's not the way it felt. There

was something bold about the way they spun around in our yard and then very calmly drove right up to our front door, took aim at my head, and pulled the trigger. They wanted to be seen. They wanted to be feared," she said slowly, thinking aloud. "Vandals usually sweep in when they're sure no one will be home. They leave a mess and run away, anonymous. Right? But these guys," she shook her head, "were making a point."

"I don't understand."

She didn't want to scare Margaret, but it was better to be aware of the danger than oblivious, wasn't it? "It may have something to do with Handel's case."

The door opened at the top of the stairs and Sally yelled down. "Billie? You down there?"

She hurried over. "What's up?"

"I thought I saw you sneaking around the back way," Sally said with a look of satisfaction as though she'd solved a Time's crossword puzzle. "We've got a problem out there."

"Is Hazel complaining about the noise again?" she asked, starting up the stairs.

"Noise? I don't think she'll have a problem with that today." Sally leaned against the doorjamb and crossed her arms. "The band didn't show. I called the number we had for them, but the guy I talked to on the phone said they were sick with the flu. Sounded more like they were all hung over to me. I looked at their website and they played for a wedding party last night."

"Awesome." Billie put her hands on her head and groaned. "If it's not one thing, it's another. The one venue that seems to bring in money is canceled due to lack of entertainment. I hope those people don't want a refund on the wine they bought for the concert."

Margaret followed her up the stairs. "Maybe you could ask Adam to fill in."

Sally snorted. "That'll be the day!"

"Hey! I resent that," Billie said, leading the way down the hall to the front office. "I have no problem asking Adam to fill in. I think he's an excellent choice. I just don't want to impose on him anymore than I already have."

The office door was open and leaning back in Sally's leather desk chair, feet up on the desk, was Adam. He grinned smugly. "I'm flattered," he said, folding his hands behind his head and rocking the chair as he leaned. "I didn't know you thought so highly of my talents."

She narrowed her eyes at Sally. "Thanks a lot," she said in a stage whisper.

"Bringing families together," she said, spreading her arms wide. "It's what I do."

Margaret stepped in front of Billie, shielding her from Adam's smug grin. "This is your winery, Billie. Your responsibility. We get that. But we're also your family. We're ready and willing to do whatever it takes to get people out here and bring Fredrickson's sales up." She glanced back and gave Adam a soft smile. "Trust me, if anyone can serenade those people and get the wine flowing, it's your brother."

"Sounds like he's already been serenading somebody in this room," Sally said from her perch on the corner of the desk.

Billie stepped around Margaret and leaned over the desk, meeting her brother's grin with one of her own. "Well, don't just sit there, little brother. We've got wine to sell."

"Thought you'd never ask." He got up, smoothed his hair back and picked up the guitar he'd propped in the corner. It was almost as though they'd planned the whole thing. At the door, he hooked a thumb over his shoulder toward the tasting room. "Better get Loren some extra help in there. He's gonna need it," he promised, and strutted off singing, "I'm coming up, so you better get this party started."

They all laughed when he was out of earshot and Margaret covered her face with her hands. "I can't believe what that man does to me when he plays. I swear, I feel like I'm sixteen again at an 'N Sync concert."

Sally leaned in and lowered her voice to a whisper. "I'll lie and deny it like a politician if he ever hears this from either of you. But," she met Billie's eyes and winked, "your brother is one hot…"

Billie covered her ears. "mmmmmmmmmmmm," she hummed loudly enough to block out the last words.

Margaret grabbed Sally's hand and pulled her toward the door. "Come on. Let's go catch the show. Maybe he'll do that thing he did last night."

Billie released a sigh once they'd gone. This was obviously going to be one of those days. She shut off the office light and pulled the door closed before following the sound of voices and laughter to the tasting room. Loren and Sammie were in full swing, filling glasses and chatting up the customers. About twenty people were wandering around, or sitting at the tables talking and drinking. Not bad.

Loren looked up and waved when he saw her.

"Billie. Didn't expect to see you around here today," he said as she approached the bar. His long black hair was pulled into a ponytail and he wore a faded blue biker scarf over his head. He must have ridden his bike in today. He owned an Indian Chief vintage motorcycle and had already talked Sally into taking a road trip with him after harvest. Billie couldn't imagine Sally riding on the back of a cruiser down the Interstate. She'd be much too worried about messing up her hair.

He poured a glass of wine for a middle-aged woman in plaid shorts and a red shirt, and waited for her to rejoin her friends before asking, "How's Handel doing? Was the party too much for him Monday night?"

"No, he's fine," she said, and smiled. "The party was a pleasant surprise. He really enjoyed it. I'm glad you and Sally could be part of it."

"No problem. Sally wouldn't have it any other way. She's known Handel a long time. She was really worried about him there for a while." He leaned over the bar, palms planted on the smooth top. His eyes roamed the room off and on keeping track of his customers. "Ever wonder what coma patients think about? I've always thought it would be like a higher state of consciousness, like my ancestors found in their sweat lodge ceremonies."

Billie raised her brows. "You mean after smoking the peace pipe?" she teased.

He reached for a bar towel and wiped the walnut counter until it gleamed. "I think the brain is too complex to just be sitting on idle, you know?"

A young blonde woman rushed up to the counter to purchase a bottle for the concert outside.

Her friends waited by the door, carrying a blanket and tiny cooler. She paid her bill, took the bottle and some of the free disposable wine glasses and headed out.

"I guess I'll go check out the entertainment. It seems to be quite popular with the younger crowd," she said, watching more young women enter the door.

"I'm surprised. Usually the jazz bands bring in yuppyish forty-somethings."

"You're right. But the group I had booked didn't show."

"No kidding. What are you going to do?" He poured a glass with his own special blend of Sangria and slid it toward Billie.

"Thanks." Taking a sip, she looked around. Another group of young women peered in the door. She frowned. This was certainly a younger crowd than usual. She told Loren, "We're using talent from within today. Our very own Adam Fredrickson is at the mic."

Loren's smile lit up his dark eyes. "I think I better take a break and go keep an eye on my lady. I assume Sally ran right out there to gawk at him." He signaled Sammie, who was busy clearing glasses left by departing guests, to take his place behind the bar.

Sammie hurried over. Or at least he hurried as quickly as Sammie ever did. He had retired from the navy and set up residence in the valley so he could be near his adult children. Two of them lived in Calistoga and one in San Francisco. Like most retired men, he was bored, so he worked part time at the winery.

"Ma'am," he saluted her as though she were his

senior officer.

"How's it going, Sammie?"

"Pretty damn good," he said, as usual. "Say, how's your husband doing? I heard he was out of the hospital and back home." He slipped behind the bar and set the tray of dirty glasses down under the counter. "That was some accident, huh? One of my pals in the navy once fell off the…"

Loren interrupted him with a hand on his arm. "We're going outside. Could you handle the dispensing of firewater on your own for a bit?" He flipped the bar towel over Sammie's shoulder.

"Yeah, sure, chief."

Loren followed Billie out the open front doors into the bright afternoon sun. They were both surprised to see a line of cars slowly turning into the winery. The parking lot was nearly full and cars were pulling off the driveway onto the grass shoulder.

Under a clear blue sky, the sun glinted off windshields and people in shorts and t-shirts meandered through the vehicles making their way toward the winery. Most had come prepared with lawn chairs or blankets. Apparently word had gone out. But how?

"What is going on?" Billie stood with her hands on her hips looking around at the robust crowd like she'd fallen into Oz.

She heard Adam over the speakers, strumming an old classic Paul Anka song. *A steel guitar and a glass of wine.* She recognized it right away. Their mother used to play it on the record player when they were kids. Sabrina wasn't really from that era of music, but she loved it all the same and had shared her love of it with them.

Billie smiled, and decided Adam was a genius. "I think it's about time I witnessed my brother's charisma."

They turned the corner of the building as he was belting out the chorus. *"Bring me wine! Make the music mine..."* Women, young and old alike, were swaying to the beat, all eyes on the auburn haired guitar god on stage.

Billie laughed out loud, unable to keep it in. Her brother really was something.

He segwayed into another of Anka's hits. The mellow, romantic love song had every woman wishing to share a glass of wine with the man on stage. *"...in a room where passions flow..."*

Loren was scanning the crowd for a glimpse of Sally. He pointed up front, close to the stage. Margaret and Sally were in the thick of things, dancing and laughing, making sure they were Adam's biggest fans. Loren leaned in and spoke close to her ear so she could hear over the music. "How does it feel to have a brother wanted by so many women?"

Billie grinned and sang along, *"...and I need you. I love you so. And I want you..."*

He shook his head. "Needs drums," he grumbled.

••••

When Adam took a break to rest his throat, women swarmed up front to meet him and no doubt told him just how wonderful he was. Loren had already returned to his post at the bar by that time, but Billie watched from a distance, arms crossed, a small smile on her face.

Margaret and Sally broke away from the mob and joined her. They were both starry eyed and pink-cheeked from their enthusiastic support of her brother. She saw Adam look up over the heads of his admirers and catch her eye. She grinned and blew him a kiss.

"Whew!" Sally fanned her hand in front of her face. "My oh my," she said in a terrible southern belle accent, "that boy can sing. He sent my blood pressure skyrocketing."

"Hey!" Margaret said, "That's my man you're talking about. Don't get any ideas."

"That's my brother you're both drooling over and it's making me a little nauseous," Billie said, but she couldn't hide how proud she was. Too bad Sabrina couldn't have been here to see him perform. She would have loved it.

"I better get in there and make sure the boys are keeping up with the customers," Sally said. "This is a great crowd for a Saturday."

Billie waited until she was gone before confronting Margaret with her suspicions. "So which one of you canceled Jimmy's Jazz Crew? You, Adam, or Sally? And how did you manage to get all these people here," she asked, waving a hand to encompass the grounds.

Margaret pulled out her cell phone. "Adam and I sent out an invitation. He's been amassing a lot of local followers on his Facebook and Twitter pages," she said, and laughed. "I can't believe it worked! Look at all these people!" She grabbed Billie's arms and pulled her into a hug.

"Thank you," Billie said in her ear. "I owe you both."

Margaret pulled back with a smile. "You don't owe us anything, Billie. That's the beauty of family."

Adam finally managed to break away from his fans and join them. He threw his arms around them both and squeezed. "Group hug!"

"Hey lady!"

Billie turned around at the loud voice behind them. A young Hispanic man stood a few yards away, arms crossed, regarding them coolly from behind red shades. His sleeveless shirt revealed arms heavy in ink and muscle.

"Are you talking to me?" she asked, raising her brows.

"You the wine chick?"

Adam stepped forward. "Can we help you?" he asked, protectively putting his six-foot-two frame between her and the stranger.

The man smirked and shook his head. "Naw. I don't need no help. I come to give help. Maybe you need a strong Mexican worker to replant those smashed flowerbeds for you," he offered. His grin revealed a diamond inset in his front tooth. It caught the light and sparkled in odd contrast to the skull and crossbones tattoo on his neck.

Adam glanced back at Billie. "Something going on here I should know about?"

"We had vandals last night," she said, moving around Adam and confronting the young man face to face, despite the creeping fear that inched up her spine. "What do you know about that?" she asked him.

He gave a slight shrug and pushed his shades up on the top of his head. His dark gaze swept boldly over her body before finally meeting her eyes. "Somebody must not like you very much, chica. Why else would they run over your pretty flowers?"

"I'd like to know the answer to that myself," she said. "Perhaps you could enlighten me."

He laughed. "No. I don't know nothin'." He turned as if to leave and then looked back. "But if I were you, I would stay indoors where it's safe. Can't be too careful these days."

"Hey!" Adam called after him. "Was that a threat?" He started to follow, but Billie grasped his arm and stopped him.

"Let him go," she said.

They watched the man move through the parked cars until he opened the door of a black SUV and climbed in on the passenger side. The truck backed out and drove away, tinted windows reflecting the winery back at them.

"What kind of truck is that?" she asked, squinting.

"I think it's a Lexus. Why?"

"Because someone in a black SUV drove in here Monday night, tore up my flowerbeds and shot at me through our front window."

"What?" Adam grabbed her by the shoulders. "Why am I just hearing about this now?" he asked, practically shaking her.

She pulled away. "We called the police. What exactly do you think you could have done that they didn't?"

"They shot at you?" he said again, unable to fathom the idea. "Why would anyone...? Do you even know that dude?"

Billie shook her head. "It's a mystery to me." She smiled reassuringly and changed the subject. "Thanks for doing all this, guys," she said, waving a hand toward the crowd and the stage. "I really appreciate it. But I need to talk to Handel."

She started walking toward the house taking slow, easy strides in spite of her inner desire to run. She dared a glance back and saw her brother making his way up to the stage again with Margaret following close behind. With no one watching, she broke into a jog. This whole thing scared her a lot more than she wanted to admit. Why would a stranger threaten her? What did they have to gain? Was it really a result of Handel's case or someone with a vendetta against her? It didn't make any sense.

CHAPTER FOUR

Margaret curled against Adam's chest where they sat on the couch, pretending to be interested in the movie he'd chosen for the evening. It was definitely a guy movie, with explosions, gunfire, and short, terse dialogue that peppered the action without actually having a storyline or character development. Davy sat at their feet on the floor, completely entranced. He hadn't even asked for popcorn or a snack.

She wanted to ask Adam what he thought about Billie's latest troubles but it would have to wait until Davy was tucked in bed for the night. She didn't want to frighten him after what he'd gone through a year ago. Sometimes he still had nightmares and woke up crying out. Hearing that his aunt might have a killer gunning for her would not be a good bedtime conversation.

Rambo, the tomcat Davy had adopted from the local shelter after begging for a pet for months on end, came padding in from the kitchen where he had been eating his dinner. He licked his whiskers and leaped up to the back of the couch with hardly any effort. After walking along the entire length and back, he settled down on the far end, curled into a rumbling black and white ball of fur and closed his eyes.

Margaret reached up and rubbed her palm along Adam's whiskered cheek and pulled his face down for a kiss. His lips pooched out as though to kiss her but his eyes remained glued on the television screen. She sighed and extricated herself from his arm.

"I can't compete with a superhero," she grumbled. "I'm going down to the cellar to work."

When she was halfway to the kitchen, they both exploded in laughter and she turned around. Davy had climbed up on the couch beside Adam and they were grinning at the screen like twin zombies. Tweedledee and Tweedledum.

Her cell rang and she picked it up where she'd left it on the kitchen table. "Hello."

"Margaret Parker?"

The voice sent shivers down her spine. She pulled the phone away and glanced at caller I.D. but it said Unknown. He was dead. There was no way he could be calling.

"Hello?" the voice asked again, the Italian accent so familiar and yet... a slight deepening, as if more years had been added. "Are you there?"

"Yes," she said, barely able to breathe. "Who is this?"

"*Scusami*. I didn't mean to upset you. I have been told that my son and I sound much alike. Did sound much alike," he corrected, and cleared his throat. "I am Edoardo Salvatore. Your son's grandfather."

He couldn't have said anything more terrifying.

Margaret glanced back into the den and saw Adam watching her. He always seemed to be attuned to her mood swings. Apparently, he wasn't as oblivious as she'd assumed. He stood up and crossed the room toward her.

"Is everything all right?" he asked softly, eyes narrowed with interest.

She pressed her lips together and nodded.

"What can I do for you?" she asked the stranger on the line, the man whom she'd once blamed for Agosto's desertion, and the man Agosto said he hated, but respected more than any other. The only grandparent her son had left.

"I was hoping to meet my grandson," he said. When there was no immediate response from her, he continued. "Perhaps we should meet first. Alone. Discuss boundaries and expectations?" He put it as a question, but she knew that just as Agosto was unable to take no for an answer, his father would be unaccustomed to the process as well. It would be better to meet with him one on one and get it over with.

"Are you coming to the states soon?" she asked, wondering how much time she had to prepare herself. She moved to the sliding door and flipped the outside patio light on. A small rodent went scurrying off into the bushes.

"As a matter of fact, I flew into San Francisco this morning. My day is wide open tomorrow," he said, leaving the ball in her court.

"I see." She turned around to find Adam still watching. His concern was sweet, but distracting.

"Can you meet me in Yountville at Antonio's? Say, two o'clock?" She was delivering Carl's monthly order of wine anyway and she would feel more comfortable knowing her brother's friend was within calling distance.

"Perfect. I was planning to make a trip out to see my nephew sometime while I was here. Now I can kill two birds with one stone."

The old idiom was not comforting. In fact, it was rather insulting. She swallowed down the harsh retort that came to mind. "Fine. I look forward to meeting you," she lied, and ended the call.

Adam leaned on one hip, eating a leftover slice of pizza from the box on the table. "You don't sound very excited about the date you just made," he said, curious but not wanting to probe.

Sometimes she wondered how men survived, unable to ask direct questions. They'd wander aimlessly for days instead of asking directions and Adam would apparently chew off his own right arm before asking her who she was meeting.

She glanced into the den. Davy now lay stretched out on the couch with Rambo curled next to him, watching the end of the movie. There was plenty of movie noise to block their conversation, but her son was a curious sort himself and he might just be listening without appearing to do so. She lowered her voice. "I'm not. Agosto's father is in town," she said, her voice tense with worry.

Adam swallowed the last bite of pizza and licked his lips. "Is this the first time he's contacted you since…"

"Yes." She shook her head slowly, trying to understand a father who would have strangers ship his son's body home to Italy and never inquire as to the circumstances of his death. Or maybe he did and he just couldn't handle seeing her or Davy at that point, knowing they were the reason his son came to America in the first place.

"What did he say?"

Margaret stepped into Adam's embrace and slowly released the breath she was holding, allowing her fears to dissipate into the comfort of her kitchen in the arms of the man she loved. After soaking in the realization that she'd just admitted to herself something she'd refused to acknowledge up till now, she leaned her head back and smiled. She wasn't sure about being the one to say the words first, but she was positive the feeling wasn't going away. "You know," she said matter-of-factly, basking in the warmth of his brown eyes, "I've fallen in love with you."

She couldn't have surprised him more if she'd announced her engagement to Sammie. His mouth dropped open and she felt his arms go slack for a moment before he pulled her close and planted a kiss on the top of her head. "I can't believe you're finally telling me this now – with your son watching from the next room," he muttered softly.

She giggled and tried to peer over his shoulder to see if Davy was actually paying any attention to them, but Adam caught her face between his palms and kissed her until she was breathless. Rambo suddenly appeared below them, rubbing against her leg and purring his contentment at the situation.

"You guys missed the best part of the movie," Davy said from across the room. Taking a quick run, he slid across the kitchen tile in his socks, bumping into them and sending them tottering. "Whoa! Did you see how far I slid? That was awesome!"

"Sorry bud, I was a little busy," Adam admitted, slowly releasing Margaret back to reality. "Your mom and I were discussing dessert."

Margaret pulled away and started straightening up the kitchen, throwing away the pizza scraps and napkins and putting their glasses in the sink. She hummed as she worked and didn't realize until she saw Adam's grin stretch wide, that she was humming the song he'd written and sung for her at Handel and Billie's engagement party.

"Dessert?" Davy made a funny face. "I thought we only get dessert on Sundays."

"Sometimes we need to make exceptions to the rules," she said, wondering if she'd always been so rigid or if she'd gotten worse after Davy's kidnapping. Seeing his face light up at the simple suggestion to have dessert on a different night, she decided it was time to loosen up. She didn't want her son to grow up thinking life was only about following rules and being safe. Sometimes you had to take chances, to choose extraordinary rather than ordinary. "Who wants ice cream?" she asked, holding up the metal scoop like a sword.

"I do," they both said simultaneously and Davy yelled, "Jinx!"

It was an hour past his usual bedtime, following bowls of chocolate ice cream all around and lots of laughter, that Davy finally trudged off to bed. He was so tired that when Margaret went up to check on him, he was already fast asleep with the light left on in his room.

She turned off the lamp and shut his door on

her way out. The clock at the end of the hall chimed the half hour as she slowly descended the stairs. Adam was stretched out on the couch in the den, his hands clasped behind his head. A sappy grin turned up the corners of his mouth, his gaze following her crossing the room.

"I see you've made yourself comfortable," she said, shutting off the television. "It is getting pretty late. I mean, if you're too tired to go home, I guess you can crash here on the couch." He'd taken an apartment in town to be closer to the clubs where he played at night and to give Billie and Handel the privacy they deserved as newlyweds. He told her that living in his sister's extra room was awkward enough before the wedding.

"I'm not tired," he said, reaching for her as she laid the controller down on the coffee table. He grasped her wrist and gently tugged her toward him. "In fact, I'm rather wide awake." He pulled her down until she was leaning over him, her hands braced on the cushion seat on either side of his lean, hard body. He reached up to release her hair from the clip that held it off the back of her neck. Long blonde strands fell between them, brushing his chest. "You are so beautiful, Meg. I'll never be able to get enough of you."

His words could have been the words of any number of young men hot for some girl, and in the past she would have brushed them off as nothing more than sexual desire talking. But tonight her heart heard what he was trying to say rather than what he was saying. She smiled and lowered her head to kiss him.

"Wait," he said, covering her lips with two

fingers. "I need to say this. I've wanted to say this for a long time, but you weren't ready to hear it."

She sighed, eased back to sit on the coffee table facing him and waited.

He scrambled up to a sitting position and pushed his hands through his hair as though to tame the mess, but it had grown out a bit too long and unruly for that. If he had on a kilt he would've looked like a wild highlander from the hills of Scotland. She gave him an encouraging smile.

He hesitated as though searching for the right words before taking her hands in his. His dark eyes glistened in the lamplight. "I never thought I'd find a woman like you, Meg. You've encouraged me to be the best I can be, to take chances and follow my heart. You have an inner strength that I admire tremendously; an ability to survive whatever is thrown your way, and yet even with all you've been through, you still possess a gentle, loving heart that makes you even more amazing."

Feeling a bit embarrassed by his glowing praise, she opened her mouth to say something.

He shook his head. "It's my turn. You already sent my world spinning off its axis tonight. Let me finish." He lifted a hand and gently brushed a lock of hair from her cheek. "I've never fallen for a girl so quickly, so thoroughly, and so finally. I love you, Margaret Parker."

"Are you done?" she whispered, tentatively leaning in toward him.

His lips covered hers and she moaned as his kisses deepened into desire. It had been so long since she'd felt this way about any man. She ran her fingers through his hair and drew him closer still, craving his touch like a sandy beach craves the incoming tide. Logically she knew this feeling wasn't sustainable. Love had different moods, different seasons, just like wine grapes. The passion of first love was all consuming but didn't have to be the beginning and the end. Time would tell whether their lives would merge into a deeper blend of love that could be savored, but right now she wanted more than a sip. She wanted…

He suddenly pulled back and looked down into her face. A slow grin turned up his lips and then he was laughing.

Margaret looked at him in bewilderment, her brain still spinning, emotions spiraling into annoyance. "What?"

"You were doing it, weren't you?" he said, still amused at something beyond her comprehension. "You were thinking about wine and how it relates to our relationship. I could actually hear the wheels spinning in that crazy winemaking head of yours."

She felt a blush rise up her cheeks, giving her away. There was no use trying to deny it. Adam had heard her hypothesizing more than once about the similarities between love and wine. "What if I was? Wine is romantic after all. More than I can say for you. Laughing at me while we're…we're…" she sputtered to an end, jumped up, and stalked off to the kitchen.

"I'm sorry," Adam called, laughter still edging his voice. He followed her and tried to put his arms around her again, but she shrugged him off.

"I'm tired," she said, which was true now that her hormones had lost that loving feeling. "I think we should just call it a night."

"I didn't mean to hurt your feelings, babe. I actually think it's pretty cool how the craft of winemaking is so much a part of you that you even process situations accordingly. That's how I am about my music. " He regarded her crossed arms pose with a crooked smile. "Would it make you feel better if I told you I was singing *Jungle Love* in my head while I was kissing you?"

She laughed and shook her head, unable to stay miffed at him for long.

He started playing an air guitar and singing, "Jungle love, it's driving me mad. It's making me crazy, crazy…"

Rambo had been asleep on his bed in the corner of the kitchen, but their intrusion had not gone unnoticed. He got up, obviously indignant, stretched, and coolly stalked off to the den where it was quieter.

Margaret put a finger to her lips. "Shhh! Now look what you've done. You've woken up the cat. Next, Davy will be down here singing along."

"He could use the practice if he's going to be a winemaking musician someday."

Davy's newest career path was to combine the best of both worlds. He loved winemaking and had already learned a lot from both her and Billie, but since he'd heard Adam play on stage, he thought that would be an awesome choice as well. Thankfully, he still had a good eight years to dream before the specter of college entered his world.

She glanced at the clock on the wall.

Adam followed her gaze and grimaced. "All right," he said, "I'm leaving." He gave her a quick kiss and headed for the front door. "But don't think I won't be back to try again. And next time, Jungle love may just rock your winemaking world," he teased.

"I'm counting on it." Smiling, she closed the door softly and turned the deadbolt.

She parted the drapes and watched him through the front window. He waved before climbing in his car. She waved back, and then pulled the drapes closed and shut off the lights. As she climbed the stairs to her room she remembered her appointment with Edoardo Salvatore the next day and a sense of doom temporarily overshadowed the thrill of being in love.

CHAPTER FIVE

Despite the bright noon sun outside, the cellar was dark and quiet, and just what she needed to be able to think. Billie moved across the room to the work counter where she'd first learned about winemaking from her uncle. She reached beneath to the racks of dusty bottles and let her fingers brush past each one like a child walking along a picket fence.

Dr. Berger had warned her back in the early days of her therapy that if she wanted to banish the bad memories of the cellar and reestablish the joy that was lost, she would have to return to the scene of the crime day after day and make new memories. Sweet memories. Memories that far outweighed the bad. And she'd done just that. She'd brought Davy here and taught him how to stomp grapes and mix wine and all the things her uncle had taught her. They'd laughed and talked and teased and slowly but surely the cellar was redeemed.

The room was much different than it was when she'd first returned to the winery. The old desk and antiquated machines were gone now and the crates had all been sorted through, their contents given away or disposed of. Billie had purchased a new desk, all metal and glass, no drawers or secrets anywhere. Her keyboard and mouse sat on top for when she brought her laptop down to work. She also had a comfortable reclining chair where she sat sometimes to read wine industry magazines or just to rest her eyes.

Davy insisted he needed a beanbag chair for when he dropped in to chat for a while, so they'd shopped for just the right one. It was black and white like a checkerboard, and when he brought Rambo with him, the cat seemed to blend right in.

Out of respect for her uncle, she'd hung one of Jack's paintings on the wall behind the desk, but was glad her back was mostly to it. She didn't understand why a man with so much talent painted the way he did. Couldn't he have whipped up a nice landscape of the vineyard or something?

She sat now in her comfy over-stuffed chair and leaned her head back. Track lighting had been installed above the work area so that the naked bulb that once graced the middle of the ceiling was no longer needed. A reading lamp stood beside her chair but she left it off.

Other than financial woes that kept cropping up every quarter, the winery had become a place of comfort and peace for her. She no longer worried that she'd made the wrong decision moving to California and leaving her law practice behind. The sweet smell of ripening grapes, heavy on the vines, was like ambrosia to her heart.

Why then did it suddenly feel as though a black cloud had settled around her? After speaking with

Handel about the man at the winery and his implied threat, they'd called Officer Torn again. He reassured them that he would look into it. Whatever that meant.

Someone wanted her scared and hiding and she didn't know why. Handel spoke with his client on the phone but Mr. Kawasaki had no idea why she would be targeted. He found the idea ludicrous; told Handel that if someone had that kind of vendetta against him, they'd kill him in jail, not have his attorney's wife tormented.

Handel had tried to lighten the situation, to convince her that it was a fluke, but she could see he was worried. This morning he'd once again gone into his office to work, but this time he shut the door. She heard him on the phone, his voice abnormally tense and angry, and wondered who he was speaking with. Instead of confronting him, she left the house to come here.

So much for the messy junk drawer of their lives. Whoever was targeting her had already nixed that idea. She and Handel were holed up in separate places, trying to solve a mutual problem… apart.

"Hey, babe."

She raised her head; surprised she hadn't heard Handel come down the stairs. He was wearing exercise shorts and dripping sweat from head to toe. "You weren't out running, were you?" she asked, pushing up from the chair. "I thought we were going to go for a walk together. Later. The doctor has not signed off on you exercising hard yet."

"Don't worry, I ran out of steam real quick. I was sweating and exhausted after a hundred yards and headed back to the house."

"Serves you right, going without me."

"You're a marked woman. I don't want to get hit by a stray bullet," he teased.

"That's not funny, because if someone shoots at me, you're supposed to jump in front of the bullet."

He pushed damp hair off his forehead and wiped his hands on his shorts. "That would be a secret service agent – or Superman – of which I'm neither."

"Then remind me… why did I marry you?" she asked, standing close enough to feel the heat radiating off his bare chest.

The left side of his mouth lifted in a sexy grin. "Dare I say, love? Or were you thinking of something a little more carnal?" he asked, pulling her against his sweaty chest and covering her mouth with his own.

Not that she didn't enjoy a little love in the afternoon and all, but she had a strong suspicion she was being manipulated. She reluctantly pulled back and looked him in the eye. "I thought we agreed to share everything from now on. What aren't you telling me? It must be bad or you wouldn't have rushed down here all sweaty before you took a shower."

His eyes narrowed but he definitely looked guilty of something. "Can't a guy visit his wife without…?"

"No. He can't. Because his wife knows him better than that. Handy, you're scaring me. What is going on?"

He reached out and brushed his fingertips along her cheek in a soft caress, his lips pulled into a thin line to keep his emotions in check. "Manny called. He said he heard through one of his contacts that someone took a contract out on you," he said, blinking rapidly.

"What? Why? That's crazy." She shook her head trying to comprehend the incomprehensible. "Who... wha...it doesn't make sense," she stammered.

"I know. I know." He pulled her back into his arms and held her tight. The only place in the world she always felt safe.

Until now.

••••

Margaret drove up to Antonio's and parked outside the restaurant's back door. She checked her watch. It was still twenty minutes before her scheduled meeting with Mr. Salvatore. If he were as punctual as she imagined him to be, he would probably show up a bit early. Other than employee cars parked in back, there were no other vehicles in sight, so she was pretty certain he wasn't here yet.

Her little red pickup made a funny squealing sound when she stopped. She hoped it wasn't the brakes again. She'd just had new brake pads installed last year. Handel told her she drove too fast and used her brakes too liberally, but the traffic was always so terrible and she was always in a hurry. Of course she rode the brakes half the time.

She beeped the horn before she got out of the cab. Carl was expecting her but he always liked her to alert them when she arrived so he could send someone out right away to carry the wine in for her. She climbed out, flipped the tailgate down and started to scoot the cases closer to the edge when she heard the door open.

"Hey, hold on, Miss Parker. I got'em." A skinny young man with stringy blonde hair hurried over and picked up the first case. He grinned at her and shook his head. "You know Carl wants me to carry these. Are you trying to take my job?"

She threw her hands up in surrender. "I wouldn't dream of it," she said with feigned seriousness. "Put a mediocre busboy out of work? No way!"

"Hey!" he said, turning at the door, his eyes narrowed. "Mediocre? I'm at least a half step above that. I'd say my talents are adequate."

"You're right. Sorry to offend you, Dirk." She held the door open for him. "Your carrying technique is also truly amazing."

At the sound of their voices, Carl looked up from the table where he was going over his accounts. "Ciao Bella!" he called from across the kitchen. He scooted his chair back and came over to kiss her cheek. "I never see your beautiful face these days unless you're delivering wine. I guess we should order more often."

Dirk set the case down and went off to retrieve the other one from the pickup.

"I'd love to sell you more wine, but my other customers might get jealous." She looked around the kitchen. Carl's cooks were already busy whipping up culinary Italian masterpieces. The air was heady with onion and garlic, basil and olive oil. She took a deep breath and released it. "Smells delicious! Coming here always makes me hungry," she said.

"What do you want? Let me fix you something," he offered, already moving toward the cutting board.

She put a hand on his arm. "Carl. Have you heard from your uncle?" she asked when he turned around.

"Uncle Salvatore?"

"He called me last night," she began.

"What?" Carl picked up the chopping knife and started slicing a Portobello mushroom. "Why? He has never contacted you before, right?"

She shook her head. "He wanted to meet, so I told him here at two o'clock. I hope that's alright."

He scraped the mushroom into a heated skillet. "He's coming here? Now?" he glanced at the clock on the wall above the stoves. "I didn't even know he was in the country."

"I thought it would be better to meet him somewhere semi-private... but with backup." She gave him a tight smile. "I'm sorry if you feel like you're being thrust in the middle, but I didn't know what else to do."

"It's fine. I know my uncle can be intimidating." He stirred the mushrooms and turned the heat down. "Juan, finish the sauce!" he yelled across the room at a Mexican man with a long Fu Manchu mustache. He was busy making egg noodles. He looked up from his work and nodded.

Carl took her arm and led her to the dining room. "The only way to ensure a pleasant meeting with my uncle is to satisfy his palate. The best food and wine available and a beautiful woman as his dinner companion. I'll supply the food and wine." He motioned toward a corner table, already set and ready for guests. "Sit. Try to look relaxed and confident. He's like a Piranha, always looking for weakness. Don't let him consume you."

If he was trying to instill confidence in her, it wasn't working. Fear, on the other hand... "Carl," she started, but he was already hurrying back through the swinging door into the kitchen. She sighed and tried to relax, shaking her arms loosely at her sides. "You will not be consumed," she muttered softly.

"Miss Parker," Dirk said, coming through the door, the pickup key in his outstretched hand. "You left your truck running."

"Oh, thanks. What would I do without you?" She took the key and flashed him a smile.

His face flushed red at her simple flattery. He scratched at his chin covered with thin boyish beard fuzz. "I noticed your power steering belt is going bad. It was squealing, so I looked under the hood. You should get that replaced soon."

"A belt? I thought it was the brakes. Well, just one more thing to worry about."

"I can do it for you if you want," he offered, tucking his hands in the back pockets of his jeans. "I work on my car all the time."

"That's really nice of you, but I can't ask you to do that. I'll take it to a garage when I have time." She sat down at the table and folded her hands in her lap.

"It's no problem. Really." He backed away toward the door. "You have a nice lunch, Miss Parker."

"Thanks Dirk."

She closed her eyes and tried to feel relaxed and confident as Carl had instructed, but at the sound of an unfamiliar voice booming behind the closed kitchen door she jumped. Her eyes flew open as a handsome, distinguished looking man pushed through the doors following Carl into the dining room.

Edoardo Salvatore wore a charcoal suit with a

white shirt and slate blue tie. He was taller than his son, and broader through the shoulders. He must have been nearing sixty, but his hair was still dark and thick with just a sprinkling of grey. Of course that could have been the work of a talented hairdresser.

His eyes held hers as he approached, his gaze icy cold. But at Carl's introduction, he took her hand and was all suave charm and kind words. She thought perhaps it was those pale blue eyes beneath dark lashes that made her think of ice. Agosto's eyes had been so dark they were almost black. He must have taken after his mother in that regard.

"Ms. Parker," he said, holding her hand a bit longer than necessary. "My son always did attract the most beautiful women."

Carl clasped his uncle's shoulder. "Please have a seat, Uncle. I'll bring a bottle of wine." He gave Margaret a reassuring smile and hurried off.

Edoardo Salvatore took the chair across from her, straightening his jacket as he did. "So, we finally meet," he said, his eyes resting somewhere south of her chin for long seconds making her decidedly uncomfortable. "Agosto should have brought you home to Italia years ago. He always was a playboy, unwilling to compromise his enjoyment for a wife and children. He refused to see the bigger picture." He sighed and lifted his shoulders in an expressive shrug. "Without heirs, we work for nothing. Sons are the future. They are our legacy."

Margaret thought about all the hurtful things Agosto had said before he deserted her and his unborn son all those years ago. He was more than just a playboy; he was a cruel, heartless bastard. He thought the world revolved around his needs and everyone should fall into line and enjoy being used. They certainly shouldn't expect anything in return. She squeezed her hands together nervously in her lap, fearful of saying something to offend this man, but not willing to let him roll right over her and Davy like a freight train. As the saying goes, the apple never falls far from the tree.

"Mr. Salvatore, I hope you won't consider me rude, but as a single mother I do have responsibilities and a full-time job. May I be direct? What is it that you want?"

He chuckled low in his throat. The sound reminded her of a cartoon tiger getting ready to pounce. "What do I want? That is a good question and certainly direct."

Carl took that moment to bring the wine. A 2011 bottle of Chardonnay from Margaret's cellar. He poured a bit for his uncle to taste. "How's this?" he asked, eagerly awaiting a show of appreciation.

Edoardo swirled the wine, his lips pursed seductively as he watched the legs cling to the glass. He breathed in the bouquet and sipped. His brows lifted in a pleasantly surprised expression. "Hmm. I don't recognize the label and it's not from Italia but..." He took another sip and nodded.

Carl filled Margaret's glass and then his uncle's. His lips curved up happily. "I was confident you would appreciate this fine wine. It's made by a genius local winemaker with whom I have a special purchasing agreement."

Margaret shot Carl a warning look.

Edoardo drained the glass and set it down. "Full-bodied, well-balanced, and vivacious," he said, his gaze on Margaret.

His flirtatious manner was creeping her out. Even Carl seemed to find it disturbing. He tried to divert his uncle's attention. "I hope you're hungry. I have fresh Tortellini and Zucchini soup or Wild Mushroom and Red Wine Risotto. What is your pleasure?"

Margaret hadn't planned on staying long enough to eat, but the man had yet to discuss what he came here for. She smiled up at Carl. "A bowl of your soup would be wonderful, thank you."

"The risotto for me," Edoardo said, his eyes never leaving her face.

Carl hesitated as though unsure whether to leave them alone together. A clatter of pots and pans from the kitchen, followed by cursing, decided the issue. "*Scusi*," he said and disappeared through the swinging doors again.

Angry voices rose and fell behind the doors until the disagreement had been settled and then only a low rumble could be heard now and then.

"Where were we?" Edoardo took another sip of wine and licked his lips.

"You were going to tell me what brought you here. I know you said you wanted to meet Davy, but why now?"

"Why now?" he shrugged. "Because there is no better time than the present to take care of the mistakes of the past. My son was taken from me. A grandson would be balm to my soul."

A tiny flicker of guilt made her stomach flip-flop. After Agosto was killed, she had the chance to reach out to his family, Carl even offered to be the liaison, but she chose to burn those bridges forever. She decided to be truthful. "Agosto said I was a diversion, nothing more. He wanted me to abort my son. Said that we weren't good enough for his family tree. That you wouldn't accept me or Davy. He had no intention of acknowledging us. How did you..."

"Agosto never told me that he fathered a child, if that's what you're asking. Not that I didn't know. My sister," he tipped his chin toward the kitchen, "Carl's mother, informed me of the situation not long after Agosto returned to Italia."

"Yet for ten years you never asked to see Davy."

"No. Because it was Agosto's private business. He was young, sowing a few wild oats as you Americans like to say, and he had many years left to sire the right heir."

The right heir. The words sparked immediate outrage. "How dare you?" She rose from the table, throwing her napkin aside. "Your arrogance knows no bounds. Do you truly believe I would allow my son to be in your company for even five minutes? You obviously destroyed any goodness that Agosto may have had as a boy and turned him into a conniving, self-centered human being. You will not do the same to my son." She strode toward the kitchen and nearly collided with Carl entering with their entrees on a platter. She dodged him and pushed through the door, leaving him staring after her.

"Miss Parker!" Dirk called from across the kitchen where he was washing dishes. "I can change that belt for you anytime. Just give me a call!"

She threw open the back door of the restaurant without responding and let it slam behind her. Anger rose up until she thought she would scream. The sun beat down upon the pavement and glared off the windshield of the shiny, new, black Jaguar parked in the middle of the driving lane, directly in her path. Unbelievable! Did the man expect a valet to show up and park his car?

She hurried past, climbed into her pickup and turned the ignition. A faint squeal accompanied the sound of the engine. "Arrogant, son of a..." she muttered and tore out of the parking lot, belatedly seeing Carl in the rearview mirror trying to wave her down. She thought about turning around and going back, after all Carl was a family friend, but her anger drove her on.

••••

Adam pulled into the school parking lot to pick Davy up from soccer camp. Boys and girls wandered all over the place, some with blue shorts and others with red. All wore jerseys that said *Shin Kickers* across the front and the kid's name printed on the back. Parents waited in hot cars with windows rolled down or stood outside talking with other parents while their kids got their gear together.

He saw Davy coming down the hill from the field behind the school. His blonde hair was so pale from hours in the sun that it looked almost white. A girl, about four inches taller and as dark as he was light, walked beside him. They were laughing and reenacting some kind of silly play they'd made in the game. The girl gave Davy a high five when they neared the parking lot and took off at a trot toward a mini van parked farther down the line of cars.

Adam opened the door and waved. Davy wasn't expecting him and was probably looking for his mom's pickup. He usually drove the BMW that Uncle Jack left to Billie when he died. She still had the

Mazda she brought from Minnesota and preferred to run around in that, but since Handel's wreck Adam figured they needed the second car. So, he'd gone car shopping. As fate would have it, he didn't find what he was looking for at a dealer, but rather parked out front of the club last night with a FOR SALE sign in the side window. The perfect vehicle.

"Adam!" Davy ran toward him, his eyes huge with excitement. "I don't believe it! You bought a Vette?" He yanked open the passenger door and jumped in, dumping his duffel bag on the floor. "Wow! Wait till Mom sees this. She'll freak out." He slammed the door closed, grinning like he'd won the lottery.

"Why would she freak out? Doesn't she like Corvettes," Adam asked, turning the key in the ignition. Had he made a terrible mistake? He wanted Margaret to know that he respected her opinion. If she really hated it...

Davy laughed, touching everything on the dash like he was taking a ride in a helicopter for the first time. "No, she doesn't hate them. She *loves* Vettes! Especially old ones like this. Uncle Handel had an old Shark when he was in college but he couldn't afford to keep it. She told me she was pretty mad at him when he sold it cause she thought she'd get it when he bought a new car."

Adam grinned. "Cool. A girl who appreciates the classics."

He pulled out onto the street and accelerated, shifting into second. The purr of the engine was music to his ears. Davy was too busy checking out every nook and cranny to ask why his mom hadn't picked him up.

"So who's the girl?" Adam asked, casual as a tornado touchdown in Oklahoma. But Davy didn't seem to notice.

He swiped his hand over the black and red leather seat. "What girl?" he asked, totally zoning on what was at hand. "This is awesome. Will you let me drive it when I'm old enough?"

Adam laughed. "You bet. In fact, when you get your permit, I'll teach you to drive this baby myself."

"Cool!"

When they pulled into the Parker driveway, Adam saw that Margaret had beat him home. Her pickup was parked outside in front of the garage. He wondered how the meeting with Salvatore went, but he knew she wouldn't want to discuss it in front of Davy, so he put it on the back burner of his mind to ask about later.

Davy reluctantly climbed out of the car, slowly lifting his bag after him. "Can you drive me to soccer camp tomorrow morning too?" he asked.

"I don't know. Have to ask your mom."

"Can't *you*?" He wistfully shut the door and followed Adam toward the front porch. "She might not understand."

Adam turned around. "Understand what?" he asked, pushing his sunglasses up on top his head.

Davy shrugged and flashed a guilty looking smile. "I want Heidi to see me pull up in the Vette."

"Heidi?" Adam waggled his brows up and down. "So this is about that girl I saw you with. I knew it." He poked Davy playfully in the chest and then bumped his finger under his chin. "You got a girlfriend!"

"Sshhh! Not so loud. She might hear," he

warned, looking up at the house.

"Why don't you want your mom to know? Is this girl wanted by the FBI or something?"

"No," Davy shook his head, serious as a Cadillac salesman. "She doesn't have a record or nothin'. Mom just gets so worried about me all the time. She says I'm her first love. I don't want her to feel bad if I like Heidi too."

Adam put his arm around Davy's shoulders. "Come on. Your mom is pretty understanding. I think you can trust her not to get too upset about another woman in your life." He turned Davy around so they both faced the car. "And once we show her this baby…" he began.

"Oh my God!" Margaret flew out the front door and down the steps. "You didn't! A 1981 Shark!" She hesitated the briefest of seconds, kissed Adam on the mouth, patted Davy on the cheek and ran to fondle the blue muscle car.

Adam watched her slip behind the wheel like she was taking up residence. To think he was worried she wouldn't like it. Now he worried he might never get her out of it.

He looked down at Davy. "I think she may want a ride to soccer camp tomorrow too."

••••

"Why didn't you tell me you were coming to America?" Carl asked, sitting across from his uncle. After Margaret ran out the back, Edoardo insisted he sit and catch up as though nothing noteworthy had just happened. Carl pushed the bowl of tortellini soup aside and placed his crossed arms on the tabletop. "It would have been nice to be forewarned. I could have prepared something special," he said, tipping his chin toward the plate of risotto his uncle was picking over.

Edoardo gulped the rest of the wine in his glass and reached for the bottle. He'd already had two glasses since Carl sat down with him and it didn't look as though he planned on slowing down. "If I called, it wouldn't have been a surprise. And this is perfect. I'm just not very hungry." He lifted his glass. "Di famiglial!"

"To family," Carl echoed. "It is good to see you, Uncle. Ever since Antonio went home to Tuscany last year, I admit I've been a little lonely for family."

"You should marry and have sons. Who is going to run this place when you are old?"

The question was rhetorical and Carl just shrugged.

Edoardo set his glass down and sat back in his chair with a contented sigh. "Marriage doesn't mean you can't do a little tasting on the side." He hooked a thumb over his shoulder toward the kitchen door. "Like with that one. Don't tell me you haven't bedded her. Life is too short not to take what you want."

"Uncle, please don't speak about Margaret that way. She is my friend. Nothing more." Not that he wasn't attracted to her. He was. So were Dirk, Juan, and his entire kitchen crew. Maybe even Abby. He wasn't quite sure about her. But nonetheless, Margaret was off limits. She was Handel's sister and as such, his family.

"Really? Well then you won't mind if I —" he broke off and laughed at the look on Carl's face. "You do want her for yourself."

"No. Not like that." He shook his head in disgust. It was never good when his uncle let the wine speak for him. He'd already drunk one bottle and was starting on another. "What did you say to make her so angry?" he asked, suspicious. He hoped his uncle hadn't propositioned her like a common call girl. Margaret would probably forgive him in time, but she might just withhold her wine orders in retribution. He couldn't afford to lose her friendship or her product.

Edoardo unbuttoned his jacket and laced his fingers over his flat stomach, a look of concern drawing his brows together. "I only asked to meet my grandson. She is a volatile woman. Seems a bit unstable to me. Perhaps she's bi-polar. Are you sure that the boy is safe living with her?"

"Of course," Carl said. "She's very protective, that's all. Like a mother lion." He hesitated, unsure whether he was overstepping his bounds. His uncle, as head of the family, had always insisted on total capitulation to his wishes. Which was the main reason Agosto had come to America all those years ago – to get away from his father. Finally he asked, "Why did you decide to come and meet Davy after all this time?"

Edoardo threw up his hands in disgust. "Why does everyone ask me *why*?" he bellowed. "He's my grandson for god's sake! Isn't that self-explanatory? I have every right to know my own flesh and blood!" He jerked out of his chair, threw his napkin over his plate and stalked away toward the restroom.

Carl leaned back in his chair and groaned. "Mama Mia."

CHAPTER SIX

Billie insisted on driving Handel to San Francisco to meet with Manny. She tried to talk him out of going at all, told him to ask Manny to come to the winery for a conference, but he just laughed.

"You want me to pay that guy fifty bucks an hour to drive out to the most beautiful vineyard in Napa?" He put his arms around her and kissed the top of her head. She was still standing in her underwear, deciding what to wear and he was already fully dressed. "He should pay us for that enjoyment," he teased and smacked her butt when he released her.

"That may be true, but you should be taking it easy. The doctors haven't even signed off on you driving alone yet."

He quirked an eyebrow. "I didn't know I needed their permission."

"Well, you aren't going to be in top form for trial next week if you don't rest," she sputtered, unable to think of anything else that would cause him to worry.

"I'll rest after the trial. I promise."

"Then I'm going with you."

Handel sighed and picked up his wallet where he'd left it on the bedside table the night before. He slid it into his inside suit jacket pocket and crossed the room to get his pain medication from the bathroom. "I don't think that's a very good idea. Until we know more, you should stay inside."

She crossed her arms and glared at him. "I'll stay inside if you stay with me, otherwise I'm going."

"I never thought I'd marry a woman who brings murder out in people – not once, but twice," Handel said, his voice droll, "but I'm beginning to see it from their side of things."

Billie knew he was trying to make her angry so she would stay home. He had another think coming. She quickly pulled a pink t-shirt over her bra and snatched on a pair of skinny jeans, all while he watched from the other side of the room.

She stepped past him into the bathroom. "Don't you dare leave without me," she warned, pointing her hairbrush. "I'll be ready in five minutes."

"That's never happened before."

"And it may never happen again."

The drive to the city was quiet. Handel brought along his laptop and was busy typing notes while she drove. They passed vineyards bearing fruit much farther along than should be in July. With the weird weather they'd had this year – early rains followed by months of warm, dry days – the grapes were ripening at an alarming speed. Harvest would be early this year and they had so much to do at Fredrickson's before crush.

Billie glanced at her husband. "I hope this trial

is over quickly, so we can get away together," she
said. "How do you feel about the Bahamas?"

He looked up, a pleased smile turning up the
corners of his mouth. "You in a bikini twenty-four
hours a day? I'd say I feel pretty good about it."

"Who says I'll be in a bikini?"

"Even better."

The drive took a little over two hours, but they
finally pulled into the parking lot of a tacky looking
strip mall. A pizza joint, nail salon, and coffee shop
took up most of the building, but on the far end was
an office with the sign, **Alvarez Investigations**. A
low riding car drove past filled with Hispanic
teenagers, blaring music that seemed to consist of
thumping bass and nothing more. Sitting on the
sidewalk against the building, directly in front of
Manny's office, was a homeless man. Clothed in
layers of shirts and pants, despite the warm afternoon
temperature, he clutched a bag of belongings to his
side and seemed to be dozing in the shade of the
overhang.

Billie looked tentatively around. "Are you sure
this is a good idea? Couldn't we meet him at a
restaurant or something?"

"We're already here now." He slipped his
laptop in his shoulder bag and opened the door. "It'll
be fine. Come on."

She followed, clicking her lock button twice for
good measure. The man on the sidewalk didn't move
or acknowledge their presence. He was definitely
asleep. She could hear him snoring. Handel held open
the door and they entered a tiny reception area with
three molded plastic chairs and a low table covered in
outdated magazines. A stand in the corner of the

room held a coffee pot and cups. The pot was still half full; the contents black as sludge. The stench of burned coffee permeated the air.

The back office door stood open and they could see Manny sitting at his desk talking on a cell phone. He ended the call, jumped up and hurried out to greet them. "Hola!" He glanced from Handel to Billie, a flicker of concern in his eyes. "I didn't expect to see you, Ms. Parker," he said. He waved a hand toward the chairs. "Have a seat. Would you like some coffee?"

Billie glanced at the pot and shook her head. "No thanks."

Handel set his bag down on the table and took the chair next to Billie. "My wife thinks I'm still a helpless invalid. She insisted on coming along to take care of me," he explained, flashing her a teasing grin, "even if it puts her own life in jeopardy."

"You told her what we discussed," Manny asked, glancing at Billie.

"I know someone was paid to kill me, if that's what you're referring to," she said, sitting back in the chair and crossing her legs. "I also know that if they had really wanted to kill me, I would be dead by now."

His eyes narrowed. "What makes you think so?"

"They missed, but then one of them came back on Saturday and spoke with me directly."

"What?" he looked totally baffled.

"Exactly. What kind of paid killers want to be identified? These guys may have tried to terrorize me, I'm not so sure they actually tried to kill me," she said. She'd been trying to come up with a logical scenario, but it made absolutely no sense.

Through the front window she saw two young men approach her Mazda. She stood up to get a better look. One of them had a crowbar in his hand. She was sure of it. She moved toward the door, but Manny got there first.

He put up his hand to ward her off. "You should have parked in my two designated spots. They know not to bother my clients." He opened the door and shouted, "Angel! No es que uno de ellos."

Billie glanced at Handel. He gave her a crooked smile and shrugged.

"Sorry about that," Manny said, rejoining them. "Young men need an occupation."

"Breaking into cars isn't their occupation?"

"It has been lately. They both lost their jobs at the cannery. Now they're a breath away from joining up with the Maras. I try to talk sense to them but they don't listen so good." He shook his head. "The gang is seductive to young men. It promises everything they long for. Family. Women. Violence. It's a hard drug to fight against. Believe me, I know."

Billie found her eyes straying to the tattoos on Manny's neck and arms. His green t-shirt did little to hide the fact that he was covered in ink. Much like the young man at the winery the other day – covered in skulls, barbed wire, and gang signs – he was a walking advertisement for death and violence without saying a word. "Did you get all those while you were in the gang?" she asked.

He held out his arms. "Sí. Except for this one." He pointed at a set of numbers. "It used to say, MS-13, but when I left the gang I had it changed." He rubbed his fingers lightly over the new numbers, 08-

18. "My mother's birthday. She pleaded with God every day that I would leave the Maras."

"She must be very proud of how you've turned your life around," Billie said.

"Sadly, she never saw the answer to her prayers. She died of a stroke ten months too soon."

"I'm sorry."

He pressed his lips firmly together and nodded. "We should get down to business."

"So the person who tipped you off about the hit on Billie is a member of the Maras," Handel began, pulling out his laptop. He'd left it on, so he just started typing.

Manny put up his hand. "Sorry, that's off the record. Loyalty is the glue that holds these guys together. They'll kill to prove it. Without a second thought. I'd rather not be the guy they take out next."

"Okay, but how do you know this information is accurate?"

"Besides the fact that your wife was shot at? I trust him. We've exchanged favors before."

"What did you give him?" Billie asked, leaning an elbow on the arm of the plastic chair.

He ignored her question and got up to pour himself a cup of black ooze. He took a sip and cleared his throat. "You have an enemy who wants you dead. Let's concentrate on that reality."

"What can we do?" Handel asked, closing the lid on his computer. "Can you talk to them? Get them to call it off?"

"It's not that simple." Manny set his cup down on the cover of a People magazine and crossed his arms over his chest. "If members of the Maras were paid to take out your wife, then they won't stop until [ff

the job is *terminado*."

"That's comforting," Billie murmured. "At least your people have a great work ethic."

"My people?"

"Excuse my wife," Handel said by way of apology, putting a hand on her arm. "She's a bit stressed, as you can imagine."

"I don't have to imagine. I've had people gunning for me before too. It's not a pleasant feeling." He took a slip of paper out of his pocket and slid it across the table. "I wrote his number down before you came in. He comes highly recommended."

"Thanks." Handel took the paper and slipped it into the side pocket of his bag.

"Whose number?" Billie asked, feeling like she was being left out of something important.

Handel shot her a quick smile. "Nothing for you to worry about. Just trial stuff."

"Let me get copies of the files you wanted." Manny got up and went into his office. They could hear him opening and shutting drawers.

There was something not right here, but Billie couldn't put her finger on it. She watched Manny come back in with a file folder in hand. "I finally talked with the guy who was working at the gas station when Sloane stopped that night. He was out of the country visiting family in Pakistan. His statement is in here with my other reports."

"And your extravagant bill, no doubt." Handel took the file and shook Manny's hand. "Appreciate your hard work. I'll look through all this tonight and get back to you."

"No problem. Let me know if you need any follow up."

Back in the car, Billie turned to face Handel, one arm along the back of the seat. "Are you hiding something from me again?" she asked, trying to read his mind and getting nothing.

"How could I hide something from you? You've been here the whole time."

She shook her head. "How do moms do this? I'm coming up empty."

"What are you talking about now?" He was clearly confused. At least she could decipher that much.

She expelled a frustrated breath, turned the key in the ignition, and pulled out of the parking lot. "Never mind. I'll ask my mother next time I speak with her."

••••

Carl unlocked the back door of the restaurant and entered the unlit kitchen. He flipped the switch and fluorescent bulbs blinked on, reflecting off stainless steel appliances and countertops. He was running a little late this morning. Had nearly missed catching the seafood guy in the parking lot ready to drive off with his order of lobsters. Louie had scowled from the cab of his refrigerated truck before climbing down and pulling out the box from the back.

"You're lucky I was still here," he grouched, and shoved the box at him. "I got other restaurants to deliver to, ya know."

Carl set the box of fresh lobsters on the counter now and looked around. He liked arriving before everyone else when the kitchen was still immaculate from a thorough cleaning the night before, and it was so quiet he could hear the tick of the clock and the growl of his own stomach.

He opened the refrigerator and pulled out a plate of leftover spaghetti. Cold pasta was often his breakfast of choice. It was always available and he didn't have to go out for it. He sat down at the table to eat and look over his inventory books. He still hadn't put everything on the computer. Writing things out in neat rows with a #2 pencil just felt right.

He was glad his uncle hadn't asked to stay with him while he was in town. That would have been a nightmare. They were both comfortable with the lives they'd built. He led a simple life that was not conducive to Edoardo's natural expectations. Bellhops, maids, and a professional masseuse were not in Carl's household budget.

Edoardo Salvatore didn't go out of his way to flaunt his wealth as his son once had, buying extravagant items just to impress people. He bought them to please himself. He was rich and that was a fact. As with many wealthy individuals, he chose to believe, despite his disdain for anyone beneath them, that it was his magnetic personality that attracted others to him.

He had booked the largest suite at Harvest House, a small luxury hotel that catered to every whim of the rich and privileged. Carl imagined by this time of day he was soaking in a hot tub and having a manicure while taking care of overseas business online. Even while relaxing, his uncle was always busy working. No wonder he'd become one of the wealthiest men in Italy.

Carl's restaurant business wouldn't have gotten off the ground if it weren't for Uncle Salvatore. He owed him much. When he couldn't afford to pay for his last year of college, when he'd needed a loan for the restaurant, when he'd needed help getting specialty foods and wine brought in from Italy...Uncle Salvatore had been there paying the bills, loaning the funds, smoothing the way. That's why he couldn't bring himself to discount everything he said about Margaret and Handel the evening before when they'd met again for dinner.

"I know you consider this *Avvocato*, to be family. Like a brother." Edoardo set down his forkful of linguini and shook his head. "Family is blood. You have a brother. Antonio. I'm telling you this because I think you are trusting the wrong people. Your mother tells me that last year when Antonio wanted to buy out of the business and dissolve the partnership that you asked this Mr. Parker to help you and he turned you down. What kind of brother turns his back on family when they need help? Eh?" He lifted his wine glass and drained it in one gulp.

"He didn't turn me down exactly," Carl argued halfheartedly. He'd been a little miffed when Handel pushed him off onto a firm that specialized in partnership law. Sure, he was a criminal attorney, but he could have taken care of it if he'd wanted to. "He was friends with both of us, so filing the paperwork would have pushed the envelope of good ethics. He didn't want to be accused of favoritism," he said, repeating the gist of what Handel had explained to them.

Edoardo poured his glass full again and tipped the bottle toward Carl.

He covered the rim of his glass and shook his head.

"Favoritism," his uncle scoffed. "Sounds like a

weak excuse to me."

"He's a good man, Uncle," he said, feeling as though he should take up Handel's side of things. "It takes a lot of time to get a law practice up and running as he has. He's a hard worker. I think you would like him."

"Is that so?" Edoardo raised his brows, clearly amused.

"Yes, that's so. In fact, he was in a terrible car accident recently and just got out of the hospital. Did that stop him? No. According to Margaret, he's already busy working on the murder trial again." He threw up his hands. "It's a huge media spectacle. On the news every night. And someone is so upset about Handel defending this Kawasaki guy that they actually shot at Billie through their front window the other night."

"Really," his uncle said, his brow now knit with concern. "I certainly hope they find the culprits."

"Me too." Carl nodded, getting back on track. "We do see less of one another since he got married, which is only natural. But Handel would do anything for me, as I would for him."

"And what of his sister? This Margaret. She is, after all, the reason Agosto was murdered. He came here to meet his son and she obstructed him at every turn. Those two come from bad genes. I read the news stories about their father. A *pervertire* on the run from the law. They still have not located him. Can you really say with assurance that my grandson is safe in that family?

"Uncle…" he said, uncomfortable with the direction the conversation was flowing.

Edoardo waved off his unspoken words. "That

kind of sickness is often repeated in the next generation. I've seen it before. I won't allow my grandson to suffer needlessly when I could keep him from it."

"What are you saying?" Carl asked, his mouth going dry. His uncle had the power and means to pull off a court-approved custody reversal or a child abduction if he so wished. Edoardo's plan – if he indeed had one – to take Davy out of the country, would not be thwarted as easily as Agosto's had been.

"I'm saying that there may be a time when you need to choose."

Edoardo sat back in his chair and folded his arms over his chest, his gaze piercing Carl's heart like a laser. He knew his uncle grieved the loss of his only son, and was desperate to be a part of his grandson's life now, but could he really be asking him to choose between his friends and his family?

Loyalty to family meant everything to men like his uncle. His ancestors had fought and died generation after generation for nothing more than a crumbling castle and a family crest. Edoardo would fight for much more. Flesh and blood. An heir to continue the family line and take up the reins of his empire when the time came that he could no longer control things.

Carl often thought that if he'd just given Agosto the benefit of the doubt, showed him that he was on his side, that he understood and supported his longing to know his son, everything would have turned out differently. Maybe all he needed was family to come alongside and turn him away from the bad choices he made. Margaret may have listened if he'd stepped forward and pleaded Agosto's case. Instead, she and Handel refused to consider Agosto's side at all, and he'd stayed out of it, not wanting to anger his friends.

He hadn't said it in so many words last night, but Carl was afraid that his uncle expected him to prove his loyalty by helping him wrest Davy from his own mother. In all good conscience, how could he do such a thing?

Carl released a pent-up breath and rose from the table. Davy was a good kid, smart and athletic for his age. He was definitely a Salvatore. But he was also as much a part of the winery and vineyard as one of those seventy-year-old vines his mom made her best wine from. He opened the cupboard and took out the bottle of DiSaronno he kept there, plunked in ice and poured himself a shot. The sweet, almond flavored liqueur blazed a trail of warmth to his belly. He didn't normally drink hard liquor but the situation was making him decidedly uncomfortable.

He heard a car pull up outside, a radio blaring country music. Dirk was here. Time to pull himself together. He placed the bottle in the cupboard and sat down at the table to finish going over his inventory. Thoughts of family ties and friendships on the brink would have to wait until after restaurant hours.

CHAPTER SEVEN

The moon was no more than a sliver, but it glowed bright against a midnight blue sky. The air was cool and dry with the sweet, seductive scent of ripening wine berries. Handel laced his fingers with Billie's and pulled her close where they stood in the middle of the south vineyard listening to the neighbor's Great Dane bark in the distance.

"I'll never tire of this," he said, slipping his hands up her arms and over her shoulders, "or forget that this is where I fell in love with you."

Billie pressed her cheek against the soft cotton of his shirt and relaxed into his embrace. She murmured a wordless agreement and breathed him in, still unable to believe that he was alive and whole after seeing his wrecked Porsche that afternoon.

The familiar car so crushed and twisted, shattered glass sprinkled liberally over leather seats, had made her heart pound with dread just thinking of what he must have gone through. Handel insisted on emptying the glove box and prying open the trunk to look for personal items. After that he took pictures with his cell phone before he signed off on the insurance papers. The Porsche was the first big item he'd purchased when he started making money as an attorney and it obviously held sentimental value. She was just glad it was made from solid German engineering. If he'd been driving her little Mazda, as the insurance agent pointed out, Handel probably would have been crushed to death.

She pulled back and peered up into his shadowed face. "Do you think you were spared for a reason… other than the fact that God was probably tired of my constant pleading?"

He brushed his fingers lightly over her hair, his voice low and thoughtful. "My mom used to say, 'God allows everything for a reason. Being God, he doesn't necessarily have to let us in on it.' In spite of what she put up with – my father's drinking, abuse, and then her cancer – she wasn't bitter. Just matter-of-fact. Like she knew the end of the story would change everything."

"I believe there's a master plan too," she agreed. "One we can't see or comprehend from our viewpoint, but I have to believe God is working behind the scenes turning the pain and suffering of this world into something beautiful."

"I hope so. But let's not waste a minute of the second chance he's given us now."

"I wouldn't dream of it," she said, stretching up on tiptoe to kiss him. His lips soon moved from her mouth to her neck, his whiskers rough and scratchy on sensitive skin, quickening the anticipation. She pulled him closer still.

He suddenly lifted his head, kissed her lightly

on the lips and turned her firmly toward home. "Come on. That's quite enough moonlight for one night. I want you in bed, wife."

"Your wish is my command," she said, eager to please and be pleased.

Together they hurried down the rutted trail, stepping over rocks and uneven ground, their gaze fixed on the porch light glowing like a beacon in the night. The neighbor's dog had decided to rest his bark and save it for another day. The only sound was the scuffing of their shoes and the distant drone of a small plane flying overhead.

Light flashed from across the field, headlights bouncing crazily in Margaret's yard. They both stopped and looked. The high whine of an engine reached them as someone accelerated and then slammed their brakes. Were the same vandals at work in Margaret's yard now?

"What the –" Handel took off at a run, sprinting down the field.

"Handel!" Billie yelled after him, but he didn't slow. He kept right on going to the end of the row, then turned and ran toward the Parker field. His ribs were barely healed and he was going directly into danger. She whipped around and ran in the opposite direction, toward the garage and her car.

If those vandals were as blatant as last time, they would be tearing around for a few more minutes. The fact that they might have a gun and that Handel was unarmed, gave her an extra burst of speed. Panting and winded, she opened the garage, yanked open the door of her car and jumped in. Thank God her key was still above the visor and she hadn't listened to Handel when he warned her that one of these days someone was going to walk right in and drive away with her car.

She backed out and whipped around in the driveway sending a spray of gravel dust flying out from under her tires. The motion sensors caused all the lights on the house and garage to come on as she shot up the driveway to the road. There was no traffic at this time of night and she hit the gas, sending the speedometer up to eighty miles per hour within seconds. The half-mile distance to Margaret's turnoff was covered so fast she had to slam her brakes on to make the turn, no doubt leaving a nice skid mark behind on the asphalt as she whipped into the driveway and turned her car sideways to block the vandals from getting away. Gravel crunched and flew, pinging the underbody of her vehicle as she skidded to a stop. She shut off the ignition, threw open the door, and jumped out.

She heard Handel shout, and the sound of a vehicle roaring toward her. Headlights bounced over the bump in Margaret's driveway and blinded her as she stood in the middle of the road, caught and held in the beam.

The truck ground to a halt within a few feet of her position. She couldn't see who was driving or even the make and model of the vehicle. She just knew it was a truck or SUV by the sound of the engine. Frozen in place as though her tennis shoes had taken up roots, she stared into the blinding glare while dust settled around her and waited helplessly for whatever was going to happen next.

"Billie!" she heard Handel yell from somewhere back by the house and then the driver of the truck hit the gas again, swerved around her and the car, bounced down into the shallow ditch and came up on the other side. As quick as they had come, they roared away into the night.

Handel pounded toward her, breathing hard and heavy. He grabbed her and pulled her against him, regardless of the pain to his ribs. Huffing and panting into her ear, his heart beating raggedly against her breasts, he gasped out a warning, "Don't ever…do…anything…like that…again."

"I'm sorry," she said against his shirt, now damp with sweat. She felt him tense as another car slowed at the driveway and turned in, stopping behind her Mazda.

They pulled apart and stared into the glare of headlights, lower than the truck's and partially blocked by her taller vehicle. The door of the mystery car opened and a shadowed form stepped out.

"Billie? Handel? What are you doing here?"

"Adam?" She ran toward her brother. "Are Margaret and Davy with you?" she asked, worried that they hadn't heard anything from them since the commotion began.

"Margaret is, but what…"

Handel hurried to the other side of the car and yanked the door open. "Margaret. You're all right," he said, relief flooding his voice.

"Of course I'm all right," she said. "But now you're scaring me. What is going on?"

"Where's Davy?"

"He's staying with a friend tonight."

Still breathing hard, he bent over holding his side. "Thank God."

Billie circled the vehicle, her attention diverted. "What's this?"

"What do you think it is? It's my new ride," her brother said proudly.

Margaret climbed out of the Corvette and pulled Handel toward the house. "You two get these cars out of my driveway. I'm taking Handel inside. He doesn't sound very good."

••••

"I'm fine," Handel reassured them for the third time. "The doctor said I'm healthy as a horse. A little running is not going to kill me. I was just out of breath."

"Healthy as a horse and stubborn as a mule," Margaret muttered, waiting for him to drink the glass of water she'd handed him.

He obediently slugged it down and grinned as he held out the empty glass. "Happy?"

"Ecstatic."

"So what's going on?" Adam asked, dropping onto the couch and looking from Handel to Billie and back again. "You raced over here after midnight and blocked off Meg's driveway just to catch us coming home from the club?"

Handel explained what had happened and they both looked plenty concerned. He glanced at Billie. "We thought someone was targeting us because of the trial, but now –" he shook his head. "I don't know what's going on. Since there's nothing the police can do tonight, except keep us up later than we already are, I'll call Officer Torn in the morning and fill him in on tonight's adventures."

"Maybe it's someone with a grudge against Fredrickson's," said Adam, "and not any one in particular. After all, everyone around here knows that Margaret works for you as chief winemaker, and now you've both been harassed."

"That's true." Billie yawned widely. "Babe, let's go home and get some rest.

They said goodnight and went out to the car. Billie backed up and turned the car around. "I hope the police catch these creeps soon. I think I've had about enough of their..." her words trailed off as the car's headlights swept the field below Margaret's shed. A dirt trail led to the vineyard beyond and in the light she saw that the truck had obviously taken the trail at some point, plowing down a section of vines like so much kindling. She hit the brakes and stared. "Oh no."

"What?"

She reached across the console and grasped his arm. "They ran right over Margaret's vines. The ones your grandfather planted in the Forties."

••••

No one managed to get to bed after they went back in to inform Margaret about the vines. She ran right out, ordering everyone to find flashlights and follow. Handel parked the car closer and left the headlights on so they could better inspect the damage.

Billie gazed around at the broken vines, crushed grapes, and deep grooves in the field made by truck tires. It was so senseless. Why would anyone destroy something so beautiful and productive, something that had stood the test of time, survived decades of weather and disease?

Margaret knelt over a knarled, thick uprooted vine and shook her head, tears of misery glistening in her eyes. Adam leaned in, rubbing circles over her back, and murmuring comforting words that Billie couldn't hear from where she stood.

"At least they didn't uproot them all," Handel confirmed, raising his flashlight to the end of the row. "We can take cuttings from the toppled vines and start a new vineyard. That way we'll always have Grandfather's Tocai Friulano if something should happen to the others."

"Nothing's going to happen to the others, because I won't let it." Margaret's voice was fiery. She raised her eyes to her brother. "Has anyone else thought that perhaps this kind of harassment is right up our father's alley?"

"No." Billie said immediately, unwilling to even contemplate such a thought. "Sean Parker is dead. The Mexican cartel killed him. Mario would not have let him live after what he did to his sister. He sent me the pictures back as proof. You know that."

"Sure," Margaret said. She turned and stalked back to the house, Adam following in her wake. He turned and cast Billie a worried look, but left Handel to smooth things over.

Handel released a heavy sigh and put an arm around her as they trudged back to the car. "She's just upset. Don't mind what she says. We're all overtired and looking for answers. There's no way my father could survive the cartel. And if he did… someone else would kill him. He made a lot of enemies in his life."

"I know." She paused and looked up at the night sky, shot full of stars. "In my head I know it's not possible. In my heart… even the thought makes me feel ill."

They climbed in the car and drove home. Outside lights blinked on again as they pulled into the garage. The hoot of an owl in the trees behind the house was a reminder that predators did manage to survive best in the shadows. The thought came unbidden to her mind that if Sean Parker were alive he would do well to remain hidden. She'd been taught that God would judge evil one day, but if that man were in her sights she wouldn't hesitate to send him to kingdom come, by whatever means she had available. A pocket of sadness filled her heart, knowing he had changed her, made her less trusting, more vengeful. Would that she could go back to the girl she once was and start over. But that was impossible.

She glanced across the yard to the winery and sheds, now dark silhouettes against a star-strewn sky, and told herself that he was absolutely, positively dead.

After Handel made sure everything was secure, he took her hand and they hurried around to the back of the house. The screen door was all that separated them from the comforts of home.

"Worrying about whether or not you lock the garage is pretty silly when we left the back door wide open," she reminded him.

"True." He opened the screen just wide enough to stick his arm in and flip the light switch up on the wall, then laced his fingers together like he was posing for a Charlie's Angels poster. "I'll go first," he said and jerked his head toward the door. "Follow me."

She rolled her eyes and entered the kitchen right behind him, glancing around to see if anything was amiss. Nothing was and she started to open the refrigerator to get a glass of juice, but he pulled her away from the door and put a finger to his lips.

"Keep one hand on my back. No matter what,

stay behind me."

"Right," she said, ignoring his silly order. "I'm thirsty. We can play cops and robbers after I get a drink."

He turned and looked at her, a crooked grin on his face, and lowered his loaded finger. "Sorry. You're tired. I was just trying to lighten things up."

She shook her head and poured apple juice in her morning coffee cup still sitting on the counter. "Don't be sorry. You make a very sexy angel. I can't wait to see what you look like in a bikini."

"Thanks, but I draw the line at imaginary guns."

"All for the best. I've had enough drama for one day." She drained the juice and rinsed her cup in the sink.

"Me too."

He followed her to the bedroom, flipping lights on and then off as they went. Whether to keep from stubbing a toe or in search of an elusive intruder she didn't know. While she brushed her teeth she thought she heard him talking to her and stuck her head out the door to catch what he was saying. He stood at the window across the bedroom, peeking through the blinds into the backyard. His cell phone was pressed to his ear and he was saying something about canceling services. What was that about?

She finished in the bathroom and climbed into bed. He was already there, checking email on his phone. It was already half past one and she was exhausted. When she curled up beside him, he set the phone on the bedside table and shut off the lamp. He put his arm around her, pulling her close.

"Be careful of your ribs," she warned.

"Don't worry. I'll scream like a little girl if it hurts. I'm fine."

She rested her head in the crook of his arm, her cheek against his chest and listened to the beat of his heart, steady and reassuring. After a minute or two she asked, "Who were you talking to?"

Was it her imagination or did his heartbeat speed up?

"When?"

"Are you really going to counter with a question?"

He breathed out a laugh and ran his fingers up and down her arm. "Sorry. I don't want you to get upset."

She waited, wondering what he could have done that would make her upset.

"Manny gave me the name of a man in security. I called him earlier today to set up an appointment and discuss our situation, but now after the vandals hit Margaret's yard as well…" he trailed off.

She pushed up on an elbow to look down at him. "Security. Is that code for bodyguard?"

"Maybe."

"You've got to be kidding me. You thought it would be a good idea to hire someone to follow me around without my knowing, when I'm already paranoid?"

He sighed and reached up to stroke her hair hanging over his chest. "Honestly, I didn't think of that. I'm sorry. I should have talked to you about it first, but I couldn't stand the thought that someone would try to hurt you because of me."

She relaxed against him once more. "I get it. But I'm glad you called it off. I've been thinking. The guy who came by Saturday… I think he was warning me."

"Yeah?"

"No, I mean he was warning me – not threatening me. Remember I thought the truck was an older midsize SUV? The truck the guy came in Saturday was a brand new Lexus."

"Okay, but you never really got a good look at the first truck or anyone in it."

"Exactly!" she said, smacking the bed with the palm of her hand. "They got away with it. No one could identify them. So why would they show up the next day in broad daylight just to gloat? Do they have a secret wish for a new home in cellblock 6?"

He chuckled. "I don't know. There are a lot of stupid criminals out there or the jails wouldn't be so full."

"True."

"It's late, babe. Let's sleep on it, okay?"

"G'night," she murmured and pulled back to her side of the bed. She heard him trying to get situated comfortably. His ribs were probably aching more than he let on. She reached out and clasped his hand. "Love you," she whispered.

He squeezed her fingers.

She rolled over and tried to relax but the face of the man on Saturday was stuck in her head. Many of the tattoos covering his arms and neck were similar to ones Manny sported. She knew that identifying a suspect by a specific tattoo could be nearly as damning as a clear set of fingerprints. Why then did criminals tend to have so many? Maybe it was like Handel said – there were just a lot of stupid criminals out there. She rolled onto her back and stared up at the dark ceiling until her eyes grew heavy. The last thing she thought of before drifting off to sleep was Manny's tattoo. A simple overwriting of numbers symbolized a change of heart from the violence and death that MS-13 stood for to the love and forgiveness his mother had prayed for. She wondered if the sentiments had pierced more than skin deep.

CHAPTER EIGHT

Handel bolted straight up from the bed and then groaned loudly, scaring her awake. "What?" she looked wildly around, wondering what had startled him. The alarm clock on the dresser said 7:17, but it felt as if they'd just fallen asleep.

He threw his legs over the side of the bed and groaned again. "I forgot about my ribs. Sorry for waking you. I remembered something important. At least I think it's important."

Billie rubbed sleep out of her eyes and watched him reach out for his cell phone on the bedside table. "It's kind of early to be making a call, isn't it?"

"I'm not. Someone called me right before the accident. I completely forgot until now. You know how when you're half asleep things just pop into your mind sometimes?"

"Mmm hmm." She dropped her head against the pillow. "I've heard that's when we're most creative. If you come back to bed, I'll show you how creative I can be when I'm half asleep," she said in a husky voice that was supposed to be seductive, but didn't even win a glance from her husband.

Handel scrolled through his calls, his back to her. "You didn't erase anything from my phone, did you?" he asked finally.

She sighed and reluctantly scooted up to a sitting position, leaning against the headboard. "No, I never did anything with your phone, other than plug it in and charge it when you were in the hospital. The nurse found it in your suit pocket when they undressed you before surgery."

"That makes no sense," he mumbled, shaking his head. "All of my incoming calls and texts are gone. Deleted. Anything before I was released from the hospital... gone." He turned around and looked at her as though he thought maybe he was losing his mind.

She remembered the daily texts she'd sent him when he was still in a coma. "There should be at least seven texts from me. I sent you one every day."

"Gone." He narrowed his eyes. "Who had access to my room, other than you and the nurses?"

"I don't know." She shook her head. "The doctors, interns, Margaret and Davy. You can't think someone snuck into your hospital room just to delete your list of calls and texts, do you?"

"I don't know what to think. I just know they're gone and that makes me wonder why."

"You can always go online and look at your account. The calls will be listed and you can see where they came from, unless the number was blocked. But then why would anyone worry about deleting them?" She yawned and climbed from the bed. "I'm taking a shower. Feel free to join me when you figure this all out."

He didn't look up. His mind was definitely somewhere else.

When she came out ten minutes later, wrapped in a fluffy white towel, her hair dripping down her back, he was gone. "I guess the honeymoon is over," she muttered.

••••

She'd dried her hair, applied a little makeup, and dressed in jeans and a bright purple tank top before joining him in his office. He sat at his desk, his laptop open and running, watching the printer in the corner of the room. It made a whirring sound and whipped into motion, rolling out two printed sheets of paper.

"I'm printing the list of incoming calls from the phone company. There were a couple of out-of-state numbers, but I think those were just telemarketers. They didn't last more than a few seconds." Handel took the printouts, marked some lines with a yellow highlighter and held them out for her to see. "There are three numbers I don't recognize. Any of them look familiar to you?"

She shook her head. "Nope."

After the excitement of the night before Billie hoped he would take it easy today, that maybe they could get out for a while, take a drive, relax. Yeah right. Handel was in his element. In baggy sweatpants and a ratty old t-shirt, he was ready to take on the bad guys, whoever they were. He still looked tired, but there was no use telling him so. She might as well join the fun. "So, what's next?" she asked.

"The phone company won't give me the info on blocked calls or unidentified numbers, but they'll give it to the police." He picked up his cell. "I'm calling Officer Torn. I think he might help us out."

"Why?"

"Because he mentioned the other day that his sister was recently arrested for assault and he was looking for a good lawyer to handle her case."

She raised her brows. "How opportunistic of you."

"Oh, it's not for me." He grinned. "I thought you might like this one. Isn't it time to get your feet wet in the California court system? Her ex-husband filed assault charges after he broke into the house and tried to rape her. She hit him with a lamp."

"So you thought that was right up my alley." She tried to look peeved, but the thought of getting back into law, helping women who really needed her, sounded pretty appealing with all the financial woes at the winery.

"Yep. That's what I thought."

She slipped a leg over the edge of his desk and swung her foot back and forth. "Okay, call him," she said, before she had time to change her mind. "And then you can tell me about this mystery caller and why it's so important somebody wanted you to forget all about it."

••••

"The cell number belongs to Hosea Garcia," Handel said as he got off the phone later that morning with Officer Torn. They were in the kitchen having a late breakfast. "Frank said he did a quick search and found out the guy has been a member of MS-13 for the past eighteen years, has done two stints in the state pen and has quite a colorful arrest record. In fact, he was arrested for driving by and shooting out someone's front window two years ago. He spent a week in jail and served the rest in community service… planting flowers in city parks."

"You don't say." She put their empty plates in the dishwasher and turned around, crossing her arms. "He doesn't have a skull and crossbones on the side of his neck, does he?"

"Frank said he'd email over a photo."

She raised her brows. "Frank?"

"Officer Torn and I are like this." He crossed his fingers. "Two law men fighting for the common good."

"You're so full of it." Billie smiled and reached for his cup. "More coffee?"

"No thanks," he said, already opening the email on his phone. "Here it is."

She stepped behind his chair to look over his shoulder. "That's him! The guy from last Saturday. See! There's the tattoo. That one is hard to forget. Creepy."

Handel sat back in his chair and rubbed a hand over his jaw the way he always did when he was deep in thought. "Now we just have to figure out whether he's trying to warn us or threaten us. And what does he know about Jimena's murder?"

"Have you thought about calling Manny and asking him about this guy? Since they were in the same gang and his sister was supposedly seeing him?"

He got up and kissed her cheek. "I'm going to do that right now," he said, and headed back to his office.

••••

When Handel called, Manny was in his car driving. He said he was on his way to see Sloane at county lockup. "I'll only keep you a minute," he said. "I remembered a call I received right before my accident."

"A call?" Manny turned his radio down.

"From Hosea Garcia. I think you might know him."

He didn't answer right away. "Yeah, I know him," he finally said. He didn't sound too excited about admitting it.

"How well do you know him?"

"We both joined the gang when we were fourteen. We were like brothers back then. But things change. I went my way and he stayed with the Maras."

"So you guys go way back," Handel pushed, eyes narrowed, listening for the clues that were never volunteered.

"Yeah, way back. So what did he say?"

"He said he knew who killed your sister."

"Really. And who would that be?"

Handel expelled a laugh. "Hell if I know. I crashed before he told me."

Manny swore and said, "People are driving crazier than usual. Someone just cut in front of me. Was there something else you wanted to ask?"

"No. Drive safe."

"Adiós."

Handel sat back in his desk chair and sighed. Why didn't Manny mention the fact that he had warned Hosea away from his sister? Was he protecting his sister's reputation or trying to keep himself out of the suspect pool?

••••

Margaret squatted beside her grandfather's original vine, now uprooted and laying in the dirt. It had been her prized possession. A family heritage worth preserving, unlike other aspects she'd rather forget. She took some cuttings and sat back on her heels with a sigh. The seventy-six-year-old trunk was as thick as a telephone pole and as twisted and weathered as an aged seaman. "If vines could talk," she said to herself.

Her grandfather had been in Italy during the war and when he came home, he brought clippings from the Friulia region. He had dreams of growing his own vineyards, making his own wine, and raising his children in the sun. His dreams were uprooted just as this vine, when he had to sell most of the vineyard to the Sanchez family in the Fifties. But he kept this small vineyard, short rows of Tocai Friulano, French Colombard, Malbec, and Cabernet Franc, that he used in his wineblending. She hated to lose this piece of living history.

She cut the top of the clippings at a slant, cut off the bottom end straight through the lower bud and sliced off all but the two top bud nodes for growth. It was best to plant cuttings in the fall, but if she wanted to preserve these old vines she had to work fast. Unable to sleep after what happened, other than to toss and turn, she'd gotten up at the first rays of light, and stayed busy all morning, preparing soil mixture and filling pots. Now she pushed a fresh clipping into each pot, documenting which vine it came from in the vineyard journal she kept.

A car turned up the driveway as she was pulling the thick vine stump toward the back of the shed.

Gravel crunched under tires as it approached. She looked up from under the brim of her baseball cap. Handel climbed out of Billie's Mazda, looked around, and spotted her. He waved and started down the hill.

Margaret dropped the vine behind the shed and turned back, pulling her gloves off as she came. "What are you doing here?" she asked. "I thought you were busy working on that murder trial."

He gave her a half smile. "I was, but... Billie went to the winery to take care of business and I found myself thinking about you over here working so hard to preserve Grandfather's vines. Thought I'd come offer a hand."

"Thanks, but I'm pretty much done. You can help carry the dead vines behind the shed if you want. There's a pair of gloves over there on the bench," she said, tipping her chin toward the greenhouse working area. She pointed at the dozens of pots lining the row, filled with starter clippings. "I took some from every vine that was uprooted. Besides the original Tocai vine Grandfather brought back from Italy, a couple of our oldest French Colombard vines were run over as well."

"I'm sorry if my case caused this trouble." He stuffed his hands in the front pockets of his jeans and gazed around, shaking his head. "I became a lawyer to help people. Thought I could make a difference. Set wrongs right and all that." He blew the breath of a laugh through his nose. "Not sure what has changed, but I'm beginning to suspect that setting wrongs right is for someone bigger than me."

She slapped his shoulder with her dirty gloves. "Hey! Who's bigger than my big brother? It's not your fault your case brought out the crazies. I blame

the media for that. If they didn't make murder and
mayhem so damn titillating –" she broke off. "How
do you know it's about your case anyway? I know I
kind of lost it last night, but Billie's wrong. Those
pictures aren't proof of anything. Dad could still be
very much alive. I'm not saying he is or that this," she
waved a hand at the vineyard, "was his doing, but you
must have him on your list of suspects. Am I right?"

"I didn't want to say it in front of Billie. She's
suffered enough at his hand. But sure. It is possible. I
don't think it's probable but I'm not ruling him out
until we catch whoever is responsible."

She didn't know how to feel at first about
Handel saying the words out loud, but it actually put
some of her fears to rest. She wasn't the only one
expecting Sean Parker to pop out from behind a tree
one night. With her brother's admission, the threat
seemed much more insignificant. If their father ever
showed up, they would deal with him together.

He moved to the bench and pulled on the extra
pair of work gloves. "Let's clean up this mess and
then you can tell me what it is I missed while I was in
the hospital."

"What are you talking about?" she asked,
dusting off her bare knees. Little indentations in her
skin showed where she'd knelt on gravel while she cut
the vines. It was a hot day, but she probably should
have worn long pants. "Nothing much happened
around here. We've just been getting ready for an
early harvest. What with all this crazy weather." She
glanced around at the smashed clusters on the
ground. "Another week or two and I would have
harvested this crop for another batch. Carl's been
asking for more cases of Margaret's Wine every year

and I have a couple of private cellars to stock as well."

"I didn't realize you were such an entrepreneur," he said, wresting a vine from the tangle on the ground. A clump of smashed grape flew up and hit him in the face, leaving a smudge of rosy juice behind. He raised his shoulder and wiped it off on the sleeve of his shirt. "Actually, I was talking about you and Adam. You two looked pretty cozy last night. Thought you were going to take it slow. Did something change?"

He asked the question casually but she could tell he was concerned. After her track record with Davy's father, he probably thought she wasn't qualified to make romantic decisions without help. She picked up some vines and followed behind him as he carried his load toward the pile behind the shed. "We have been taking it slow. I know you've been busy with your new wife and this big murder case of yours, but the rest of us do carry on with our lives even when you're not paying attention," she said, and then was immediately ashamed. Handel had been in a coma for a week and she didn't know if he would make it. She would have given her right arm to guarantee her brother's recovery and yet now she was irritated with him because he was worried about her.

She threw the armload of vines on the pile and put a hand on his arm to stop him from hurrying off for another load. "I'm sorry. I didn't mean it. This whole thing has me on edge."

He shrugged. "You don't have to answer to me. You're not a kid anymore and I should stop thinking of you that way. You're a smart business woman, a great mom, and a passable sister. I just want you to be happy."

"I am happy." She grinned. "I'm happy being Davy's mom. I'm happy being your sister. I'm happy being chief winemaker at Fredrickson's." She paused and cleared her throat for emphasis. "And I'm really happy to tell you that I'm in love with your brother-in-law."

He was quiet for a moment as he digested the news. Then he pulled her into his arms and patted her awkwardly on the back. "That's great, Meg. I'm happy for you too." He pulled back momentarily and held her at arms length, smiling into her eyes. "Really, I am. But that won't stop me from telling Adam that if he does anything to hurt you, he will answer to me."

"I'm sure he'll take your threats very seriously," she said, trying not to grin.

"Come on. Let's finish cleaning this up and I'll take you out for a celebratory iced mocha."

"You're on."

●●●●

Billie sat at her desk in her winery office and stared at the closed door. Sally had called on the intercom and asked if she wanted to eat pizza with everybody in the conference room, but she really wasn't hungry after the late breakfast she had with Handel. There was mail she needed to go through and bills to pay, but she couldn't stop replaying Handel's phone conversation with Hosea Garcia over and over in her head.

At the winery music festival on Saturday, Garcia had seemed very intimidating, almost threatening. But Handel said that on the phone he was quite the opposite. Was it possible that the voice on the phone and the man she'd spoken with were actually two different people? Could someone have used Garcia's phone to make the call so that he wouldn't be identified? Or was Garcia playing both sides of the fence, wanting to have revenge on whoever killed his lover but not wanting to get himself fingered in the process?

Loud voices in the hallway outside her office alerted her to trouble two seconds before Sally threw open the door, her eyes wide with excitement. "Billie, there's a fire at Margaret's place. Looks like her potting shed. I already called the fire department, but I sent the boys over to see if they could help," she said, obviously referring to Ernesto, Sammie, and Loren. "They took the pickup."

Billie was out of her chair and running down the hall before Sally had finished. She flew out the front door, and ran across the parking lot, staring toward the south vineyards and the Parker house. Smoke billowed up from the back end of the shed, thick and black. She opened the side door of the garage and pushed the button. The garage door went up and she stood there staring at the empty space where her Mazda usually sat. Handel must have gone out somewhere.

She opened the door of the BMW, but remembered she didn't have the key. It was hanging in the house on the key holder beside the refrigerator. Sirens wailed from about a mile away. Good. The fire truck was nearly here.

Sally caught up with her, panting like a middle-aged woman carrying fifty extra pounds, although she was only twenty-nine and skinny as a rail. "Billie!" she stopped to catch her breath. "Loren called on his cell. The fire's not as bad as it looks. It was lucky the wood behind the shed was still green and Margaret has an extra large hose hooked up down there. He said there's a lot more smoke than fire."

"Thank God." Billie breathed a sigh of relief. "I don't think Margaret can handle any more damage to her vines. She was pretty upset last night."

"Why, what happened?" Sally suddenly perked up, eager to know the latest. "I had to hear secondhand about the vandals shooting through your window. Come on, what gives? If I don't know what's going on around here, how am I supposed to spread juicy rumors?"

Billie shared the latest vandal action with her overeager secretary as she headed for the back door of the house. Sally followed, not wanting to miss a thing. When she had the key to the car in hand, they both got in and she drove to Margaret's, not far behind the fire truck just turning in the driveway.

"Holy moly," Sally said, using her favorite corny phrase for anytime something was out of the ordinary. "This just keeps getting more and more bizarre."

Smoke was still billowing up from the back of the shed but the fire truck was completely unnecessary, because by the time they had their boots on the ground, Sammie and Ernesto had taken out the fire with the garden hose. After making sure everything was thoroughly doused, the firefighters climbed back in their truck and backed away.

Loren ran up to where Sally and Billie were watching from a distance, trying to stay out of the way of the firefighters, but mostly trying to avoid the smoke. "The men in yellow said it was a good thing we got here so quick. The back wall of Margaret's shed is damaged but it could have been much worse. Luckily, it didn't spread to the vineyard."

"That is good news." Billie shot Loren a thankful smile. "You guys were great." She glanced around and up at the house. "Has anyone seen Margaret? It's strange she wasn't outside working in the vineyard." A niggling worry inched its way up her spine. With all the strange things that had been happening, it wouldn't be surprising to find that the fire was not an accident.

Loren hooked a thumb over his shoulder. "She was out here earlier cause she's been planting new clippings in pots down there. Looks like she took out some of the old vines for some reason." He frowned. "With hanging fruit on them."

"She didn't take them out," Billie said, her voice grim.

"What do you mean?"

She glanced at Sally. "Cue the information secretary. I'm gonna go down and talk to Ernesto and Sammie."

"Don't worry. I'll fill him in," Sally promised.

Billie glanced at the dozens of pots Margaret had filled and set in a row. A couple of them had been tipped over in the rush to put out the fire. She bent down and scooped dirt back in before arranging the cuttings upright once again.

"Miss Fredrickson," Ernesto called from the corner of the potting shed, waving a hand for her join them. He was always so formal, refusing to call her by her first name, but seemed to forget that Parker was her married name now.

When she hurried over, he pointed at a lump of melted red plastic in a pile of charred and still smoking vine stumps. She squinted as acrid smoke bellowed up in her eyes and pulled the neckline of her shirt up to cover her mouth and nose. "What is it?" she asked against the thin material.

He coughed and poked at it with a stick, turning it over. "A gas container. See. The nozzle is melted flat."

Sammie was still spraying water here and there, making sure no spark rekindled the flames. He nodded toward the burned back wall of the shed. Fire had burned through in spots, but the structural damage was minute. "I doubt Margaret left that container down here. There's no tools in there powered by gas. So, whoever did this brought his own fuel."

"Are you sure?" Billie hated to think the winery was being targeted but that's what it looked like. At least when it was supposedly connected to the murder trial, it made more sense. Now, she didn't know what to think.

Sammie pointed up the hill. Handel and Margaret were just climbing out of the Mazda. "Ask her yourself," he said.

Margaret didn't wait for Loren's retelling of the story, but ran down the hill toward the scene of the crime, blonde ponytail swinging behind her. "What happened?" she yelled, zoning in on the newly potted cuttings, eyes flashing over her vineyard and back to the shed.

Billie stepped forward, dipping her chin toward the pots. "It's okay. None of your vines were damaged. The guys knocked over a couple pots getting back here is all. The fire started in your rubbish pile and climbed the back wall of the shed."

"Started how?" Margaret rounded the shed and stopped, staring at the smoldering, damp mess. She put her hands on her hips and shook her head. "Handel and I just pulled those dead vines back here before we left to get coffee. We weren't gone that long." She pointed at the melted, red container. "And I don't own a gas can like that."

Ernesto poked at it with his stick again.

"If I get my hands on them," Sammie muttered under his breath.

When Handel joined them the guys repeated their earlier assessment of the situation, then he walked carefully around the scene and took pictures of the damage with his cell phone. "I'll call Officer Torn. He's already working on this vandal problem and knows what we've been dealing with." He put a hand on Margaret's back. "Come on. There's nothing to do here now. The guys have it under control."

They trudged back up to the house. "When is Davy coming home?" Billie asked.

Margaret pushed a wisp of stray hair behind her ear. "Joan said she'd get all the boys back home by four," she said. "It was his first sleepover. He was pretty excited. They were going to the county fair today."

"Well, when he gets home why don't you two come over for dinner?" She glanced at Handel and he nodded. Not that it would keep the vandals from more destruction but she knew Handel would feel better about having his family nearby.

"I don't know. They showed up both times when I was gone. Someone needs to be home to keep an eye out." Her voice turned droll. "Maybe I should trade Rambo in for a guard dog."

"If you change your mind you know where we are."

Sally rode back to the winery with them, but Loren stayed behind to drive Ernesto and Sammie. She was unusually quiet in the back seat until they pulled up to the winery's front door to let her out. "You two be careful now. I don't know what's going on around here but someone clearly has it in for your family."

"We will. Thanks, Sally." Handel waved and drove the short distance to the garage, pulled in and shut off the ignition. They both just sat there as though unsure what to do next.

In the lengthening silence he reached out and clasped her hand.

••••

In spite of the early impromptu barbecue at Margaret's place that afternoon, Handel decided to cook outside on the grill for dinner. Like his sister, he excelled at the perfect steak, so Billie was happy to let him take care of business.

It was a beautiful evening. The air was warm and heady with the scent of ripe grapes and a gentle breeze played over leaves on nearby vines and trees. A blur of bright red caught Billie's attention as a cardinal flitted from branch to branch calling his mate.

She heard voices and looked across the field. Margaret had called earlier to say she'd changed her mind about joining them for dinner. She and Davy came bearing gifts; Davy carried a bottle of Dr. Pepper and Margaret a bottle of her wine. She wore a blue and white sundress with white flip flops, her hair tied loosely back with a ribbon, and looked more like a Disney princess than a mom.

Davy was eager to share all his adventures from the fair and kept on talking until it was time to eat. He proudly wore his 4-H t-shirt and was upset when he accidentally dropped a blob of mustard in the middle of it. "Aww, shoot! I was going to wear this tomorrow too," he said, pulling his shirt up to lick at the spot.

Margaret rolled her eyes. "I think you'll survive one day while it's in the wash. Besides, you have soccer again tomorrow and you'll be wearing your jersey."

He stuffed the rest of his hotdog into his mouth and tried to talk while chewing. "Can Adam drive me tomorrow too? He said he'd drive me everyday if you gave the okay."

Billie laughed at the ironic picture they made. Margaret was simply beautiful without trying. Her son, his mouth stuffed full and mustard staining his shirt, was a mess without trying. Adam fit into that mix perfectly. A beautiful mess.

"We'll talk about this later. Corvette or no Corvette, you can't just ask Adam to drive you around like he's your chauffeur." She handed him a napkin.

Davy sighed heavily before taking the napkin from her hand as though using it would offend his sensibilities. Instead of cleaning the catsup and mustard on the corner of his mouth he used it to wipe at the spot on his shirt again, leaving traces of white paper behind. "He said he didn't mind," he said, continuing the argument. "I told Heidi that he might let her have a ride."

"Davy!" She shook her head. "You can't make promises over something in which you have no say.

Even if Adam were to agree to that, Heidi's mom would probably not. And I wouldn't blame her."

Billie intervened. "Davy, could you go inside and get the black olives? I completely forgot them. They're in the side door of the refrigerator."

"Sure." He hopped up from the picnic table and ran toward the back door.

"Nice. Instant obedience. How do you do that?" Margaret asked.

Billie shrugged. "Easy. I'm not his mom. You've got a tough job and kids are never truly grateful until they have to go through parenting themselves." She tipped her head to the side and made a face. "At least that's what my mom tells me."

"Oh, I forgot," Handel said. "She called."

"When?"

"This afternoon when Margaret and I were at the coffee hut," Handel slipped a bite of T-bone steak into his mouth and chewed around his words. "Said she wanted to check up on me cause you hadn't called her back."

"I hope you didn't tell her about the vandals. You know how she is. If she thought I needed her, she'd be out here in a flash. That's the last thing we need." Billie set her fork down. "She's been acting odd lately as it is. Bungee jumping, going to stock car races, Jet-skiing. Do you think it's a late mid-life crisis or an early second childhood?"

Davy ran out the back door with the jar of olives, Adam following on his heels. "Adam's here!" he shouted unnecessarily.

A soft blush stole over Margaret's cheeks when Adam stopped behind her. She turned her face up for a kiss. "I didn't think you'd make it. Thought you had to rehearse or something," she said.

Billie moved over to make room for him on the bench across from Margaret. He slipped his long legs over the seat and leaned with his elbows on the table, his smile directed at the girl in blue. "I got hungry," he said simply.

She blushed deeper.

"Okay then." Billie handed him a plate with a grilled steak and baked potato, then pushed salad and pasta bowls toward him. "Have at it."

He wolfed down a few bites of steak as though he hadn't eaten all day before pausing to ask, "Did you get those cuttings done that you talked about?"

Margaret nodded, her face pensive. She glanced toward Davy who was busy trying to juggle walnuts fallen from a nearby tree. "It's been a busy day," she said.

Handel picked up his empty plate and jars of condiments and moved toward the house. "Davy! Make yourself useful."

When they were both in the house putting things away, Billie told Adam about the fire. "No one was in any serious danger," she was quick to point out, seeing the way he reached for Margaret's hand. "The back wall of the shed will need to be repaired but other than that..." she shrugged.

"What did the police say? Are they doing anything about it? What do they need before they make an arrest – a dead body?" He sat back, anger quickly replacing worry in his eyes.

Margaret pushed her plate aside. "We've seen this guy. He was at the music festival." She looked at Billie. "Why aren't they arresting him? Didn't you tell them he was the one?" she asked, joining forces with

Adam. Apparently she'd decided her father was no longer her top suspect.

Billie stood up and went to the grill to make sure Handel had shut off the gas. "I don't know that he is *the one*," she said, "He didn't come right out and admit it and it was too dark to see anyone that night. So unless he turns himself in and confesses, the police have no case against him."

"Figures," Adam huffed and crossed his arms. "He can shoot at you, destroy seventy-year-old vines, and set fire to Margaret's property and no one can touch him. Where's the justice in that?"

Handel strode out, bearing dessert on a tray. Strawberry shortcake piled with berries and whipped cream. "Justice is in a fair and open trial with evidence to prove beyond a shadow of a doubt a suspect's guilt. Or would you rather punish the accused first and then find out later he was the wrong guy?"

"Well if I get my hands on him while he's in the middle of another act of *alleged*," Adam put his fingers up as quotation marks, "vandalism, I'll let you know."

The sun was setting and shadows were deepening. Margaret kept glancing toward her house in the distance. "Where's Davy," she asked, when they were done with dessert.

"I left him inside. He wanted to watch some weird reality show about hunting crocodiles or something."

"We should get going." She started cleaning up the rest of the picnic supplies. "Can you drive us over, Adam?"

Billie shook her head. "Go on. I've got this."

"Thanks."

When Billie was putting the rest of the things on the tray and folding the tablecloth, she heard the Corvette hot rod down the driveway. She smiled, knowing that Adam wasn't just showing off for Davy, but for his girl. He was such a big kid.

Handel rounded the corner of the house. "Need any help, babe?" he offered, taking the tray from her hands and following her into the kitchen.

He poured them each a glass of wine while she filled the dishwasher, then stood leaning against the counter beside her. "Frank thinks I should call Hosea and ask him point blank if he's involved in these acts of vandalism or if he knows who is."

She slanted her eyes at him. "Frank does, does he? Did he also deputize you in case you need to make a citizen's arrest?"

"I didn't think to ask him. Now I wish I had." He stepped behind her and began massaging her neck and shoulders, his hands moving gently, kneading out the knots and warming her skin. "You always have the best ideas," he said. He kissed the side of her neck, right below her ear, sending a shiver down her spine.

She turned into his arms and slid wet hands up over his chest and around his neck, dampening his shirt. "Seems like you're the one with the best idea now," she murmured as he lowered his head to kiss her.

His cell phone interrupted the moment once again. He tried to ignore the ringing in his pocket but she finally pulled back, pressing her hands against his chest. "Go. Answer it."

Handel took it out of his pocket and looked at caller ID. "It's Frank," he said, trying not to look eager.

She picked up her wine glass and poured it down the drain. "I'll be in bed if you need me," she said, and left him with his new best friend.

Handel's conversation lasted longer than expected, or he decided to go in his office and work, because by the time she finished reading a chapter in her book, he was still missing in action and she was finding it quite impossible to keep her eyes open. She finally gave up, clicked off the lamp and went to sleep.

CHAPTER NINE

Margaret stood on the front step and waved as Davy drove off with Adam the next morning on his way to soccer camp. Her son had a knack for getting his own way. She was a little jealous of the buddy friendship the two of them had built up in such a short time, but only because sometimes it seemed like he was pulling away from her.

She shook her head and went back inside. Of course Davy was pulling away from her. He was growing up. A ten-year-old didn't need his mother hovering all the time. She was glad he and Adam had formed a bond of mutual respect. A boy needed the right kind of male mentors. She couldn't ask for better examples than her brother and Adam.

She cleaned up their few breakfast dishes and then remembered to throw Davy's new favorite shirt in a load of laundry before changing into loose khaki pants and an old faded tank top to work outside. The burned wall of the shed needed to be torn off and replaced with new wood. First she had to move everything inside the shed, out.

She pulled her long braid through the hole in the back of her cap, slipped her cell phone into her pocket and went out through the garage. Adam had recently installed a keypad entry, so she punched in the numbers and closed the door behind her. After the last two days, she certainly didn't want vandals sneaking into the house or wine cellar while she was out of sight.

Halfway down the hill to the shed, she heard a car approach. She turned around, her hand up to the bill of her cap to block the glare of sun shooting through the branches of the elms. The same black Jaguar that had been parked outside Antonio's back door the other day was now parked in her driveway.

"Damn." She should have known she couldn't escape this man so easily. His son thought he ran the world. The father probably thought he ran the universe. Hands on her hips, she waited.

Edoardo stepped out of the car and turned slowly, looking around at the house and fields. His gaze swept over her and then came back to rest. He lifted a hand in greeting. "Buon giorno, Margaret!" he called.

Grudgingly, she started back up the hill pulling off her gloves as she went. She stuffed them in the utility pocket of her khakis and stopped a few feet away. "Hello, Mr. Salvatore," she said, her voice clipped and formal. "What can I do for you?"

She was glad Davy was not at home so she could deal with this man without further emotional complications. Agosto had put Davy in the middle, trying to use his innate longing for a father as a ploy to force her hand. Davy was not a bargaining chip in a board meeting. He was flesh and blood and soul, and he had already been hurt enough by the Salvatores.

Edoardo gave a low chuckle, his mouth slanted in a rueful smile as his eyes caught and held hers. She could see where Agosto had gotten his hard-to-resist charm. The father wasn't as devilishly handsome as the son had been, but like an aging Bruce Willis, he was no slouch to look at. He'd come in more casual attire – black slacks and an open collared violet colored shirt – but still gave off that aura of self-made millionaire.

"Perhaps there is something I can do for you," he said, tipping his head slightly as he regarded her. "I heard about the recent trouble you have had with vandals."

She narrowed her gaze. "Where did you hear that?" she asked, crossing her arms over her chest. The police had not been dispatched for the fire because Loren had told them it was just a shed fire, away from the house and no one was injured.

"At my hotel. The woman at the desk was speaking with the postman. He said there was a fire and damage to your vineyard. Carl mentioned the other night that someone had shot through the front window of your sister-in-law's house as well." He shrugged. "A tight community. People talk."

It was true, her mail carrier had noticed the broken vines yesterday and asked her about them. Apparently he was good at distributing more than mail. And Carl was probably just making conversation, but she wished he'd make it with someone else. She didn't want this man knowing anything about her personal business.

"What is it that you think you can help with?" she asked.

"The idea that you and my grandson live way out here without proper protection is appalling to me. I will pay for a home alarm system and a security guard to patrol your property for a few days in case the vandal returns."

She was shaking her head before he finished his over-reaching pompous speech. "We don't need your money, Mr. Salvatore. And it doesn't really matter whether you like that we live out here. This is our home. If I feel that we need more security, then I'll take care of the matter. Thank you very much," she said, her voice firm and strong despite the fearful quiver in her gut at his commandeering manner. She reminded herself that she was no longer the insecure young girl that Agosto once ruled in that same arrogant fashion, but she was a talented, strong woman who had found her niche in life and excelled at what she did. She didn't need this man to approve of how she lived.

"I'm sorry you feel that way," he said. "Frankly, I find it quite disturbing that you would turn my offer down. A single mother like yourself," he said lifting a hand toward her, "should be eager to prove to the courts that she is able to keep her son safe."

"I am his mother," she said, trying to appear unmoved by the subtle threat. She shoved shaking hands in the front pockets of her khakis. "I have raised and protected him for the past ten years and I will continue to do it to the best of my ability until he's an adult. I have no need to prove anything to anyone!"

"When people find out he is my grandson, he

will no longer be a nobody. He will be high profile, like one of your American celebrities. With that in mind, security must be high as well, for his continued well-being."

"In that case," she said, letting a tinge of anger color her voice, "the wise thing to do is make sure no one ever knows he's your grandson."

His mouth pulled tight and he glared his disapproval. "You don't know who you are dealing with, young lady."

"I think it's time for you to leave."

But he wasn't finished yet. He stepped closer and pointed a finger in her face. "I will not be so easy to dispose of as my son proved to be. I've read all of the police reports that said your father murdered Agosto." He paused, breathing heavily through his nostrils like an angry stallion about to rear and trample whoever got in his way. For a moment she thought he might strike her and she took a step back. When he continued his eyes were still hard, but he'd lost the crazy look. "But I know who is really responsible for my son's death."

Margaret didn't respond. The implied accusation was too much to register. She stared after him as he turned abruptly and got back into his fancy sports car. He didn't even glance her way when he backed out and drove off. Gravel dust settled around her and she breathed a huge sigh of relief that he was gone. Watching the black car disappear down the highway, relief soon turned to dread. Could this be the beginning of a power struggle for Davy's custody? The man did not look like a quitter. He would absolutely make her life miserable to the end.

How far was he willing to go? He was already

accumulating info to use against her in family court, trying to prove that her home was unsafe for a minor. What else had he learned? Did he have someone spying on her? She turned around, pulling her gloves back on. She could only deal with one demolition at a time. Salvatore would have to wait.

••••

Handel typed Hosea's number into his phone and stared at it on the screen for long seconds before pressing send. He'd waited until Billie was at the winery working; he wanted to be able to concentrate on every nuance of the conversation. Sometimes when his wife was around he had a hard time keeping a clear head. Logic was often overridden by emotion, especially since his accident. He didn't know if the head trauma had damaged some emotional cortex or something, but he just didn't feel like himself.

It rang once. Twice. Someone picked up but there was only silence.

"Hello? Hosea?"

"Who is this?" a low voice asked, giving nothing away but his Mexican heritage.

"Handel Parker. You called me a few weeks ago. Remember? Due to an unfortunate set of circumstances we were unable to finish our conversation."

"I got nothin' to say."

"Wait!" Handel said, afraid he'd hang up before he had time to ask his questions. "You said you know who killed Jimena. Were you there?"

The man muttered a string of swear words in Spanish. "You lawyers are all the same. You don't want the truth, you just want to win. When your own family is threatened, then you get all uptight and want justice right now. Where's the justice for Jimena? Huh?" he broke out into swearing again.

"Hosea," he interrupted, speaking calmly, despite his desire to reach through the connection and grab the man by the throat. "I understand you cared about Jimena. I admit I didn't know her, but I do care about justice. That's why I'm asking you for the facts."

"So you can twist them in court? Nah! I don't think so. I'm already walkin' a thin line. If he finds out I —" he swore loudly.

"If who finds out? Jimena's killer? Don't you want to see him pay for what he did?"

Handel heard him sniff. "She was going off on him when she heard he was knee deep in aqua for Las Boyz. I just wanted my money before we left for Mexico. That's all I wanted. Now she's dead and he'll never pay. You'll make sure of that."

"There can be no justice if good people won't come forward with the truth," Handel said, trying to eek out the little bit of humanity that might still be hidden behind the man's angry defenses.

Hosea was silent for a few seconds and Handel wondered if the line had been disconnected, but the time counter was still ticking down on his call. "There is no justice for people like us," he finally said, his voice hollow with regret. "Only vengeance."

"Taking the law into your own hands is a dangerous occupation, Hosea."

"This world is a dangerous place. You want some free advice, Mr. Lawyer? I'd get a gun if I were you. A big gun."

"Is that a threat? Because I don't like threats. Especially against my family."

These gang members killed with no scruples. Hosea might have loved Jimena Kawasaki, but that didn't mean he was completely innocent of her death. He'd already admitted he'd been there at the time. So to him shooting a stranger would be like smashing a bug on the sidewalk.

The man's high-pitched laughter reminded Handel of a nervous hyena. He wondered if he was doing drugs again. "I'm not the one you need to worry about. I warned your chica. Look closer to home. And don't call me again." He hung up.

Handel disconnected the device he'd used to record the call and sat back in his desk chair with a sigh. The recording may not be admissible in a court of law but he planned to have Officer Torn listen to it anyway. Frank had some experience with gangs in his early days of walking a beat in San Francisco. Maybe he'd pick up on something in Hosea's words that he was missing.

He replayed the conversation through once more and then stopped to rewind the last part again. *"I'm not the one you need to worry about. I warned your chica. Look closer to home."*

Handel leaned with his elbows on the desk and stared at the framed wedding photo of Billie on the shelf across the room. How close to home was the man referring? Someone connected to the trial? Someone Billie and Margaret worked with at the winery? He shook his head. None of this made sense. Were they targeting his family to keep him distracted because they thought he was too close to identifying the real killer or because they didn't like the idea that he might get Kawasaki off? *Now she's dead and he'll never pay. You'll make sure of that.* The trial was set to resume on Monday and he was starting to wonder if his client was innocent after all.

••••

Sally stepped into Billie's office, a huge grin on her face. "I think you might want to see this," she said, hooking a thumb behind her. She snorted a laugh as though unable to keep it in and led the way down the hall.

Billie squinted, stepping out the door into the full sun. Loren was ogling somebody's new Harley. He walked around it, his fingers lightly brushing the leather saddle. "This is a hot ride, Mamma," he said appreciatively.

The woman stood with her back to the door. In jeans, boots, and a bright pink and black leather jacket, she was most definitely hot, whether or not she was a mamma. The temperature had to be eighty degrees out. Billie thought Loren was just using his slang a little too liberally until the woman pulled off a matching helmet and fluffed shoulder-length dark brown hair with a shake of her head.

"Mom?" Her mouth dropped open when Sabrina twirled around.

"Wilhemina!" She handed Loren her helmet and pulled Billie into a leather-clad hug. "I missed you!" She slowly drew back and looked at her daughter as though she hadn't seen her for years. Her eyes were red and moist. Probably from buffeting the wind with her face. "I just had a feeling that I needed to be here," she said, as dramatic as ever.

"A feeling, huh? Does it come and go like hot flashes, Mom?" she waved an arm at the bike. "Cause riding a motorcycle all the way from Minnesota seems like more than a feeling. Have you lost your freaking mind?"

Sabrina looked confused, a line of worry between her brows. "Are you all right, honey? You don't look so good. Maybe we should go inside where it's cool and discuss this." She took Billie's arm and tugged her gently toward the door.

Sally was biting her lip to keep from laughing, but her eyes were nearly popping out of her head from the pressure. Billie glared her way, but as soon as the door closed behind them she heard Sally and Loren explode into gales of laughter.

Sabrina followed her down the hall to her office and tugged her jacket off. She hung it on the coat hook behind the door. "Your office looks so professional, Billie. Like a real business owner," she said, smiling brightly.

"I am a real business owner, Mother," she said, sitting on the edge of her desk and crossing her arms. "Now are you going to tell me what in the world is going on with you?"

Her mom cocked her head to the side and rubbed the side of her neck. "I'm a little stiff after that ride," she said, "and I could use a drink."

"A drink? What? Are you a beer guzzling biker chick now?"

"No, silly. I need some water. It's hot out there."

"Stay right here," she ordered and hurried down to the lunchroom for a bottle of water. She pulled two out of the refrigerator and strode back to her office.

Sabrina was sitting behind the desk, leaning back in Billie's chair with her hands laced behind her head. She reached out for the bottle. "Thanks, honey.

I feel like a camel with an empty hump."

Billie twisted the cap off her water and took a long drink. Eyes closed, she counted to ten. When she opened them her mother was fiddling with the things on her desk, straightening everything into neat piles and groupings. She sat down in one of the facing chairs and sighed. "Okay, now start at the beginning and tell me exactly what has been going on in your life that has led you down this path of insanity. A motorcycle? Really, Mom?"

Sabrina waved a hand at her as though brushing away a pesky fly. "I didn't ride it all the way from Minnesota. I rented it when I got here. I know I told you when you were in high school that motorcycles were deathtraps and if you ever got on one I would never forgive you, but I've changed my mind." She shrugged. "Oh, they're deathtraps all right, but if you've got nothing to lose, they're a heck of a lot of fun."

"Wha–?" she couldn't find the words. She just looked at her mother and shook her head. The woman had the audacity to actually look refreshingly flushed and happy. Billie didn't know whether to applaud her new adventuresome spirit or smack some sense into her. Until her Mother's last words registered. She covered her mouth with her hands. Nothing to lose. What did that mean? Was she dying?

Sabrina gasped and jumped up. "Oh, no, I didn't mean that. I meant that at my age, I have less to lose. You and Adam are grown, I have no husband, no one relying on me."

"Mother, don't ever scare me like that again," Billie said, grasping the arms of the chair. "We have enough going on around here without..." she stopped, her inward editor shushing her, but it was too late.

Sabrina sat back down, her gaze narrowed. "I knew it!" she said, pointing her finger. "It was not just a random hot flash moment, as you so colorfully expressed." A small smile flitted over her lips. "And I think I know what it is," she said smugly.

"No you don't."

"I think I do."

Billie rolled her eyes. "Mother, you do not have ESP."

"I don't know what it's called, but every mother has a connection with her children. When they need her, she just knows. So here I am." She looked at her hands folded on the desktop and made a sound of disgust. "First I need a hot bath and about a quart of moisturizer. Then we'll talk."

••••

Once Sabrina was cleaned up and had a bite to eat, Handel and Billie got to hear a play by play of her recent adventures. After relating all the details about how she'd learned to ride a motorcycle when she was kid – something obviously never shared with Adam and Billie when they were growing up – Sabrina explained that she'd taken a refresher course a month earlier and purchased a Harley. She'd been riding around Minnesota, seeing the state from a different perspective for the last few weeks, but riding all the way to California had still seemed a bit daunting.

"I shipped my suitcase and just brought my riding gear and overnight bag. That way when I got off the plane, I could ride straight out here on my rented Harley and really smell the vineyards. It was amazing," she said with a nod.

"You really bought a motorcycle?" That was the last thing Billie heard. "What are you going to do with a Harley, Mother? Join the Hell's Angels?" She couldn't imagine her mother riding around alone. She would be too bored.

"Speaking of Hell's Angels, there's a really nice group of bikers at the new church I'm going to. They invited me to join them on their rides." She brushed a hand through her still damp hair. "Now, enough about me. What is going on around here?"

Handel exchanged a look with Billie and jumped up. "Who wants a glass of wine?" he asked, moving toward the kitchen.

"Hold on there," Sabrina said. "You should be resting. You've only been out of the hospital for a week and a half," she reminded him. She looked at Billie with a quirk of her dark brows. "I'll have a glass of that nice Tocai Friulano you sent me for Christmas."

"Sorry, Mother. I don't have any of that on hand. That's some of Margaret's special crop." Now she might not have any for years. It would take a while for the cuttings to become strong vines with a fruitful harvest. "How about some nice Cabernet Franc?"

"Sounds lovely." Her mother patted the sofa cushion next to her. "Come sit back down, Handel, and we'll have a little chat."

Billie tried to hide the smile as she passed him, but failed.

She pulled open the door of the little Thermo-electric wine cooler they'd gotten for a wedding gift and selected a bottle of Cabernet Franc. She had to go to the dishwasher to find clean glassware and then sliced some cheese and bread. After arranging it all on a tray, she drew a deep breath and slowly released it. "Time to party with the Hell's Angel."

"I thought maybe you'd be hungry," she said, setting the tray on the glass coffee table. She poured the wine. "So, what have you two been chatting about?" she asked, sitting across from them.

"Your mother wanted to know what I was thinking while I was in a coma," Handel said, throwing an arm along the back of the couch. "I said I was thinking about you, of course."

"Smooth."

Sabrina patted Handel's leg. "I knew you were the one for Billie the moment I set eyes on you."

"As I recall," Billie said, waving a piece of cheese in the air, "you were still trying to get me back together with what's-his-name."

"You mean that sportscaster? He was never right for you. What kind of mother would name their son after a cigarette?"

Handel's blank look made Billie laugh. "His name was Kent."

"Ahh. Makes perfect sense now." His eyes were laughing over the rim of his wine glass.

"Which brings me back to the present," her mother said.

Billie waited with bated breath. If she really had ESP it would be revealed now.

"Has Adam got up the nerve to propose to Margaret yet?" she asked.

The doorbell rang and Billie put up her hand. "Hold that thought," she said, a smile teasing at the corners of her mouth. She hurried to the front door and pulled it open.

"I'm glad you three could join us," she said brightly and waved them in.

"Is that Loren's Harley out there? I thought he had an Indian," Adam stepped in the door but was glancing back at the sleek red Fat Boy softtail.

Davy was the first to notice their guest sitting next to Handel. "Sabrina!" He ran over and gave her a hug. "You said next time you came you'd bring me a Minnesota Wild jersey."

"Davy," Margaret reprimanded, looking embarrassed, "that's no way to greet a guest."

"It's all right," Sabrina said, "This one says what he's thinking and I'm all for that." She looked him up and down. "You have really grown up, young man. I hope that jersey is going to fit."

"You brought it?"

"Not exactly. I shipped it. It should come tomorrow."

"Cool."

Adam pulled his mother into a hug, his eyes questioning Billie from across the room. "What are you doing here?" he asked.

"Now that's no way to greet your mother," Sabrina said, pulling back. She squeezed his cheeks playfully like she used to when he was a boy. "You should say, 'It's great to see you, Mom.'"

"It's great to see you, Mom. So what are you doing here?"

"I came for a visit, of course. I missed my kids. Is that a crime?"

"No, but it is kind of short notice."

Billie laughed. "You mean no notice. She just showed up here like hell on wheels."

Adam glanced toward the window and back.

He shook his head. "You aren't saying that bike is Mom's," he argued before she had time to say anything at all.

"Can I go sit on it?" Davy asked Sabrina.

"Sure, kiddo. Just be careful. It's a rental."

He ran outside, slamming the door behind him. Margaret cringed. "Sorry. He gets a little exuberant sometimes."

Adam was staring at his mother like she'd just announced she was a member of NASA and was flying to the moon on Friday. Billie waved him and Margaret toward the matching love seat. "Sit. Have some wine and cheese. I'll get a couple extra glasses." She smiled innocently toward her mother. "What was it you wanted to ask Adam, Mom?"

Handel choked on his cracker and downed it with the rest of his wine. "Let me help you," he offered, rising from the couch and following.

In the kitchen she pressed her lips tightly together while her chest shook with restrained laughter. Handel sighed. "You are a trouble maker. Adam and Margaret are gonna kill you."

"Not if the Maras get to me first."

"Don't even joke about that," he said, pulling her into his arms.

They heard laughter from the other room. Billie eased back and smiled. "You think she's telling them her story about seeing William H. Macy at the airport and calling him a wild hog?"

••••

Margaret had debated since the day before whether or not to tell Handel about the threats from Edoardo Salvatore. She knew he would want to jump right in the middle and try to take care of everything as he always did, but he had enough to deal with. The trial would resume in just a few days and he was still recuperating from his accident.

Billie would be a better option. She knew about family law and could at least suggest a course of action. But since Sabrina showed up the day before, she had not had an opportunity to discuss anything with anyone, not even Adam.

She stuck the wine thief into the bung hole, put her thumb over the hole on the end of the glass tube and drew a sample of the Chardonnay from the barrel. In the glass the white wine still looked a bit cloudy, but she took a sip and rolled it around her tongue. It was beginning to get that creamy rich feel that Chardonnay always had. Good.

The door at the top of the stairs opened and she heard footsteps descending. She peeked through the barrels and saw a pair of red heels. "Margaret, are you down here?" Sally called.

"Yeah, hold on a minute." Margaret stood up from her stool and set the glass down. She stepped out from between the barrels. "What's up?"

"Billie brought over a huge chicken salad her mom made for lunch and wondered if you were hungry. She said to join her in her office so you two could talk about harvest week."

"Sure, I'll be right up."

She straightened up her work area, washed her tools and headed up the stairs. Billie's door was open and she had the salads sitting on her desk waiting. She looked up from her computer and smiled.

"Glad you could join me. My mother usually makes enough to feed an army and Handel's appetite still isn't what it was before. He decided to go to his

office in town today. Said he needed to get Patty up
to speed on everything before next week, but I think
he may have just wanted to get a break from his
mother-in-law."

Margaret gave a short laugh. "She is very…"

"Melodramatic?" Billie offered.

"I like her," Margaret hurried to add, "She just
takes so much energy to be around. Sometimes I feel
like she's twenty-something and I'm middle-aged."

"That is so accurate. Believe me, I've felt the
same. Even when I was fifteen." She shrugged. "But
she's my mom and I love her."

Margaret pulled a chair close to the desk and sat
down. She took the bowl of salad Billie pushed
toward her. Chunks of crunchy fried chicken were
tossed on a bed of lettuce, tomato, cucumber and
sweet onion. She drizzled dressing over the top. "Sally
said you wanted to talk about harvest."

"Oh, that can wait. Actually, I was interested in
your visit with Edoardo Salvatore yesterday." Billie
took a bite of salad and waited.

"How did you know – ? Never mind. Sally,
right?"

"She is the resident gossipmonger. Seems
Ernesto was in the field not too far away and
overheard raised voices."

Margaret set her fork down and sat back with a
sigh. "Well, I wanted to talk to you about it anyway."
She told Billie everything that had transpired since her
visit with Edoardo at Carl's restaurant and how she
was afraid he was planning to use underhanded tactics
to get some sort of custody or visitation rights with
Davy. "He as much as threatened me. Said my place
wasn't a safe environment for *his grandson*. As if that

trumps the fact that Davy is my son."

Billie shook her head. "Unbelievable. If I didn't know how sweet Carl could be, I'd think the whole family was nuts."

"Yeah. I feel bad that Carl is thrown in the middle again. Handel and he have been close friends for so many years. I'd hate if their relationship was ruined over my problems with his uncle."

"That can't be helped." Billie picked up a pen and wrote something on a sheet of notepaper. "If Salvatore plans to fight for visitation rights he will first have to prove that he has rights. Davy's paternity was never recorded on a legal document. Am I right?"

She nodded. "Handel said it would be best to just put *unknown*. I know that sounds creepy, but now I'm beginning to see the wisdom in it."

"It will definitely give us more time to prepare, if and when he files with the court." She tilted her head to the side, her eyes slanted. "Have you told Davy his grandfather is in town?"

"No. After everything that happened last year, I don't think he's ready to handle another crazy relative."

They ate their salads and chatted about the harvest, what preparations they needed to make and how many seasonal workers to hire. Margaret discussed the progress of the barreled wine and Billie suggested a by-invitation-only barrel tasting party to ratchet up interest in the Fredrickson brand.

Margaret nodded. "Sounds like a plan. I think if we send out invites to about fifty of our best customers, the word will spread. The Chardonnay is very promising this year."

"I'm sure it won't be as popular as Margaret's

Wine but I hope it will come in a close second," Billie said. She picked up her phone and smiled. "It's Handel. He sent a text asking if my mother is back yet."

"Where's she off to now?" Margaret still couldn't believe the woman rented a Harley and rode in from San Francisco. She would never forget the look of shock on Adam's face. It was priceless.

"She borrowed the BMW. Said she wanted to do some shopping and she was going to stop by and say hello to Carl." Billie frowned. "I hope she doesn't expect Antonio to be back from Italy. Carl said he was seeing someone over there and it was serious. She doesn't show her true feelings much, so I'm not sure if this mid-life crisis is a direct result of a broken heart or a hormone mix-up."

"Maybe it's just your mom's wild side coming out after all these years," Margaret teased. "You should have heard Adam last night after he took me home. He's really worried about her. Thinks she might need a psychiatric evaluation."

Billie waved a hand. "My mother? Not on your life. The rest of us may need one though by the time she flies back home to Minnesota."

CHAPTER TEN

Handel was meeting Frank at Charley's Coffee House. There were a few empty tables this time of the afternoon, so he chose one away from other customers. He took a sip of espresso and looked around. The black, cream and turquoise décor was retro enough to bring in the baby boomers, yet avant-garde enough to attract the young artsy crowd that populated the area.

Handel had known Charley since high school. She was always outgoing and loved connecting with people. He watched her leaning over the coffee bar, talking with a customer, her hands moving as quickly as her lips. She reminded him of Carl. They'd make a great pair. She glanced his way and called across the room. "Hey, Handel. Need a refill on that espresso yet?"

He shook his head with a smile. "Not yet, Charley."

"Let me know when you do." She turned back to her customer, handing her a pastry from beneath the counter.

Frank came in the front door, looked around, and caught his eye. He nodded in acknowledgment then ordered a coffee before joining Handel at the table. "Hey, counselor. How's it going?"

"Good." Handel shook his hand. "You're not in uniform. Day off?"

"Yep, I'm supposed to be out running errands for my wife." He grinned. "Thought she'd probably like me to pick her up some of Charley's sticky rolls."

"Good call." He pulled the tiny recorder out of his suit coat pocket and slid it across the table. "That's the conversation I told you about. I'm not up on my gangbanger jargon," he said, picking up his espresso. "With your background maybe you can interpret for me."

Frank slipped the buds into his ears and pressed play. Handel sipped espresso and watched customers come and go while Frank listened to the recording, his eyes closed in concentration. He pressed rewind and listened again before shutting it off and pulling out the buds.

"Interesting," he said, picking up his coffee cup. He took a sip and licked his lips. "I won't bother to tell you that it's illegal to record a phone call in California without getting the permission of the other party involved. Because of course, being a lawyer and all, you already know that."

Handel nodded. "I do indeed. But hypothetically... if I were to record a phone call and that individual said something about aqua – which I know is Spanish for water – what would that mean in gangspeak?"

"Knee-deep in aqua means someone is

producing meth in large quantities."

"Terrific." He closed his eyes for a second and blew out a breath. "I like to think what I do is more than just keeping innocent people out of jail. It's about being a part of justice in action. That means something, you know?" He rubbed a hand over his chin and shook his head. "Sure you do. You're in the justice game too."

"I arrest them. You release them." Frank shrugged. "Doesn't mean we're not both serving justice."

"Yeah, well now I'm wondering if my keeping innocent people out of jail is actually stretching the truth."

Frank frowned, his forehead rippled like waves on a lake. "People lie, counselor. I've heard confessions from men who had nothing to do with a crime and I've heard elaborate stories of innocence from men who had committed heinous acts of violence. People will lie to protect themselves, their friends, to get a warm room for the night, or to cover up something worse." He waved a hand. "Just about anything. You seem like a pretty astute judge of character. If you believed your client when you took him on, then you have nothing to beat yourself up about. If he does have something to do with," he lowered his voice, "aqua, it doesn't mean he's guilty of the crime he's being tried for."

"Maybe, but I hate the thought of..." he broke off. "Sorry. I don't mean to throw my problems in your lap. I really do appreciate your help."

"What goes around comes around."

Handel chuckled. "Is that a subtle reminder of your sister's court case?"

"Maybe a little one."

"Don't worry. Billie agreed to handle it. I told you she would. She sees a woman or children in trouble and she's compelled to come to the rescue."

"I don't think my sister needs to be rescued exactly," Frank said, running a hand over his blonde buzz cut. "I taught her self-defense after all. She wanted to be a cop too, but that husband of hers talked her out of it. Maybe once this crap gets settled she'll revisit the idea. She'd make a good one."

"She does have a great head-bashing technique," Handel said, holding back a grin.

"That she does."

Frank purchased a box of caramel rolls and another coffee before he left, saying he was buying his wife's forgiveness for another week. Handel slipped into Billie's little Mazda and turned the key. He'd found a parking spot directly in front of the shop and someone was already waiting for him to move so she could occupy it. He pulled away from the curb and moved into traffic. His hand automatically slipped down to shift gears, but came up empty. He really missed his Porsche. After the trial, he needed to go car shopping.

His cell phone rang in his pocket. He'd forgotten to sync it with the Bluetooth in Billie's car earlier. He slipped it out and glanced at the screen. Sloane Kawasaki was calling. He'd let his answering service pick up. Before he spoke with his client again, he needed to get some facts straight. He dropped the phone into the cup holder and pushed his foot down on the gas.

••••

Handel pulled into the garage and shut off the

engine. The BMW was gone. Maybe Billie had decided to take her mom shopping or something. He climbed out of the car, grabbed his briefcase and went around to the back door. He was just about to put the key in the lock when the door was yanked open and Billie stood there wild-eyed, looking as though someone just told her the world would end at 6:30. He glanced at his watch. Luckily, they had a good twenty minutes to spare.

She backed up and let him in, then took his briefcase and set it on the table. "You're not going to believe what is going on," she began, following him to the refrigerator for a beer.

He pulled open the door and selected a bottle, twisted the cap and took a long drink before saying, "What now? Your mom decide to join the circus?"

Billie crossed her arms tightly over her chest and bit at her lip. Never a good sign. She shook her head, clearly agitated. "Margaret just got done telling me about her run-in with Salvatore yesterday and today Mom stops to see Carl and ends up accepting an invitation to the symphony with his evil uncle. She didn't even bother to ask me what I thought." She threw her hands up in the air. "What is wrong with that woman?"

He took another pull on his beer and leaned against the counter. "Settle down, babe. I'm sure... What did you say about Margaret?"

"Salvatore stopped by her place yesterday. They apparently did not see eye-to-eye on anything. He told her that living out here was unsafe for his grandson."

He muttered a curse.

"Yep. That about says it all."

"And what does your mother have to do with

any of this?" he asked, rubbing a knot in the base of his neck.

Billie moved behind him and massaged the muscles, talking over his shoulder. "She wanted to stop and see Carl while she was in town. His uncle happened to be there at the time. According to Margaret he's a real ladies' man. Or at least he imagines himself to be. He probably threw a bucket-load of flattery at her and she swooned at his feet."

"Swooned?" he said with a grin, turning to face her.

She slid her arms up around his neck and smiled back. "What can I say? I've been reading a book set during the Civil War."

"Sounds like we may have a civil war around here pretty soon. What is your mother thinking?"

"Thinking?" She pulled away again and stalked to the door and back. "I don't believe thinking is one of her many action-packed activities these days. Although," she said with a twist of her lips, "I can't really blame her for accepting a date with the man. It's not as if she knew the circumstances. As usual, she blindly jumped in with both feet then called to tell me why she wouldn't be home till late. I'm a little ashamed to say that I blew a gasket."

"Naw. You?"

"I tried to tell her it was a bad idea and she wouldn't listen. Then she hung up on me. Can you believe it? My own mother cut me off in the middle of a tirade." She gave a self-deprecating laugh. "When will I learn?"

He reached out and pulled her back into his arms, resting his chin atop her head. "I think you've learned a lot. Think of the change in your relationship from when you first came here. You and your mom are practically on the same wave-length these days," he teased. "A little more togetherness and you won't even have to speak. You'll just know what the other one is going to say."

She raised her face to his. "You're so not getting any tonight."

"How about right now?" He kissed her until she melted against him and then took her hand and tugged her toward the bedroom.

••••

Later, with Billie lounging in his office easy chair reading her Civil War novel, Handel worked at the desk preparing for the trial. Whether Sloane was a drug dealer or not, he was on trial for murder and it was his job to focus on that. Handel hoped he wasn't wrong about the man's innocence in the death of his wife. He sighed and rested his eyes a moment, rubbing his temples.

"Are you all right?" Billie asked, closing her book with her finger marking the page. "I didn't even give you a chance to tell me about your day when you came home. Seems like our pact to share the messy junk drawer of our lives has been put on the back burner."

"Sorry." He offered a tight-lipped smile. "It's coming down to the wire and I'm not sure I'm ready."

"That's hard to believe. You were ready and eager before the accident. What happened?"

He cleared his throat and leaned back in his chair. The wood creaked with his weight. "I met with Frank today. Unofficially."

"Oh? About the vandalism?"

"Not exactly." He told her about recording the

call and what Frank had told him.

Billie set the book down and pulled her legs up under her in the chair, getting comfortable. "So, Kawasaki is working with a rival gang to distribute meth on MS-13's turf and someone kills his wife as payback?" she said.

"That's one theory."

"You have a better one?"

"What if Jimena found out Sloane was producing meth in one of his warehouses? Maybe down by the wharf, right in the middle of MS-13 turf. She hates the gangs because of what it did to her family when Manny joined. She confronts Sloane and tells him to stop or she'll let the Maras know who their competition is. He can't let that happen, so he picks up whatever is handy and smashes her skull in."

She frowned. "I don't see that happening."

"Why not?"

"If Jimena was having an affair with Hosea and planned to leave with him anyway, why would she care what her husband did? She was going to be gone soon. If Hosea is to be believed, they were leaving that night."

"Maybe he killed her to stop her from leaving and it had nothing to do with drugs." He picked up his pen and tapped a soft beat on the edge of his desk, thinking. "Or, it did have to do with drugs and she was angry, because she thought he was pulling her brother back into the business of illegal activities. Manny did say that he did some work for Sloane on occasion."

"That sounds more plausible." She leaned her head back, eyes narrowed. "I imagine a fiery, Hispanic woman being protective of the only family she has left, maybe throwing objects at her husband until he gets angry enough to pick up something and hit her with it."

"Really? That's what you imagine? Or have you been watching the Spanish channel again?"

She laughed. "You got me. Sometimes I have it on at the office. It's helping me to learn Spanish, so I can communicate more easily with Ernesto and the temps he hires for harvest. I can't help that all the women in their soap operas have fiery tempers and throw things when they get angry."

He dropped the pen and crossed his arms, leaning back with a sigh of resignation. "I don't want to believe this of Sloane but it's looking worse all the time. The more I think about it, the more I doubt my initial gut feeling."

"You took on a murder suspect as a client with nothing more than a gut feeling that he was innocent?" She snickered. "Sounds like an episode of every corny cop show on television."

"Hey, I happen to like corny cop shows. The bad guys always get caught in the end, because the good guy has a gut feeling. Don't knock what works."

"So, what's next?"

He didn't want to tell her that Frank had also looked up Hosea's address for him and he planned to drive to San Francisco in the morning and speak with him directly. His gut feeling told him Hosea wasn't the enemy, so he wasn't too worried about showing up unannounced, but taking Billie along was out of the question. The neighborhood he was going into was not known for backyard barbecues or friendly neighbor chats over the fence. There were shootings and fights breaking out on a daily basis. People stayed off the street unless they were looking for trouble.

He must have hesitated a moment too long. She stood up and approached his desk, holding his gaze like a laser beam lie detector. "You are not going alone to speak with Hosea. It's too dangerous."

He opened his mouth to protest, but she glared daggers. "I mean it. I almost lost you in that accident. I won't lose you because you're out playing Private Investigator. You have one of those. Remember? Have you thought about calling Manny?"

"Sure, but I don't think it's a good idea. If Manny told Hosea to back off from his sister and finds out now that Hosea was there the night of the murder to pick her up and take her out of the country," he spread his hands and shrugged, "who knows what might happen."

"I see your point." She perched on the side of his desk, and kicked her leg back and forth. "What about Frank?"

He laughed. "Even if he agreed to go in an unofficial capacity, he wouldn't get past the front door. Hosea already made it crystal clear that he doesn't talk to cops."

"Right." She sighed and lifted her brows. "Then I guess it's just you and me, babe."

"No way!" He stood up and moved toward the door. The conversation was over. He would not take Billie into a dangerous neighborhood. It wasn't going to happen.

She followed him to the kitchen and watched as he took out the bread to make a sandwich. "What about Ernesto?"

"What about, Ernesto? He's a vineyard manager. As far as I know he doesn't have secret interrogation techniques for getting the most juice out of the grapes." He laughed at his own joke.

Billie pushed him out of the way and took over making his sandwich. She found leftover chicken in the fridge and sliced a big red tomato that was ripening on the windowsill. "Maybe he could go along as an interpreter, like Tonto did for the Lone Ranger when they went into Indian territory."

"I don't think you're old enough to have watched those shows," he said, sitting at the table.

She set the plate in front of him and crossed her arms. "Ever hear of cable television? It's where reruns reign supreme."

He took a bite of his sandwich and watched his perfect wife pour him a glass of milk. "Anticipating my every need. You're the best."

She took the seat across the table and slid the glass toward him. "Don't get used to it. As soon as you're completely recuperated you're on your own," she threatened with a smile.

"You're a tough nurse, but you do have a great bedtop manner," he said smoothly.

She flushed all the way up to her eyebrows.

Sometimes she surprised him with how innocent she could be, a fragile little girl in a woman's body. He reached out and clasped her hand. She grinned, pulled away and picked up the other half of his sandwich. Took a big bite.

"Hey! How am I going to get my strength back if you eat my food?"

"Tough."

"All right."

"All right what?" she asked, licking her lips. She took a drink of his milk too.

"You talk to Ernesto and see if he knows anyone from that neighborhood."

"That's a long shot. They're not all related, you know." She dropped the rest of his uneaten sandwich back on his plate. "But I'll see what he says. And it might be a good idea if he drove his old pickup. "

Handel finished his sandwich, watching her wipe off the counter and put away the mayonnaise and pickles. He had no intention of sticking around in the morning long enough to chat with Ernesto about coming along. He'd already be long gone.

••••

It was a quarter past two in the morning when Billie opened her eyes and looked at the clock. She'd heard something. She rolled over and saw that Handel was still asleep, snoring softly. Trying not to disturb him, she struggled out of the blankets and set her feet on the floor. Bleary-eyed and groggy, she moved to the chair and pulled Handel's sweats and t-shirt on.

At the door, she hesitated, listening. The sounds were coming from the guest room end of the house. Her mother was home. It might not be the best time to confront her about her choice in dinner companions, but they were both awake now anyway.

At her mother's door she knocked softly. Ten seconds later, the door opened and her mother stood backlit by blazing white light. Or at least it seemed that way to Billie's sleep-heavy eyes. "Can I come in?" she asked, glancing behind her mother at the bed. It was covered in store bags and open shoeboxes. No wonder she'd woken up. Her mother must have had to make three trips to carry all that inside.

Sabrina stepped back and waved an arm. "Be my guest." She quietly closed the door after her. "I'm sorry if I woke you. I tried to be as quiet as I could, but when that darn cat of yours shot through my legs outside the back door, I'm pretty sure I yelped."

"We don't have a cat."

"Even more reason to yelp." She moved bags off the bed. "Sit. Take a load off. You look exhausted."

Billie sat down and yawned widely. "I'm trying to stay half asleep so it won't be so hard to return to that fine state when I go back to bed."

"Well, don't let me stop you." She started pulling clothing items out and hanging them in the closet. "Early morning chats have never turned out well for us, honey."

"That's because I was a teenager coming home after curfew and they weren't chats. They were lectures."

Her mother released the breath of a laugh and shook her head. "Now the roles are reversed." She tipped her head to the side, hands on her hips. In navy slacks and a bright pink, lacy top, and despite it being well past most people's bedtime, she still managed to look ten years younger than her age. "So get on with the lecture and I can wash my face and go to bed. I'm exhausted. What a night," she said, moving to the closet again. "Edoardo really knows how to show a girl a good time."

Billie rolled her eyes. "I know you don't want to hear this, but…"

"Let me guess," her mother said, turning to face her as she closed the closet door. "You don't like him."

"You don't have to say it like that. It's not as if I tell you on a regular basis who you can and cannot date."

Now it was Sabrina's turn to roll her eyes. "Oh really? What about when I was dating Antonio?"

"Mother, I'm sorry he broke your heart," she began.

"He didn't break my heart," she said, shaking her head. "We mutually agreed that it would never work out. He wanted children. That part of my life is over. So he went back to Italy to find true love with a woman with working ovaries."

"I'm still sorry," she said. "I know you cared about him." A flimsy wisp of red material stuck out of a bright pink striped bag sitting beside her on the bed. She pulled it slowly out of folds of crinkly wrapping paper. It slithered from the bag and lay in a slinky gossamer pile on the plain blue bedspread like a hooker in a church pew. "Mother?"

Sabrina snatched it up and stuffed it back in the bag. "Is nothing private around here?" she asked, stomping to the dresser and shoving the bag in the top drawer. "I am your mother, you know."

"Yeah, that's what freaks me out," she mumbled. "Please tell me it has nothing to do with Edoardo."

"I'll have you know that I already bought all of these things before I met him. So you can wipe that disgusting look off your face and go to bed." She pointed to the door like a drill sergeant. "Good night."

Billie sighed. "I'm sorry, Mother. It's none of my business."

"Darn right," her mother said, arms folded tightly across her chest.

"I don't want to ruin your visit, but I thought

you should know that Mr. Salvatore is not as wonderful as he presented himself to you. He already threatened Margaret about getting custody of Davy. He's doing the exact same thing his son did before Sean murdered him last year. I'd prefer it if you stayed away from him. I don't want something to happen to you."

"I hope you're not insinuating the same thing is going to happen again. Two murders at one winery might just put you out of business." She peered in the dressing table mirror and fluffed the hair at her temples. "And as for Edoardo's interest in his grandson… well isn't that normal?" She met Billie's eyes in the mirror. "He told me he regrets the way he raised Agosto and wants to make things right with his grandson. To be a part of his life like a normal grandparent should. Does that sound like a horrible thing to ask?"

"You don't know him, Mother, or what he's capable of."

"Neither do you. You're just taking Margaret's word for it. Have you thought that perhaps she's being a bit over-protective and possessive because up until now she's been the driving force in her son's life, other than Handel of course. Davy is ten-years-old. He needs strong male leadership."

"Mother, you don't know what you're saying. Davy's father was a bastard of the highest order. Edoardo is the strong male influence that made him that way." She could see she was getting nowhere fast. She shook her head and got off the bed. "I can't do this right now. We'll talk in the morning."

"Do you want me to move into a hotel?"

"Of course not! Mother," she pleaded, "don't

make this about you. This is Margaret and Davy's lives we're talking about."

"Whatever."

Billie stopped with her hand on the knob of the door and stared in wonder at the woman occupying her mother's body. Her mother, the epitome of etiquette and manners, proponent of proper English and derider of slang, had said *whatever* like a valley girl in training. What next? *Snap?*

"Good night." She went out and closed the door behind her, too tired to continue any conversation. When she slipped quietly back into bed, Handel rolled over to face her and mumbled something that sounded like, *the defendant's guilty.* She yawned and tried to fall back to sleep but every time she'd dose off she dreamt she was fighting some old guy in court while her mother clung to his arm, swooning whenever he smiled her way. She woke repeatedly in a cold sweat.

CHAPTER ELEVEN

Billie woke to sunlight glinting through the blinds and birdsong outside the window. She turned bleary eyes toward the red digital numbers of the alarm. Eight o'clock. Handel was already out of bed and she could smell frying bacon and eggs floating toward her on a lovely cloud of fresh brewed coffee fumes.

She let her head fall back against the pillow in pure contentment. "Beautiful. A husband who cooks. I've died and gone to heaven."

Ten minutes later she was just dozing off again when she heard her mother call. "Billie, your breakfast is getting cold!" She rapped on the bedroom door. "Handel said to let you sleep, but since he's run off I figured we could talk. Get dressed and I'll warm you a plate."

Billie reluctantly slid out of bed and pulled on shorts and a t-shirt. There was no independent living when her mother was around. She was the child and always would be. She ran a brush through her hair

187

and pulled it off her neck with a clip, said a little prayer for patience, and hurried to the kitchen.

"Good morning," she said as cheerfully as she could manage before coffee.

Her mother handed her a steaming cup of java and waved her into a chair. "Your plate is in the oven. Just a sec." She put an oven mitt on and opened the door. The savory smell of bacon wafted out and made Billie realize she was ravenous.

"Wow, Handel was really busy this morning," she said, taking a bite and savoring the salty goodness. She folded two more strips of crispy bacon between crosscut slices of buttered toast. "Where did you say he went?"

Sabrina brought her coffee cup to the table and sat down across from Billie. "He said he needed to run to his office for something. After all the trouble I went to, he barely ate a thing."

"You cooked breakfast?"

"Of course. Did you think it materialized out of thin air?"

"No, I thought Handel made it."

Her mom gave a short laugh. "A man that cooks? That's what married women's dreams are made of."

"You got that right," she said, and sighed.

"I know I was angry last night, but let's put it behind us, honey," her mother began, reaching out to pat her hand.

"I'd love to." She smiled and took a sip of coffee. "So when are you taking that hog back to San Francisco and flying home?"

"Oh, I'm not leaving quite yet. I just got here. You haven't even filled me in on what's happened around here the past eight months." She raised her brows expectantly. "Adam looks happy and evidently fancies himself in love. Is he still looking for a second job? I hope he's not wasting his time in those dive bars singing for loose change, like he did in college. He has real talent with numbers. He could get a banking job or work for some big firm." Her mother paused to take a sip of coffee and Billie jumped in.

"Adam and Margaret make a great couple. I'm happy for both of them, and for Davy," she added. "He really looks up to Adam and I think that's a good thing. Adam realizes loving Margaret comes with a price. Taking on the role of a father. Being responsible for someone other than himself. I think he's ready. You should be proud of him."

"He just turned twenty-four," her mother said. "I read an article that said a boy's brain is not fully formed until he's twenty-four. What if he's slow?"

"He's not a boy. He's a man. He's old enough to drink, drive, go to war, and vote. He's old enough to be in love." Billie wondered why her mom had pushed her to date and find the right man from the day she graduated high school, but refused to encourage her son to do the same.

"I guess you're right, but he should at least have a good job before he decides to commit and settle down with a wife and child."

"Well, I think you might want to hold off on planning his future. As far as I know he hasn't proposed or anything." She didn't think it was her place to tell their mother that Adam had a job singing in a nightclub and that he was pursuing the music career that she so eloquently voiced as *wasting his time*. "But you should ask him.

"I plan to. What time does he come to work?"

She shrugged. "It varies. Depending on how much sleep he's had," she said, before her brain caught up with her mouth. "I mean – we don't need him every day."

Sabrina's gaze narrowed, but she only nodded. "Will he be in today or do I need to stop over at Margaret's place to see him?"

"Oh, he doesn't live with Margaret," she said quickly. "He has an apartment in town."

"Oh." Sabrina visibly relaxed, and smiled. "That's good. Margaret wouldn't want to set a bad example for Davy."

"No, she's pretty conservative that way." Billie swallowed a bite of eggs and washed it down with the last of her coffee. She got up to get a refill. Remembering the red negligee in her mother's shopping bag, she couldn't help asking, "And how do you feel about sex outside of marriage?"

"Billie! Why would you even ask me that?"

"After seeing that negligee, I had to ask. It's not the kind of thing a woman wears when she's alone."

"I bought that for you, silly."

"For me?" Billie frowned. "Why?"

Sabrina got up and started cleaning the dishes and putting things away. "Because it's your birthday next week and I wanted to buy you something special."

Billie wondered if special had a different meaning in her mother's world. "Wouldn't that have been a more timely gift at my bridal shower?"

"Until you have children running around this winery, I'd say a little romance is always timely." She flashed a smile over her shoulder. "I'm sure Handel will love it."

"I guess you should have bought it in his size," she said, setting her dishes on the counter. She kissed her mother's cheek. "I need to get ready and run over to the office for a bit. Are you planning to go out?"

"Mind if I use the car again?" her mother asked, rinsing a plate under the tap. "My hair gets so frizzy under that helmet and I thought I'd take Adam out for lunch. A little mother/son time."

"No. Go ahead." She assumed Handel had taken the Mazda to the office. He knew Sabrina preferred the bigger vehicle when she drove. "See you later then. Thanks for breakfast."

••••

Handel swung the hinged cityscape of San Francisco away from his built-in wall safe and punched in the digital combination. He pulled open the door and reached to the back where he'd stowed his gun and holster. He had a conceal carry license, but had never actually worn the gun anywhere except to the shooting range.

Today he was wearing it. He wasn't about to go into a gang neighborhood unarmed and vulnerable. Hosea might not want him dead, but someone did want to stop him from learning the truth. Whether it was to keep Sloane Kawasaki behind bars or to protect his own butt, he wasn't sure. He would be prepared.

He strapped on the shoulder harness, checked that the gun was loaded, then flicked on the safety and slid it into the holster. After pulling his suit coat back on, he went into the little executive bathroom and stared at his reflection. There was a small bulge under his coat, but not really obvious. The real test would be if Patty noticed.

He flipped off the lights and closed his office door. Patty was typing away at her keyboard. She glanced up with a smile. "Going home already, Mr. Parker?"

"I've got some errands to run first," he said, avoiding a direct lie. If Billie called, at least Patty would have an excuse handy for his extended absence. "I'll see you tomorrow."

Outside in the car he settled into the seat, adjusted the holster now poking him in the ribs, and put Hosea's address into his phone's GPS. In a couple of hours he would be talking to the one man who could tell him whether or not his client was guilty of murder.

••••

Billie stopped in the front office. Sally – or the office coordinator, as her secretary preferred to be called now – was still going through her morning rituals. She had her feet up on the extra chair and was drinking coffee, doing her nails in a bright shade of green, and watching an episode of whatever show she'd missed the night before, on her computer screen.

"I'm glad the business Internet account is being put to good use," she said, stepping around the desk to see what Sally was watching this morning. A bunch of decade's past stars were flaunting aged bodies in skimpy outfits while they danced the rumba. "Have you seen Ernesto around?" she asked.

Sally didn't look up from her nail polish endeavors. She shook her head. "He's been going out to check the grapes every morning." She glanced up at the clock on the wall. "Probably in the north field about now with that new kid. Trying to teach him all he knows."

"What new kid?"

"You know, the one he hired to help build the bandstand. He told him he could stay on and help with harvest too. He's been trying to find things for him to do." She finally glanced up, blowing on her nails. "He and Carlos can't do everything," she said, as though Billie had argued the point.

"No, I suppose not. That's why I gave Ernesto the job of hiring. He knows when and if we need extra help and for how long. I trust him." She stepped out into the hall. "You — I'm not so sure about."

"You can't get better help around here than me!" Sally called out belatedly. "Trust is overrated!"

Billie was already pushing through the front door. Ernesto had a cell phone with him most of the time, but he had been known to leave it in the truck. She walked behind the winery and around to the bandstand, climbed up on stage and looked toward the north fields. The platform gave her a very good view of the surrounding vineyards and she soon spotted Ernesto's pickup parked along the dirt road between fields.

She climbed down and started walking. It was going to be unusually hot today. According to the thermometer tacked to the wall of the shed she passed, the temperature was already at eighty-two degrees and rising. If this kept up, harvest would be here before they were ready. She was glad she'd put on shorts this morning.

As she drew closer, she saw the two men standing a little way inside a row of Riesling, heads down examining the berries. When Ernesto looked up, she waved. "Good morning," she said, stopping at the end of the row. "I see you're busy teaching the new kid on the block."

Ernesto nodded his head toward the younger man. "Sí, esto es Javier Hernández."

"Nice to meet you, Javier," she said and smiled. The young man didn't smile back or respond, he just stood looking at her, hands stuffed in the front pockets of his baggy jeans. He wore a long-sleeved plaid shirt, buttoned all the way up and she wondered how he could stand the heat. She thought maybe he didn't speak English, but when she turned back to Ernesto, he was giving Javier a hard look like a father reprimanding his son for being rude.

She cleared her throat. "Ernesto, could I speak with you a minute?"

"Sí." He said something to his young protégé in Spanish that Billie couldn't keep up with, but it sounded like it may have included a reprimand. Apparently, watching soap operas on Spanish television wasn't really the best way to learn the language.

Javier started walking back to the winery, kicking up little puffs of dust with every step. She squinted after him, trying to see the tattoo climbing the back of his neck. Why did all these young men want to cover themselves in ink? She was glad Handel had spent his money on education when he was younger rather than adorning his body with pictures of leopards or naked ladies. He was much too sexy in his natural skin...

"Miss Fredrickson?" Ernesto jolted her from her daydream.

"Sorry. Thinking about winery business," she

lied, even as she felt her face flush with color. "Actually, I had a question for you. Handel and I were planning to visit a friend in the city and we heard it's a bit of a dangerous neighborhood." She told him the suburb and street address and he shook his head vigorously.

"You don't want to go there. It's a bad place. I went there once to see my cousin. You couldn't pay me to go back."

"Don't you see your cousin anymore?"

He lifted his cap and scratched his head. "He was in a gang. Now he's in prison for murder."

"That's terrible."

He shrugged. "He crossed the border to get away from that life, but he couldn't escape. The gang pulled him back in."

"Were you ever tempted to join a gang, Ernesto?" she asked, her interest peaked by his family admission. "You seem pretty level-headed now."

"No. I always loved the vines. My family had a vineyard when I was a boy."

"I knew you worked at a vineyard in Sonoma before you came here, but I didn't know about your family's vineyard. What happened?"

He rubbed a hand over his chin and looked off across the field toward the Parker place. "The drug cartel wanted my padre to plant marijuana between the vines. He refused and they set it on fire. We lost every vine. He died soon after that. It was his life blood."

Billie didn't know what to say. She shook her head. "I'm sorry."

"Long time ago. Now I care for these vines," he said and moved toward the truck. "Want a ride?"

"Sure." She didn't know how to talk Handel out of going to see Hosea, but after hearing Ernesto's thoughts on the matter, she knew she had to try. There must be a way to speak with Hosea that didn't involve putting Handel at risk. She certainly couldn't ask Ernesto to go along now. He was adamant about never wanting to go there again.

They climbed in the truck and bumped over the rutted road back to the winery. When he pulled under the shade of the oaks and shut off the ignition, she thanked him and started to climb out.

The driver's side door creaked loudly when he pushed it open. "Javier is from that neighborhood," he said, moving around the back of the truck.

She stopped and waited for him.

He looked down, hands stuck in the back pockets of his cotton workpants. "I hope you won't be upset but I've been letting him stay in the woodworking shed until he gets a place."

"Ernesto, the winery could get in trouble for that. It's against regulations to have people live in those buildings. You know that."

He met her eyes. "I'm sorry. I'll find him someplace else."

The sadness in his eyes was curious. "Is Javier more than an employee to you?" she asked.

He hesitated before nodding. "He's my cousin's son. I promised his father I would look out for him, but when Vega went to prison, Javier fell in with the same gang. He was only fifteen, but there was nothing I could do. That was three years ago. He showed up a few weeks back and said he was done with that life. He wanted a fresh start." Ernesto reached in his pocket for his wallet and opened it. "I can pay you for rent," he offered.

She put out a hand, urging him to put his money away. "No. That's not the problem. It's city regulations. If it were up to me I wouldn't mind him staying here temporarily, but I can't afford to be fined or shut down because of it. You understand?"

"Sí. I will move him out."

"Can't he stay with you?"

"We don't have an extra room. My mother-in-law lives with us now," he said. "But I will talk to Mona. She will let him sleep on the couch until we find another place."

Billie took that to mean his wife was not too keen on the idea or Javier would have been there already. She probably didn't want an ex-gangbanger hanging around her two little boys.

"Thank you for understanding, Miss Fredrickson. I don't want to make trouble for you."

Billie couldn't help wondering as she walked back to the house whether trouble had already been made. Was it a coincidence that Javier showed up about the same time that Handel had his accident? Stranger still – that they'd had a rash of vandalism since he'd been living on her property.

She poured herself a cup of cold coffee and stuck it in the microwave for a few seconds. Her mother was already gone out. The garage was empty and the door left open when she walked by. She sat at the kitchen table and dialed Handel on her cell phone. He didn't pick up after four rings and his answering service picked up.

She left him a message. "Handel, when are you coming home? Did you decide to stay at the office and work a while? I spoke with Ernesto. He told me

some things you might find interesting. I'll talk to you
when you get back. Love you. Bye."

••••

Handel felt the phone vibrate in his pocket.
Probably Billie. He hoped she wouldn't be too upset
when she found out he'd left without her, but it
would be tricky enough to get in and out of Hosea's
neighborhood intact without bringing his wife along.
He flipped on the radio to pass the time.

After the weather report, news turned to the
trial. The talk radio host's glib tone made Handel
think he was announcing the release of a Hollywood
movie, rather than a trial that would decide someone's
fate. "After a lengthy continuance, San Francisco's
high profile murder case, Kawasaki versus the State of
California, resumes this Monday. Sloane Kawasaki's
lead defense, Handel Parker, was in critical condition
after an accident on I80E early last month. He has
since been released from the hospital and is reported
to be doing well."

The host's sidekick spoke up. "That's one way
to buy time to refute the state's case." Laughter.

"Yeah, the hard way. But whether he can prove
his client innocent is yet to be seen. For those of you
who have been living under a rock, here's what
happened. Multi-millionaire owner of Sakitown
Imports, Sloane Kawasaki, is on trial for murder in
the death of his wife. She was found dead last
September when police were sent to the Kawasaki
residence due to an anonymous 911 call."

"Sounds like another way of saying, the bastard
knocked his wife around then left the house and
called from a payphone so no one would know he'd
been home. Living in a house that big, so far from

other neighbors, who's gonna know?"

"True. Unless the servants speak up, and they probably don't speak English," the host said dryly. "Or have green cards. But who needs'em? This is a sanctuary city after all!" They both laughed and the host continued his version of the news. "Mr. Kawasaki has maintained his innocence, pleading not guilty and in fact put up a one hundred thousand dollar reward for information leading to the arrest and conviction of the *true* killer." He scoffed. "Might be kind of hard to find a witness in that neighborhood. They were probably all out playing golf at the country club." The sidekick laughed along and they cut to a commercial.

"Ha ha," Handel murmured. He wished the media would quit trying the case in the court of public opinion so that he could do his job. At this point, even if Sloane were acquitted, the many who believed the pontificating of the media, bloggers, and/or anyone with an opinion, would still consider him guilty.

After sitting in bumper-to-bumper traffic for an extra half an hour because of an accident up ahead, Handel finally exited the freeway and made his way through the city, following GPS directions. He was soon in a part of town he'd always managed to circumvent in the past. Rundown buildings, barred windows, and tough looking characters hanging out on street corners were a few clues that he was not in the Valley anymore.

At a stop sign he flipped on his turn signal and waited for an old pickup to make a left hand turn across from him. A group of young men lounged against the building to his right, eyeing him like a rabbit fallen into a den of wolves. One of the men stepped forward, pulling up faded, sagging jeans with one hand. "Yo, dude," he said loud enough to be heard through the closed window. "You lookin' fer something? I got what you need." He pulled the edge of his shirt up and revealed little baggies taped to his stomach.

Handel shook his head and turned the corner. He saw the man flip him off when he glanced in the rearview mirror. Two more blocks and he turned left, onto Bourbon Street. The houses were close set, peeling paint and broken shutters. Patches of dirt and chained Pitbulls claimed the area where grass should be. Two kids, not more than twelve or thirteen, sat on a front porch smoking.

House numbers were nearly obsolete, but he managed to make out the faded outline of 19457 on the mailbox of a bright turquoise house in the middle of the block. There was no killer dog in sight but there was a warning sign on the front door that said, *No Trespassing. Violators will be shot. Survivors will be shot again.*

He pulled along the curb and shut off the engine, looked around. The two boys were watching him cautiously from their stoop, necks craned. They were probably wondering if he was a cop or something. He should move quickly before Hosea realized he was here and snuck out the back before he had a chance to talk to him. Now was as good a time as any. "Relax. Deep breaths," he told himself. He drew his gun from the holster, pulled open the door and stepped out. A dog yipped a couple doors down and he glanced that way. A tiny Chihuahua stared at him through the slats of a rickety wood fence, bulbous eyes glaring as though he thought he were a Doberman. But his bark was annoying rather than frightening, and Handel wished the thing would shut up.

Holding the gun close to his side, he hurried up the crumbling blacktop driveway. An old, rusty, white, cargo van was parked there, the front passenger-side tire completely flat. He stepped over a pile of boards left stranded in the path and up to the front porch. He read the warning sign again and confidently gripped his gun, being careful to keep his finger off the trigger. He'd had plenty of hours of practice, but actually carrying a weapon and maybe having to use it in a real situation was much different than shooting at outlines of Osama Bin Laden at the firing range.

He rapped at the door, half expecting a large dog to announce his presence by lunging at him from the inside, but there was no sound. Nothing. Maybe Hosea wasn't home. He banged harder. There was a doorbell, but it was dangling from the wall on the end of exposed wires, as though someone had gotten angry at the sound and ripped it off.

Handel slipped his gun in the holster and cupped his hands to look in the front window. There was a curtain covering most of it, but a small opening was all he needed. He peered in, squinting to focus. He saw a light on in the back. It looked like the kitchen area. The front room was dark but he could make out a sagging couch and old stuffed chair.

He turned around and looked up and down the street. The boys were gone from their porch, but a woman was staring at him from the yard where the yippy little dog was still barking. He waved. "Have you seen Hosea?" he called. She picked up her dog, turned around and hurried back into her pink house. "Thanks," he said under his breath.

Before he could talk himself out of it, he put his hand on the knob and turned. Much to his surprise and more than a little disappointing to his personal safety gauge, the door opened. "Hosea?" he called softer into the gloomy room. "Are you here? I'd really like to talk to you. I come in peace," he added as an afterthought, remembering Billie's analogy of Tonto and The Lone Ranger.

Other than the soft hum of the small window air conditioner in the front room, the house remained quiet. He moved slowly toward the kitchen where he could see the side of a refrigerator covered in magnets and pet dishes in the corner against the wall. Hosea did have a pet, but the bowls were small so hopefully the dog would be small as well and easy to fend off if it showed up.

The kitchen was an L shape so until he got to the doorway, he couldn't make out the rest of the room. A soft meow startled him and he stopped and drew his gun. A white and tan cat ran out of the kitchen and straight toward him. But instead of attacking him like a good guard dog would have done, the cat ran through his legs and out the open front door. Great. Now Hosea really would have a reason to kill him.

He looked down at the carpet where the cat had just run across. The matted, green nap was certainly not the cleanest he'd ever encountered, but he could still make out little paw prints in a slightly darker shade. He turned and followed the trail into the kitchen where the tracks glistened damply red against yellowed linoleum. Blood.

He raised the gun and moved slowly, careful not to step in the trail that led directly to Hosea's body. The young man's head was braced against the bottom of the cupboards, his body sprawled on the kitchen floor as though he'd slowly slid down to rest. Blood oozed from gunshot wounds to his chest and head, puddling beneath him.

"Dear God. I'm in deep –"

The high whine of sirens alerted him to danger. He quickly holstered his gun, stepped around the murder scene, and hurried to the front door. A police cruiser was already turning into the end of the street. He sat down on the front porch and waited. When the officers stepped out of their car, he raised his hands in the air to show them he was safe.

"Get down on the ground!" one of the officers yelled, moving forward with gun in hand.

Handel put his hands behind his head and slowly eased off the porch and got down on his knees. When the officer approached, he volunteered, "I'm Attorney Handel Parker, Officer. I have a conceal carry license and am carrying my weapon in a shoulder harness."

"Lay flat on the ground, hands behind your head!" the officer yelled again.

The other officer knelt down and relieved him of his weapon and cuffed his hands behind his back. Handel remained completely still, complying with the officers. The younger officer grabbed his arm and pulled him up to a standing position. He took out his wallet and checked his identification.

"What are you doing here, Mr. Parker?" the officer demanded. "We got an anonymous call reporting a shooting." He raised Handel's gun and sniffed. "This hasn't been fired.

"I came to speak with a potential witness about the trial I'm working on and found Mr. Garcia dead on the kitchen floor. He's been shot at least twice."

The other officer called it in on his radio. "Okay, you're going to have to sit in the car and wait, sir, while we get this sorted out." They put him in the back of the patrol car, still in handcuffs, and shut the door.

Handel watched the two officers prepare to enter the house, guns drawn, one from the front, the other circling around to the back. He tried not to breath too deeply in the enclosed space. The back seat of the cruiser smelled like stale urine and vomit. He was going to have a lot of explaining to do when he got home.

CHAPTER TWELVE

After a nice, civilized lunch with her son, learning that he was doing all the things she'd hoped he'd given up, Sabrina dropped Adam off at his apartment and headed back down the highway toward the winery. He was a grown man, like Billie said, but she couldn't seem to see him that way. He was still her little boy, just taller with rougher cheeks. She knew she had to let him make his own decisions, even if they included stupid choices she didn't agree with. She'd made plenty of those herself over the years. Was it a crime to wish better choices for your children?

Her cell phone buzzed and she assumed it was Adam calling to apologize for disappointing her. She glanced down at the passenger seat where she'd dropped her phone with her purse. The screen was lit up with a number.

Edoardo. Her heart did a little flutter. She felt like a teenager when she was with him, so insecure and pulled in by his obvious mastery of the female psyche. He could say that her hair was as brown as the underside of a muskrat and she'd probably smile and giggle. What was wrong with her? She knew the man was no good, but whatever had been pulling her to make split second decisions for the past year or so had also taken over her ability to say no to bad boy types – or bad man types.

She shook her head and kept driving. Italian millionaires be damned! She would not answer the phone. When it stopped ringing, she breathed a sigh of relief. Wonderful. He'd given up. Now she could go back to Billie's place and act like the stick-in-the-mud woman she'd always been. It was certainly safer.

The phone tweeted, alerting her to an incoming text. Would the temptation never end? She pulled the car over onto the shoulder of the road and picked up her phone, opened messages and read. *Come with me to Honolulu. If we leave now, we can be there for a torch lit Luau on the beach.* "Of all that's holy…" she murmured into the quiet of the car.

She pressed her lips together and closed her eyes. A Luau on Waikiki. She could feel the sand between her toes, balmy breezes playing through her hair, and hear waves gently lapping against the shore. This was the stuff romance novels were made of. A rich, handsome man who was probably no good, enticing her to run off on a whim and live out what she'd only allowed herself to fantasize about up till now.

Dropping the phone, she glanced in her rearview, and whipped the steering wheel around, making a U-turn back onto the highway. Billie would have to pick the car up at Harvest House if she needed it. She was going to Honolulu.

••••

Billie had been back working at the office for a couple of hours before she realized that she still had not heard from Handel. She tried his cell again, but it went straight to voicemail. She turned off her computer and overhead light and pulled the door closed after her. Sally was sitting at her desk chatting with Loren when she stopped in the doorway.

"No customers in the tasting room?"

Loren shrugged. "Slow day. Sammie is watching the bar for me."

"Great. Could you tell Margaret I went home?" she said to Sally. "If she needs me I'll be around. Just give me a call."

"No problemo, boss."

Loren followed her out to the front door and held it open. "When's your mom going home? Thought maybe Sally and I could ride along to the city with her when she goes. Make sure she gets back all right and have a little adventure at the same time."

"That's very thoughtful of you, Loren," she gave him a crooked smile, "but I have no idea when she's going. I'll be sure and pass along your offer though."

He grinned. "Mother squaw getting on daughter squaw's last nerve?"

"Something like that. She's out getting on Adam's last nerve right now. I'm sure I'll be hearing from him soon."

Loren laughed and let the door swing shut.

Except for her mother's rented Harley parked along the side, the garage was still empty when she passed by. It felt strange as if she'd been deserted. Where was he? She once enjoyed her own space, felt freer alone, but since Handel came back into her life she couldn't imagine that state of existence being attractive ever again. He was more than a lover; he was her best friend. She could confide in him, share her heart with him, and just simply be with him.

She let herself in the back door and flipped on the kitchen light. He was so insistent on speaking with Hosea Garcia in person before the trial resumed that she felt sure he would have returned from the office by now. She filled the decanter with water to make coffee, and reached in the cupboard for the Hazelnut Crème coffee beans when the realization hit her like a hammer to the chest.

"He wouldn't," she told herself even while her heart raced with dread. She dropped the bag of coffee beans and picked up her cell phone. Quickly scrolled through the numbers to Handel's office. It rang only once before Patty picked up.

"Parker & Associates."

"Patty? This is Billie. Is Handel there by any chance?" She bit at her lip, expectantly hopeful, yet dreading the answer.

"I'm sorry, Billie. Mr. Parker left quite some time ago. He said he had some errands to do. I'm sure you'll be seeing him soon."

"Thank you. I'm sure I will," she said. She dropped the phone on the table and sank into a chair, feeling numb. He'd lied to her. Not right out lied to her face, but just as good as. She felt conflicted, wanting to wring his neck but at the same time desperate to know he was safe. She glanced at the clock. He would have had plenty of time to get to the city, find Hosea, and start home by now. Unless something had happened. Something bad.

She snatched up the phone and called his cell, and once again it automatically switched over to voice mail. She didn't do helpless well, but that's what she was. Without a car and without a clue. It was time to trust someone bigger than herself. Someone who knew the beginning from the end. "Please God, don't let anything happen to him," she begged.

••••

Adam picked Davy up from soccer camp same as always, but the boy was unnaturally quiet. He sat with his head pressed against the door, not saying a word. Adam noticed he had a couple huge scrapes down the side of his leg and another cut on his lip, but he decided to ignore that until Davy was ready to talk about whatever happened.

He flipped the radio on to a classic rock station and sang along. "Hot blooded, check it and see. I got a fever of a hundred and three…"

Davy turned his head to stare at him curiously. "Do you know the words to every song ever written?" he asked.

Adam laughed and turned the radio down. "Not quite. I know a lot of songs but I'm sure there are a few out there I haven't heard yet."

"Mom said you're a musical genius."

"No, she didn't," Adam shook his head, grinning. Margaret might love the way he played but she would never use those words. People like Page, Hendrix, Clapton, they were genius. He was adequate. "You must have misunderstood her," he said.

"No, I didn't. She was talking to Uncle Handel and said compared to his singing you were a musical genius."

"I liked the shorter version better." He shook

his head. "But thanks for the update." He turned into an empty corner lot where an ice cream truck had set up business. A line of customers were already waiting for popsicles and ice cream bars. He shut off the engine and rolled down the window. Ice cream always made things better. "Hungry?"

Davy nodded.

Adam pulled out a ten-dollar bill and handed it to him. "Get me whatever you're having," he said.

"Okay."

He watched Davy run to the truck and get in line behind three other kids. His cell phone rang and he picked up. "Hey," he said, seeing it was Billie calling. "What's up?"

"Are you with Mom?" she asked, without preamble.

"Nope. I just picked Davy up from soccer practice. She left hours ago. Probably two, two fifteen."

"Really?" She sounded worried.

"What's wrong, Billie?" He unbuckled his seatbelt and climbed out of the car. Keeping an eye on Davy, he walked over to stand in the shade of a group of walnut trees bordering the lot. "You know she likes to shop. Maybe she stopped somewhere and lost track of time. She's definitely been acting weird lately."

"You told her you're playing the club, right?"

"Yeah. She was disappointed, but I think she took it well."

She was quiet for a moment.

"What else is wrong?" he asked. It was Davy's turn to order so he would be running back in a minute. "It's not just Mom, is it?"

"Handel went to San Francisco without me." Billie's voice sounded husky like maybe she'd been crying.

He didn't want to sound unsympathetic, but that was the lamest reason to be upset he'd ever heard. Handel practically lived in San Francisco during a trial, and that was starting up again on Monday. His accident had apparently brought out her anxious, paranoid side. "He's always done that. Why's this time different?"

"Because he could get himself killed," she said, choking on the last word. She hated crying in front of anyone. Always had to be the strongest, the bravest, the one with airtight tear ducts. His sister had been a tough act to follow.

"Hold on. Where exactly did he go?"

Davy was walking toward him, an ice cream bar in each hand.

"He went to see that guy who was at the concert the other day. You know, the one covered in tats? He's a member of the MS-13 gang and says he knows who killed Sloane Kawasaki's wife."

"What? Shouldn't he send his private investigator or something?"

Davy handed him an ice cream bar covered in chocolate and crispy things. He took a bite and nodded his thanks. Davy apparently recognized one of the other kids cause he took off again and stood near the car eating his ice cream, talking to a big kid with freckles and long red hair pushed behind his ears.

Billie sighed, exasperation seeping through the line. "That's what I told him but he wouldn't listen. I thought he was going to wait and have someone else go with him, but he took off and isn't answering his phone. He intentionally left this morning while I was sleeping." She sniffed again.

"I'm sure he's fine. Maybe his battery went dead," he suggested, feeling the need to stick up for Handel. The man was only trying to keep Billie out of danger. That was his job after all, to protect his wife. Not that she would see it that way. Come to think of it, Margaret probably wouldn't think of it that way either. A real man didn't stand a chance these days.

"I've got to go," she said. "If you hear from Mom let me know."

"Will do."

He slid the phone in his pocket and returned to the car. Davy was done with his ice cream and was taking turns kicking a hacky sack with the other kid. He waved goodbye and climbed in the Corvette beside Adam.

"Is that a friend of yours?" He asked as he pulled out of the lot back onto the street, moving slow to keep from bottoming out his shocks on a big dip in the entrance.

Davy nodded. "He's in my class at school. He's eleven but he got held back by his mom," he said as though that were a badge of honor. "He didn't have to go to school till he was seven."

"Cool," Adam said and rolled up his window to turn the air on again.

"Who was ya talking to?"

"Billie. She was looking for Sabrina."

Adam was eager to get back to the winery, drop off Davy and drop in on his sister. He accelerated and passed a red Honda on highway 29 going five under the speed limit. Davy slipped down in his seat as though he was afraid of being seen. Adam shifted gears and pulled back into the right side. "Someone you know?" he asked.

Davy nodded.

"I thought you loved this car. Why are you acting ashamed to be seen in it?"

Davy straightened up but kept his face turned away. "I'm not."

"Looked that way to me. It wouldn't have anything to do with the cuts and scraps all over you today, would it?" He glanced in the rearview and passed another car.

Davy shrugged.

"Was that a yes?" He tapped a beat on the steering wheel. "You know your mom isn't going to accept a shrug as explanation. She'll want to know exactly what happened."

"Can't you tell her I got hurt playing soccer?"

"Did you?"

"No," he said, barely loud enough to hear.

Adam shook his head. "I won't lie to your mom and neither should you. What ever happened, she'll understand."

He was quiet. They passed vineyard after vineyard, the heady sweet scent of ripe grapes heavy in the air. Even with the air conditioner on it filled the car. Finally, they passed the sign for Fredrickson's. Davy stirred beside him, grabbing the handle of his sport bag in readiness as though he were going to jump out while the car was still in motion.

Adam slowed for the turn and glanced across the fields. Black smoke rose hazy on the still air. "What the…?"

Davy turned to look in the same direction. "It's

the wood working shed! It's on fire!" he said unnecessarily.

Adam pulled into the end of the driveway and churned up gravel as he skidded in a U-turn facing back the way they'd come. He hit the gas and peeled out, tires squealing against blacktop as they gained traction. In seconds they were turning in at the Fredrickson corner. He handed the phone to Davy. "Call 911 and tell them there's a fire at the winery."

Adam parked back by the house and honked the horn, hoping to alert anyone still around and bring them out to help. He ran toward the hose reel attached to the garden shed and started yanking it out. There was a sprayer end on it that Billie used to wash the car. He twisted the faucet on all the way, grabbed the end of the hose and ran, stretching the coil as far as it would go.

The north side of the shed was already ablaze with flames shooting toward the afternoon sky. A garden hose would probably do little to slow the progress of the fire on the building, but maybe he could put down enough water to keep sparks from spreading to the vines. The hose stopped and he looked back. He was at the end. Still not close enough to do much good. He sprayed the ground around the base of the shed, but couldn't reach the entire side of the building. "Davy! See if Billie has another hose to add on!" he yelled.

Ernesto was beside him in seconds, with another hose. This one stretched from the back of the winery. One they used for cleaning the cement floors. His sprayed farther, reaching the vines closest to the building. He kept it raining over them, a shield of protection against flying sparks.

He didn't know how much time had passed before the wail of a siren cut the air and he glanced toward the road. A bright red fire engine raced down the drive. The team of firemen jumped out and quickly attached their hose to the fire hydrant outside the winery. Working together they advanced on the flames, sending a gush of water up and over the entire wall of flame.

Adam stepped out of the way, making room for the professionals. Smoke bellowed out and he moved back some more, coughing into the crook of his arm. Billie appeared at his side. She grabbed his arm, her face filled with fear.

She saw Ernesto and ran toward him. It looked like they were arguing about something, but the vineyard manager just kept shaking his head. Adam went and pulled her away from the action. She'd told Davy to stay back by the house and he was still there, leaning against the Corvette taking a video of the whole thing with Adam's phone.

"I think I'm going to be a fireman when I grow up," he said, eyes wide with interest as he watched the men at work putting the fire out.

"Why am I not surprised?" Adam took the phone from him and pressed the red button to stop the recording. He glanced up and saw Margaret pulling around the fire truck in her little pickup. She parked on the other side of the Corvette and jumped out.

"What happened?" she asked, joining them.

Billie shook her head, her mouth tight with anger. "That's what I'd like to know. Someone is trying to sabotage this winery and I've had about enough of it."

Adam met Margaret's confused gaze. He took her arm and walked away a few yards to speak privately. Billie didn't seem to notice. She stood with arms crossed, staring toward the burning building.

"I'm not sure what started it. Apparently, Billie thinks it has something to do with the other acts of vandalism, but she went off on Ernesto a little while ago for some reason, like she thinks he has something to do with it." He shrugged.

Margaret looked around. "Where's Handel?"

"That's the other thing. Billie called me earlier. Said Handel went to San Francisco to speak with a witness. It just so happens to be that creepy guy who threatened Billie the other day."

"What?" She spun around, eyes wide. "That guy had gang tats all over his body."

He nodded. "She's really worried."

"So am I now. I'll kill him when he gets home."

"Get in line." He slanted his eyes toward Billie.

The firemen had the flames contained within fifteen minutes. They'd all once again managed to keep the fire from damaging any of the vines, but the large outbuilding was a complete loss. The fire had gutted it, destroyed the south and west wall and whatever contents and tools weren't burned in the flames were damaged beyond redemption by smoke and water.

By the time they'd poked through the charred rubble and ascertained that it was safe to leave it for the night, the sun had slipped below the horizon, leaving streaks of cotton candy pink behind. Ernesto and Sally were the only employees still hanging around and they left once the firemen had packed up and led the way.

Margaret finally managed to get Davy in the pickup. She kissed Adam and sighed. "He needs dinner and I want to check on things at my place. This stuff is really freaking me out. What next?" She shook her head. "Good night."

"Night."

He waved as they headed home. When he turned around, Billie was sitting on the front steps of the house, head in her hands. He went over and sat beside her on the step. "What a day, huh?"

She didn't respond.

He felt his phone buzz in his pocket and pulled it out. It was a text from Sabrina. *Flew to Honolulu for a luau. Be back tomorrow night. The car is parked at Harvest House Hotel. If you need it, ask at the desk. Love, Mom.*

Billie had pulled her phone out at the same time. She was staring at the small screen, her mouth open in a look of pure shock.

He tilted his phone for her to see. "She sent it to both of us."

His sister made a moaning sound like a wounded animal. "Will this hellish day never end?" she demanded.

The sound of tires on gravel interrupted their misery. Billie stood up and watched her Mazda slowly approach. Adam intuitively knew that fireworks were about to commence and decided to make himself scarce. He kissed her cheek and hurried to his car.

Before Handel had parked in the garage, Adam was already flying down the highway toward his apartment. He cranked up the radio and sang along to America, *Ventura highway in the sunshine, where the days are longer, the nights are stronger than moonshine...*

••••

Handel knew before he stepped out of the car and approached his wife – who stood on the front porch, arms crossed tightly, lips drawn into a thin line – that he was not necessarily so lucky to be alive. He glanced back at the burned out shed and knew that no matter how pressing the question was to ask, now was not the time to worry about fire insurance either.

"Hey babe," he said, moving closer. "I'm sorry–" The word was barely out of his mouth and she was in his arms crying. This was so not what he expected. So not like Billie.

"How could you do that to me?" she demanded, pressing her cheek against his chest, arms wrapped securely around his neck as though she'd never let him go. "I've been sitting around here thinking you were shot or worse."

"Worse than shot," he teased, still trying to get his mind around this new version of his wife. He half expected she'd shoot him for not taking her along. Instead, she was clinging to him like Velcro. He patted her back. "It's all right. I'm fine."

She drew slowly away and pulled his suit coat open, eyes wide with fury. "What are you doing wearing a gun?" she asked, her words a harsh whisper.

"It's not what you think."

"It's exactly what I think! You expected violence and you went anyway, without backup and without a lick of sense."

"Now you're just being mean," he said, trying to get a smile out of her. It didn't work. He put his hands gently on her arms. "Look, I couldn't take you. I did think it would be dangerous and honestly, I didn't think it would be wise to bring a woman into that situation."

"But it was perfectly safe for a man, right?" She twisted out of his grip, now going straight from worry to righteous anger. "That's why you have a gun strapped to your side. What, did you imagine you were the Terminator or something? You think being male makes you invincible?"

"Billie," he said, trying to interrupt her diatribe so he could explain.

"You made me sit here all day long sick with worry, going over and over in my head every horrible thing that could have happened…"

"Billie!" He cupped her face with his hands, bringing her eyes to his. "Hosea was already dead when I got there. Someone shot him. The police showed up and I was put into the back of a cruiser. I had to go down to the station and give my statement before I could leave."

Her eyes filled with tears. "Thank God you got there too late," she said and pressed her lips to his, kissing him hard, salty tears and all.

Handel remembered the traffic jamb that had held him up on the highway for an extra half an hour, causing him to arrive on Bourbon Street within minutes of the murder. He added his own silent prayer of thanks and held her tight.

CHAPTER THIRTEEN

After a soak in the Jacuzzi, Handel and Billie sat cuddled together on the couch reading. He was rereading an old law journal article while she lay with her head in his lap staring at the same page of the novel she'd started twenty minutes ago. She finally put in a marker and set it aside.

"I can't concentrate," she said and sighed heavily. She scooted up to a sitting position, leaning her head on his shoulder and looking down at his magazine. "When are you going to ask?"

"Hmm?"

"The fire? You didn't notice one of the sheds was missing and the air smelled like burnt toast when you got home?" She ran her fingers down his arm. "You told me all about your experience in the *barrio*. While you were gone the *barrio* came to the winery." Neighborhood was one word she'd actually picked up from Spanish television.

"What are you talking about?" He laid the magazine on the coffee table.

Billie told him about her conversation with Ernesto and how his cousin's son just happened to be living in the shed for the past few weeks unbeknownst to anyone. "He's also a member of the Maras. You think that's a coincidence?"

He frowned down at her. "What did Ernesto say?"

"When I accused him of harboring the kid who shot at me? He refused to believe it, of course."

"But you don't know for sure that this kid shot at you, or that he started the fire. Where was he when all of this happened, anyway? I thought you said he's been shadowing Ernesto."

Billie shrugged. She was not proud of herself for the way she accused her vineyard manager of knowingly harboring a criminal. He didn't deserve that. He was a good man, just trying to help a lost boy. But there was something in his eyes when she spoke to him that looked a lot like fear. So he must have suspicions of his own. "He was with him earlier, but I didn't see him when the fire broke out."

"That is curious, and it does fit with what Hosea told me on the phone."

"He told you about Javier?"

He put his feet up on the coffee table and leaned his head back. "No, not exactly. When I all but accused him of shooting at you, he said we didn't need to worry about him, but to look closer to home for the culprit."

"Closer to home. Well, the wood working shed is pretty darn close."

Handel glanced at his watch. "Where's your mother? Shouldn't she be here cooking something elaborate for us?" he asked, probably only half teasing. They hadn't eaten dinner yet.

"I can't believe I forgot," she said, shaking her head. "She had the gall to send a text message to tell Adam and me that she was on her way to Honolulu."

"An impromptu vacation?"

"You know what this means. Salvatore is wining and dining my mother to get to Margaret, and she doesn't even have enough sense to see it." She stood up and paced to the window and back, feeling the tension tighten her chest again. "She's not acting herself. There is definitely something going on with her. I think she needs an intervention."

Handel sat forward on the couch, forearms braced on thighs. His brow was creased in thought. "How do you know he's using her to get to Margaret? Maybe he wants to get to your mom. She is an attractive woman."

She glared at him. "Did you really just say that to me?"

He threw up his hands. "Sorry. Trying to see things from both sides."

"Well, stop it." She ran her hands through her hair pushing it back from her face. "She's obviously having a mental breakdown or something. Why else would a middle-aged woman get on a private jet with a rich man she hardly knows to fly spur of the moment to Hawaii for a luau on the beach?"

Handel looked at her, a crooked smile curving his lips. He didn't say anything but she could hear the words as clear as if he did. What middle-aged woman wouldn't want to live out that fantasy? Billie only hoped her mother was strong enough to say no to anything above and beyond dinner and wine.

She blew out an exasperated breath. "Forget I

asked."

He stood up and put an arm around her shoulders, turned her toward the kitchen. "Come on. Let's eat. Talk of luaus is making me very hungry."

••••

Their whirlwind flight to Honolulu didn't end there. Sabrina followed Edoardo to a helicopter pad, hair blowing like mad as blades whipped the air around them. They ducked their heads and hurried along, his arm possessively wrapped around her. The copilot held open the door and took her hand to help her in, then spoke with her host for a moment before climbing into his seat and adjusting his radio headset.

Edoardo settled in beside her and showed her how to buckle the belt. His hands were hot against her skin when he touched her throat and collarbone as he pulled it across her chest.

The pilot spoke into his radio, gave a thumbs up and they lifted off. Flying over the city was beautiful. Sabrina was entranced. Waikiki beach spread pale and white between high-rise hotels and blue green waters foaming along the shore. They flew over Pearl Harbor and the Diamondhead crater and Edoardo pointed out other places of interest, speaking close to her ear, his hand resting on her thigh. She was glad she'd dressed casually in black capris and a lacy yellow top today. She didn't know what she'd wear later but he promised on the plane that he would supply any other clothes she might need. He'd said it with a subtle hint of humor as though it was ludicrous to think she'd need anything more than a towel and hotel bathrobe. The way he looked at her made her feel both hot and cold… but that could just be her hormones acting up again.

They flew along the edge of the island for a while, passing mile after mile of powdery white beaches. Edoardo leaned across her and pointed out the coral formations coming into view. "Kaneoche Bay," he said close to her ear. "We'll have a great view of Sacred Falls soon. Have you ever seen it?" he asked, his lips nearly brushing her skin.

She shook her head.

A valley of lush, green vegetation rushed by, and he explained that it was a popular site for making Hollywood movies. She nodded, trying to enjoy the ride in spite of the uneasiness she was beginning to feel. He brushed a finger along her jaw to get her attention. She looked down at the magnificent cascade of water. Even from the sky she could feel its shear power and might.

"Gorgeous," she breathed, trying to take it all in.

They flew on until a resort lay spread out before them. Tennis courts, golf course and swimming pools were unmatched by the beauty of the surrounding beach and ocean. The pilot spoke into the radio and soon landed on a heliport away from the hotel.

A car was waiting to shuttle them the short distance to the resort. Edoardo spoke with the pilots, then stopped to read a message on his phone while she climbed into the backseat of the car. The chauffeur tipped his hat, "Aloha."

"Aloha," she said in return. She was surprised the sun was still so bright. "What time is it?" she asked.

"Half past six, ma'am."

"I forgot. We gain three more hours on the

islands, don't we."

"Yes, ma'am."

Edoardo joined her in the car and they took a narrow curving road to the resort less than a mile away. He was quiet, giving her space. Sabrina wondered if he'd tired of the game already. He didn't seem like a man who would give up easily, though. She felt sure she was going to need to be firm tonight after the luau to persuade him that she wasn't ready for anything serious. Not that he would consider casual sex serious, but she certainly did.

At the front desk he introduced himself and the staff jumped to attention. They were shown to the presidential suite where elaborate flower arrangements and bowls of fruit waited like tokens of island hospitality. But Sabrina felt sure Edoardo had more to do with the display than resort management. He waved the bellhop away after giving him a generous tip for carrying his small overnight bag and laptop case.

With the door closed, Sabrina felt rather vulnerable. She walked around the huge room, stopped to admire the flowers, and lifted a strange red fruit she'd never seen before. "This is all so beautiful, Edoardo. Have you stayed here before?" she asked, to lighten the mood he'd fallen into.

"I've stayed here once or twice," he said, hanging his suit jacket in the closet. He moved leisurely toward her loosening his tie and unbuttoning the top button of his starched blue dress shirt with one hand. "I have a bit of money invested in this resort," he admitted with a shrug.

"Really? Which part do you own," she teased half-heartedly, backing up until her hip bumped the side of a Victorian-looking fainting couch. "The golf course or the swimming pools?"

"Neither. I own the beds," he said, reaching for her.

She nearly tripped trying to circumnavigate the couch, and ended up sitting down in the middle of it to keep from falling.

"And the couches," he said smoothly, lowering himself beside her. His mouth descended on her bare shoulder and moved upward to her neck, leaving a hot tingling trail of desire over her skin. This was definitely going to be harder than she thought.

He pushed her slowly down until her head rested on the pillowed arm of the couch and then cradled her legs in his lap and leaned down to kiss her. "You're so beautiful," he murmured, letting his lips stray to her neck and collarbone.

"So are you," she couldn't help adding. "And so fit," she said, feeling hard muscle beneath his shirt.

His laughter rumbled in his chest before he captured her lips once more and she was lost in a deluge of senses. She kissed him back, liking the power she felt at the way he showed his desire for her. Middle age had sucked a lot of life out of her and made her feel unattractive, unwanted, and most of all, unneeded. But this man — handsome, rich, able to have any woman he wanted — desired her. It was a heady drug that was quickly pulling her under.

She felt something stirring between them and gasped. This was going too far, too fast. He reached down and pulled his cell phone out of his slacks pocket, glanced at it and unwound himself from her.

"I need to take this," he said, moving toward the adjoining bedroom. He closed the door between them with a soft click.

She pulled up to a sitting position and caught her breath, feeling like a prisoner on death row getting a last minute reprieve. "Thank God," she whispered. When did she start letting emotion rule her head? Now was not the time to lose control. She was a fifty-three year old woman, for heaven's sake! Not a young innocent girl on her first real date.

Sabrina got up and grabbed her purse where she'd left it sitting on a low end table. She should have insisted immediately that they have separate rooms when she realized he'd secured the suite for them both. But Edoardo insisted on the way up in the elevator that with two elaborate bedrooms and bathrooms, and separate entrances, she would be as alone as she wanted to be. And there lay the rub. How alone did she want to be?

She hurried into the other bedroom and shut the door, locking it for good measure. If Billie and Adam knew the mess she'd gotten herself into, they would be shocked. After all the times she'd harped on them to always have a back-up plan, she had run off without any plan at all.

••••

Adam played at The Screech Owl from eight to eleven, but felt as though he'd done an all-nighter. He was wasted. He drove home to his apartment and sank into his easy chair with a bottle of beer, flipped on the television and watched the end of some old black and white movie about a disembodied hand crawling around strangling people. How that worked, he wasn't sure. Really strong fingers? He clenched his hand around the neck of the bottle and flipped to the news.

There was nothing interesting. A small bit about Sloane Kawasaki's offer of a reward to anyone who had eyewitness information leading to the arrest of the real killer. Regardless, he was on trial for his life on Monday and the reporter sounded almost happy about it, like he had a vested interest. Adam shook his head. These news people seemed to believe their own suppositions whether there were facts to back them up or not. Guilty until proven innocent was the new mantra. He hoped he never got caught in a false arrest, but if he did, he hoped Handel would take the case. The man was dogged. He still couldn't believe he'd driven into a dangerous gang neighborhood of San Francisco to speak with a possible witness.

He pulled his phone out of his pocket to check messages. He'd had it turned off at the club and forgot to turn it back on. Nothing more from his mom, and he was really worried. Why would she go off on a romantic interlude with a complete stranger? Sure she'd gone out to dinner with him once and he obviously put on a great act, but according to Margaret he was a real creep, even coming on to her the first time she met him at Carl's restaurant.

The adrenalin rush of fighting the fire earlier had wiped him out. He leaned his chair back and kicked the footrest up and scrolled through Margaret's messages. *Thanks for picking up Davy today. He told me he got into a fight to protect a girl. Talk to you about it tomorrow. Love you.*

So he was right. The kid had gotten into a fight. Sometimes he felt like he was witnessing his own childhood again. Davy was a lot like him. Maybe that's why they got along so well. He rubbed a hand over his face and yawned. Sleep. That's what he needed. His finger accidentally touched the little camera icon and the video player blinked on. He hadn't slid it back to camera mode after Davy took the movie of the fire.

Curious, he played it back, squinting at the little screen. He should plug it into his laptop. It would be much easier to see. There he was running with the hose, then spraying as far as he could reach. Ernesto showing up from the winery. Who was that? Did he just see someone run out from the other side of the shed? He went back to the beginning and played it again, looking hard at the south side of the building. Yes! There he was. A guy in a long-sleeved plaid shirt and a Fredrickson Winery cap appeared on the south side of the burning building, then disappeared out of the frame into the vineyard beyond. He didn't look familiar but the guy must work there. Why else would he have a hat with the winery logo?

A glance at the time told him it was too late to call Billie. After everything she'd been through in the past twelve hours, she probably needed the rest. He'd call in the morning. He downloaded it to YouTube and sent her the link in an email. Maybe when they watched it up on a bigger screen, one of them would recognize the guy.

••••

It was over two hours later when Edoardo finally knocked on her bedroom door. Sabrina sat on the edge of the king-sized bed and stared across the room at the locked door, wondering if the man had a key. He probably did, but was biding his time. He knocked again.

"Sabrina. Are you all right? I'm sorry I took so long. I had to take the call. It was important business." He paused, then asked, "Would you like to go for a swim before dinner?"

Dinner? That had come and gone. She had been starving and finally snuck out of her room an hour ago to eat one of the complimentary bananas from a fruit basket. Maybe his plan was to get her so hungry she would do whatever he asked. She drew in a breath and went to the door. It was now or never. She needed to make it clear that she was not going to be his next conquest.

She turned the knob. He leaned casually against the doorjamb with one shoulder, as though this happened all the time. His smile was quick and magnetic.

"Thank God you opened the door," he said, his Italian accent as sexy as ever. He reminded her of Armand Assante when he played leading roles in television movies during the seventies and eighties. Trouble was, he didn't always play a good guy, but much like Salvatore's personality – the dark side of the coin. "I thought perhaps I would have to break it down."

She swept past him, trying to look cool and confident. "No need for that. I'd love to go for a swim, but as you already know," she glanced down at the outfit she wore, "I have no suit."

He followed her slowly across the room, hands in his pockets. The corner of his mouth curved up. "That does not bother me."

"Well it does me," she said and stepped securely behind the bar to get a bottle of water from the refrigerator. Biding her time, she twisted off the cap and took a sip. "Perhaps you can go alone and I'll take a nap while you're gone," she suggested.

"Oh no, I will not go without you." He took her hand and tugged her from behind the bar then twirled her around as though they were dancing. His gaze moved seductively over her figure. "An American size eight, I think," he said with more confidence than his words implied.

"Excuse me?" Sabrina was unaccustomed to a man being so blatantly accurate. "If you had a lick of decency you'd guess a smaller number."

He laughed. "American women." He moved closer and brushed a lock of hair from her cheek. "No matter how beautiful you are, you are never satisfied with your body. Always looking for perfection that does not exist. Am I correct?"

"And I suppose Italian women are all completely comfortable in their own skin, right?"

"Of course. Because Italian men make sure they admire every woman for the singular beauty that she is. We don't compare, we celebrate the differences."

Wow. Just wow. As soon as she managed to write him off as a smooth operator and get him out of her head he said something totally unpredictable. Something that almost sounded as if he cared what women thought and what they felt, not just *how* they felt pressed against him. Dear God, she needed to get away from this man.

"I will have every available size eight swimming suit brought up immediately," he said and began dialing the phone on the bar.

"You don't have to—"

He cut her off with a snap of his fingers and spoke in a quietly authoritative voice to the person on the other end of the line. When he turned around he was smiling but his eyes were hard. He sighed and shook his head. "Please forgive me for being abrupt. It always takes a bit of getting used to," he said waving a hand toward her, "this American female habit of arguing every point. I know women's rights have twisted everyone's idea of equality, but truly wasn't it better when men and women knew their place and could expect certain things from members of the opposite sex?"

"Certain things?" she said, her American female poking her nose into the conversation again. "What exactly are you expecting from me, Mr. Salvatore?"

"No, no, no." He put his hands up in surrender. "Whatever you are thinking is not what I said. Please," he extended his hand, palm up in supplication. "Sometimes my English does not translate well. Let's just have a good time. We will swim, attend the luau, and maybe go dancing before the night is over, but we will not do anything you do not want to do. Capisce?"

The way he said *want to do*, she knew he wasn't acknowledging the option of her backing out, but rather, his unarguable magnetism for the opposite sex. And yes, she had to admit she found him very attractive. And yes, she wanted him in that needy, emotional, careless, sexual sense of the word. But *want* was not the end all, be all. She was old enough to know better. A lot of things she wanted were bad for her and he was most certainly one of them.

Sabrina found herself praying for a way out. The knock at the door gave her reason to ignore his question while she went to the bar and picked up her bottle of water. He strode across the room and pulled open the door. A young woman about Billie's age, thin and tanned, moved past Edoardo holding about a dozen swimsuits over her arms. Her gaze swept the room and landed on Sabrina with a look of surprise.

She smiled tentatively. "Ma'am," she said. "Where would you like me to place these?"

Edoardo waved a hand toward her room. "Lay them on the bed," he ordered.

She hurried to do as she was told, then retraced her steps to the door, glancing briefly at Edoardo with a little batting of her eyes, but he ignored her.

"Thank you," Sabrina called as the girl went out the door.

Edoardo smiled disarmingly and winked. "I look forward to seeing your selection," he said. "Since you have so many to choose from, I will give you some time. Meet me back out here dressed for our swim." He glanced at his watch, "Say thirty minutes?"

She nodded.

He grabbed a wine cooler from the refrigerator, went into his private room and shut the door.

Sabrina released a sigh and turned back to the bar. His cell phone was lying there lit up. Someone had sent him a text. She leaned over and read the words before the screen went dark. Her gaze narrowed. What did that say? She glanced back at Edoardo's closed door before sliding her finger across the screen and opening messages. She quickly perused the conversation and gasped.

••••

Adam heard *Queen's Bohemian Rhapsody* playing beneath his head and groggily reached for his phone under the pillow. He rolled over to his back. "Yeah?" he said, his voice soft and gruff.

"Adam, I'm sorry for waking you," his mother's

voice said, briskly impatient and not that sorry. "I completely forgot that it's a three-hour time difference but this just couldn't wait. I'm worried about your Margaret and I don't have her number."

He forced his eyes open. They felt gritty as if the sandman had just come and filled them up. Rubbing a hand over his face, he cleared his throat. "Mom. It's after midnight. I just got to sleep. Why are you worried about Margaret all of a sudden?"

She lowered her voice. "Edoardo Salvatore is not who he pretends to be."

"Really." He yawned loudly and scratched his head. "Who exactly is he then? A hit man for the mob?"

"Adam, sit up right now and listen," she directed. "I saw a text come in on his phone. Someone with the initials JT."

"Justin Timberlake?"

"Well if it is, he's involved in some very nefarious plans."

Only his mother would use the word nefarious. "Mom, could you get to the point? I really need to sleep."

He heard the crinkle of paper. "I wrote it down as soon as I locked myself in my room," she said. "Edoardo instructed JT to stir up the Parker woman. The next day JT answered that the fire was contained early. No vine damage. I never heard about a fire. Do you know what he's talking about?" She didn't pause long enough for him to respond, but continued, "Edoardo then told him to get personal. JT's last text a little while ago said Parker's truck just had a tune up."

Adam was still trying to decipher the first thing

his mother said. "Why are you locked in a room?" he asked squinting into the dark. "Has that man tried... I'll kill him," he mumbled.

"Concentrate, Adam! This is important. The woman you love could be in serious danger. Don't you get it? JT has fiddled with her pickup. Maybe he put a hole in her brake line. They always cut the brake line," she said.

He heard knocking and a muffled voice in the background. "Is that him?"

"Yes. I have to go. Warn Margaret," she whispered and ended the call.

There was no way he was getting back to sleep now. He didn't think Margaret would be using her pickup in the middle of the night, so he didn't have to run straight over, but the thought that Salvatore was behind all these acts of vandalism made him too angry to lay around. He needed to vent physically.

After pulling on sweats and a t-shirt, he left his apartment and went for a run. The cooler night air felt good against his face and managed to clear the rest of the cobwebs from his mind. He turned down one street after another, running through a strange quiet world of sleeping neighborhoods where the only sound was the soft smack of his running shoes against pavement. His shirt was soaked through by the time he turned back. He cut across a baseball field to shorten his route.

He stopped to catch his breath and looked up. Red and white lights marked the wings and fuselage of a jet making its way toward San Francisco. He felt a sense of impotent anger at the thought that his mother was in the company of that creep over two thousand miles away and he couldn't do anything about it.

••••

Sabrina answered the door wearing the only one-piece bathing suit the girl had brought for her to try, in slimming black, and a sheer cover up in a dark shade of coral. Poking through the pile of string bikinis earlier in bright sapphire, hot pink, emerald green and red, she realized that the girl had expected a younger, perkier woman to be staying with Edoardo in the executive suite. Not one with body parts that hung low like overripe fruit.

Elasticity was something young women took for granted, wearing things without any kind of support until they realized too late that it was gone and it wasn't coming back. But she felt quite confident in this suit. The price tag alone made her feel a bit perkier. She'd looked in the mirror and known the old adage to be true. You really do get what you pay for. Instead of a woman well into her middle years, she saw a vibrant, put-together, sexy older woman who didn't need to be ashamed of where she was at in life. She was a knockout.

Edoardo smiled appreciatively. "I can't believe my luck. To accompany the most beautiful woman in Oahu," he said, taking her hand. He kissed the tips of her fingers and pulled her arm through his. He was wearing royal blue shorts with white stripes down the sides and a hotel robe unbelted over the top, revealing a muscular chest with a light sprinkling of curling gray hair. He obviously had no problem with confidence.

Her return smile was probably overly bright, but she couldn't let him suspect her true feelings for him or that she knew about his underhanded plans against Margaret. The man was a cad. The absolute despicable nature of what he was doing to poor Margaret! And how did he know that Davy wouldn't be in that pickup the next time she drove? Was he willing for his grandson to get hurt as well just to get his own way?

She owed Billie an apology for not believing her when she said the man was no good. But now was not the time to show her hand. She would smile and flirt and eat so much food at the luau that he would have to get a luggage trolley to carry her back upstairs. That ought to cool his ardor.

"Ready to turn heads?" he asked, opening the door into the hallway.

"Let'em spin," she quipped, a little worried that having dinner with the devil might be more dangerous than she anticipated.

On the ride down in the elevator, he faced her, one hand braced on the wall, his gaze seductively focused on her mouth. He was just moving in for a kiss when the bell rang and the doors opened. She slipped under his arm and out, hearing a soft chuckle behind her. He was not going to be easily distracted from his pursuit. She needed to find a reason to get them back on that helicopter and on their way home.

CHAPTER FOURTEEN

Margaret clipped three separate clusters of grapes from different rows in the vineyard and started toward the house. She intended to test the level of acidity and see how close to harvest they really were. The vines were heavy with fruit this year, the wine berries exorbitantly large. It would be a terrific crop. They only needed to have everything run like clockwork for magic to happen.

She heard the hum of the Corvette before she saw it turn into the drive. Adam pulled up to the garage and parked beside her pickup. He got out and looked around. When he saw her coming up the hill he waved and leaned against the car with arms folded. His long, lean legs were encased in faded jeans and he wore the green shirt she'd given him for his birthday. Her favorite color. She smiled, and quickened her pace.

He straightened up and kissed her when she stopped to open the garage door with the number pad. She wasn't taking any chances with the rash of vandalism. Her wine cellar was the thing she prized most, other than Davy, and she couldn't bear it if someone got in and trashed it. She licked her lips. "You taste like peppermint," she said, carrying the grapes inside the garage.

Adam anticipated her destination and lifted the wooden door in the floor, propping it up with a crossbar. He descended the first few steps into the cellar and turned on the light for her. She set the grapes on a low table and turned around for a proper kiss. When she pulled away she noticed the dark rings under his eyes. "What are you doing here so early, anyway? You look like you didn't get much sleep."

His brows drew together. "I got less than that. Mom called about an hour after I went to bed. Did I tell you she's in Oahu with Salvatore?"

"What?" Margaret's mouth dropped open and she shook her head.

He nodded, frustration clear in his eyes and the tenseness of his shoulders. "It was a spur of the moment thing. But I guess now that she's there she's at least seeing him for who he really is."

"What did he do?" she asked, worried that Sabrina would be used by Edoardo just like she had been used by his son. "He didn't...?"

He shook his head. "Not that I know of. If he touches her, I'll kill him."

She pointed him to a chair. "Sit. You look about ready to fall down."

"I went running after she called. For two hours," he said, slumping into the metal chair.

"Did it help?" She knew he ran when he was angry or frustrated. He said it was better than taking it out on the people he loved. She loved him for that too.

He shrugged. "A little."

She set up her testing equipment while he told
her about the call and the strange text messages his
mother had intercepted. She wiped her hands on a
towel and turned around. "Someone messed with my
truck?"

"I think you should have it looked over. By a
mechanic. Who knows what this JT guy did."

"That's crazy. Why would Salvatore do
something that could potentially hurt Davy as well?"

"He's just a rich thug. He acts like he's above
the law, that he can change things to be what he
wants them to be with a wad of money and a snap of
his fingers. We need to get proof that he's behind
these acts of violence and maybe he'll get on his
private jet and fly home… alone."

"I can't afford to have a professional mechanic
look over my entire truck. Who knows how much
they'd charge. I haven't even had the power steering
belt replaced yet and that's been squealing for a while
now."

"I'll pay for it," he offered, reaching out to pull
her onto his lap.

She went willingly, curled up against his chest
and kissed his neck where the V of his shirt was open
and inviting. "You can barely make the payments on
that car out there after paying your rent each month,"
she teased. "Don't worry. I know a guy."

"Yeah, but I don't like the idea of you asking
one of those guys for a favor."

He sounded a little jealous and she tweaked his
nose. "It's not a favor, silly. He's a friend and a very
nice kid. He offered to replace the belt for me the

other day. I'm sure he won't mind looking over the rest of my hunk of junk."

"I'm sure he won't, but I think I should be there as well. Where do we find your young mechanic genius?" he asked, rubbing a lock of her hair between his fingers.

"Carl's restaurant. Dirk is head dishwasher there," she said and grinned.

••••

Billie was already in her office at the winery by half past six. Despite Handel being just a reach away, she tossed and turned all night, managing to feel more tired when she got up than when she went to bed. She hadn't seen Ernesto yet, and wasn't necessarily looking forward to it. She owed him an apology for jumping to conclusions. Whether or not Javier had anything to do with the fire, she knew Ernesto would never knowingly let him stay here if he thought the boy would bring damage to the vineyards. He'd lived through that hell once already.

She turned on her computer and opened email. Deleting spam seemed to be a fulltime occupation anymore. She clicked through the list, opening business correspondence and taking notes to call certain people later in the morning. An email from her brother had a link to YouTube. That was weird. He sent it a little after one in the morning. Did he record himself playing the club last night?

The link opened to a video screen shot of the shed on fire. She clicked to play and watched Adam run with the hose, spraying at the already engulfed wall with what amounted to a drizzle. Then Ernesto came from the other direction, pulling the winery hose behind him and spraying the surrounding vines with a sense of desperation. His eyes were wide and anxious beneath the brim of his cap.

Davy zoomed in on the shed as flames shot through the roof and ate away at the east wall. A man moved out from the shadow of the building on the south side, glanced sharply toward the road when he heard the siren, then darted off into the vineyard out of camera range. Javier.

She pulled the time lapse bar back, sat forward in her chair and replayed the last bit.

Even with the blurry pixilated quality of the video at that distance, she recognized his shirt. He'd been wearing the same shirt when she met him in the vineyard earlier in the day. His face was not clear, but she had no doubt they'd found the culprit hell-bent on causing the winery trouble. But why? What was his motivation? If he really quit the gang and wanted a new life as he told his uncle, why would he screw it up? And if he was there on behalf of the gang, to distract Handel from looking for other suspects in Kawasaki's murder trial, then she felt really bad for Ernesto. He didn't deserve that kind of disloyalty after trying to help the kid.

She let the video play to the end. Davy turned the camera on the approaching fire truck and watched as the men jumped down and set to work pouring a deluge of water over the flames in a matter of minutes. And there she was grabbing Ernesto by the elbow and yelling into his face. She flushed with embarrassment when she watched Adam pull her away from the poor man so he could go about the business of saving her vines.

The video ended with a shot of them both walking back toward the house, Adam's arm around her and her head on his shoulder. She owed her brother big time for his quick thinking and for stepping in when she'd lost it.

Sally knocked on the open door. "Hey, boss."

"Good morning."

"I'm making some coffee right now. It should be ready in a few," she said, leaning against the doorjamb with arms crossed. "That was quite the excitement yesterday, huh? Did the firemen ever tell you how they think it started?"

Billie sent the video to Handel's email. She shut Safari down and pushed back from the desk, grabbing two notes she'd written for Sally when she came in. "No. They just assumed with power tools in there that maybe it was an electrical fire, but I'm sure they'll have an official report soon." She handed Sally the notes. "Could you call these two distributors and see what's taking so long on our orders?"

Sally nodded, but didn't budge. She apparently still had something to say. "Good thing Javier wasn't in there when it started, huh?"

"You knew he was sleeping in the shed?"

"I saw him go in and out and put two and two together."

"But you didn't think it was worthy of a mention?" she asked, putting her hands on her hips. "If the insurance company learns that he was sleeping there and was the cause of the fire, they'll not only refuse to pay but they may cancel our policies."

Sally had the sense to look chagrined. "Sorry, boss." She backed into the hall. "I really didn't know. It was just a guess. If I thought…" she shook her head.

"Never mind. It's too late now. I found out

yesterday, a few hours before the fire. I told Ernesto that Javier couldn't stay there. He was going to let him crash on his couch until he could find him another place."

"That's a strange coincidence," Sally said. "You don't think he did it in retaliation, do you?"

"That's something I need to speak with Ernesto about." She followed Sally to the front office. "Has he showed up yet?"

"I haven't seen him."

Ernesto usually came in and had coffee and one of Sally's cookies before going out to the fields, but she didn't know if he would feel comfortable about seeing her after the way she acted the day before. She peeked into the conference room where Sally left a tray of cookies on the table nearly every morning, but no one was around.

"If you do, tell him I'm looking for him. I'm going over to the house for a few minutes. I'll be back in a bit."

•••

When she left the house earlier, Handel was still sleeping, no doubt mentally worn out from his brief stint as an investigator and subsequent hours spent at the police station the day before. But when she let herself in the back door, he was sitting at the table drinking coffee and reading the news on his laptop.

"Morning, babe," he said, tilting his face up for a kiss.

She grazed his forehead and picked up his cup. "I haven't had my coffee yet," she said and sat down to finish his.

He got up and filled another cup, placed it in front of her and took his now empty one back to the counter. He refilled it, emptying the rest of the pot and shut off the warmer. "You were sure up bright and early," he remarked.

"Maybe that's why I caught the proverbial worm. Check your email," she said, blowing across the top of her steaming cup.

He sat down and clicked to the video, then watched it all the way through in silence. His eyes met hers across the lid of his laptop. "Javier?"

She nodded.

"Did you notice the way Ernesto looked at you when Adam pulled you away?"

"What do you mean?"

Handel set the video to the correct spot and turned the screen so she could watch. "The guilt on his face. He knows it was Javier."

She sighed. "I can see why he would deny it. He tried to help the kid and all he got in return was trouble. He loves his job as vineyard manager. It's what he's always wanted to do. Maybe he thinks I'll fire him because of Javier."

Handel met her eyes. "Would you?"

"Of course not! I can't believe you'd ask me that. Ernesto is part of the Fredrickson family now. Like Sally or Loren or Sammie." She propped her chin in her hands. "As soon as I see him I'll apologize for acting like he was guilty before proven innocent."

"Lot of that going around," he said, pointing at a local news article he was reading online. "They've already tried and convicted Sloane without ever hearing the facts. The more sensational the crime, the more media salivates, stirring up controversy and making personal judgments against people they know nothing about."

She reached out and covered his hand, squeezing his fingers lightly. "Doesn't matter. He has the best attorney in the state. I'm confident the truth will prevail."

"Yeah, but whose truth? Hosea's or Sloane's?"

"Maybe they're one and the same."

There was a knock on the back door and it opened. "Can I come in?" Adam asked, already closing the door behind him.

"I think you are," Handel said. He closed his laptop and pushed it to the side. "Have a seat."

Adam glanced at the empty coffee pot before taking the chair at the end of the table. "Did you guys watch Davy's video of the fire?" he asked without preamble.

Billie got up to make another pot of coffee. "I just showed it to Handel," she said, filling the decanter.

"Well?"

"It's Javier. Ernesto gave him a job a while back," she said, putting in the filter and coffee. "I haven't spoken with Ernesto yet, but Handel thinks he already knows."

"You think he was in on it?" Adam frowned and shook his head. "Ernesto is a stand-up guy. I don't think he'd be part of something like that."

"I didn't say he was." Handel pushed back from the table and went to the refrigerator. "I said he knew Javier started the fire. It was the look on his face after Billie confronted him."

Handel set a pint of half & half in front of Adam along with the sugar bowl. Her brother's taste in coffee leaned toward a hot milkshake. She poured him half a cup before the pot was completely brewed and brought it to the table. They watched him doctor it to within an inch of its life before he took a sip.

"Your coffee is always so good," he said, his eyes glinting with humor. He set his cup down and crossed his arms. "Do you think it's possible this guy, Javier, knows Edoardo Salvatore?"

"Why?"

Instead of answering her question, he asked another one of his own. "Have you heard from Mom?"

"No. But what does any of this have to do with the fire?"

"That's what I've been wondering all night." He told them about the conversation with Sabrina. "From the text messages between him and this other guy, JT, it sounds like he's been behind all of this."

"But why?" Handel asked, leaning back in his chair, a frown creasing his forehead. "I can see him causing trouble for Margaret, maybe trying to make it look like Davy isn't safe with her, but why shoot at Billie and burn the winery shed?"

"Maybe this isn't just about getting custody of Davy. Maybe it's about revenge." Adam cleared his throat, looking slightly uncomfortable. "I didn't say any of this to Margaret, but isn't it possible that Salvatore wants payback on all of us?" He pointed at Handel, "Your father murdered his son." He pointed at Billie. "Agosto was found dead in your winery dumpster." He tapped a finger against his own chest. "And I'm the new guy in Margaret's life, filling the empty space of a father in Davy's life."

"That's an interesting theory," Handel said, sounding a little annoyed with her brother's choice of words, "but Manny told us the word on the street is that someone put a hit out on Billie."

"A hit? Like in gangster movies? Why would anyone, other than Salvatore, want to do that?" Adam asked. He gulped the rest of his sweet coffee and wiped his mouth with the back of his hand. The boyish motion made Billie think of Davy and how much the two were alike. She couldn't help smiling.

"You're her brother," Handel said. "You can't think of a good reason?"

"Hey! I resent that." Billie crossed her arms and leaned against the counter waiting for the coffee to finish brewing. "So who's to say it isn't Salvatore?" she asked. "I mean, he could very well have friends in low places. Didn't you say the Las Boyz originated in Sicily?"

Handel laced his hands behind his head and looked up at the ceiling as though light bulbs really did give off ideas. "Well, the two things we know for sure is that he's behind the stuff at Margaret's place and his henchman's initials are JT. Does anyone know Javier's last name?"

Billie hadn't even thought of that. She shook her head. "No, but I'm going to find out. As soon as I speak with Ernesto."

CHAPTER FIFTEEN

Adam was a little leery about letting Margaret drive the Corvette, but when she batted those eyelashes at him and leaned in to grab the keys from his hand, he let her have them. She gave him one of her blindingly beautiful smiles and he couldn't think straight anyway. It was probably safer for her to drive, seeing as she was driving him crazy.

He clicked his seatbelt and started to direct her on how to shift slowly out of first into second because it had a little jump in the gears, but she took off and was tearing down the highway like Danica Patrick before he could get the words out. He swallowed hard and gripped the edge of his seat. "So, where did you learn to drive like this?" he asked, watching vineyards flash by in a blur as she passed car after car and continued to gain speed.

"I practiced at the track. A guy I knew in high school used to let me drive his Mustang. Then Handel had a Corvette when he was in college. Once I snuck out after he was asleep and took his car all the way to

Reno."

"How far is that?" he asked, pressing his foot
hard against the floor when she swerved into the
oncoming lane to pass another car and pulled back in
just in time to avoid being a hood ornament on a
truck.

"Oh, it's about two hundred miles, but I made
it there and back in under four hours," she said
proudly.

"Please tell me you didn't share that story with
Davy."

"Are you kidding? Do I look stupid?" She
flashed him another smile.

"No," he said, wishing she'd keep her eyes on
the road. "But you sound crazy."

They made it to Antonio's in record time.
Adam opened the door and nearly fell to his knees to
kiss the ground, but it was littered with cigarette butts
from employees sneaking outside for smoke breaks
and looked a little too unsanitary for his tastes.

"Want me to wait outside while you talk to your
other boyfriend?" he asked, leaning against the door of
the car.

"Don't you want to say hi to Carl?" She
pounded on the metal security door with her fist.
"Sometimes they can't hear over the noise in there,"
she explained.

He grinned. This girl surprised him on a daily
basis. Just when he thought he knew her, she proved
he'd only skimmed the surface. He looked forward to
digging deeper, peeling back her layers and savoring
each moment. Hopefully most of the moments
wouldn't be death-defying like that car ride. He
hurried over and banged on the door with his fist as

well.

Carl threw open the door, an angry scowl on his face, "What the…" he broke off and threw his arms wide, "Ciao Bella! I didn't expect you today." Margaret was pulled into the man's embrace while Adam watched – now with a scowl on his face.

"Sorry," she said pulling back. "I guess I should have called, but it was sort of an emergency. I didn't have Dirk's number and thought I'd just stop and talk to him," she said, glancing over his shoulder. Carl frowned and she gave him a small flirty smile, "if it's all right with you of course."

"Do you even have to ask? I can't imagine what important emergency business you could have with my pitiful dishwasher," he said, waving them past him into the kitchen, "but he's all yours."

A skinny guy with stringy blonde hair tied back in a ponytail stood at the huge stainless steel sink washing pots. He glanced back and his face immediately flushed with color when he saw Margaret standing behind him. "Hey, Miss Parker."

"Hi, Dirk. Is it all right if I take you away from all this for a little bit?"

Dirk glanced worriedly at Carl.

"Go!" Carl barked, waving him away. "The sooner you fix Margaret's emergency, the sooner you get back to work."

They went out the back door and when Dirk saw the Corvette he nearly blew the blood vessels in his eyes, they stretched so wide. "Hot damn! Did you trade that old pickup in for this baby?" he asked, moving slowly around it. "Guess you don't need me to replace that belt now, huh?"

"Actually, I need you to do more than that."

Margaret put a hand on his shoulder. "This is Adam's car," she said, nodding in his direction. "Sadly, I still have the pickup and a major problem."

He turned around, clearly excited. Apparently, fixing cars ran a close second to dating a babe who looked like Marilyn Monroe. "What is it? I can fix most any car. Just ask my dad. He's a mechanic at the Texaco station. He taught me everything I know."

She smiled. "That's what I need to hear."

They gave him directions to Margaret's house and he said he would come in the morning before work. He was still gazing longingly at the Corvette, so Adam took pity on him and let him look under the hood and sit behind the wheel for a minute. Dirk held out his cell phone. "Would you mind taking a picture of me for my Facebook?" he asked, hopefully.

"Of course he will," Margaret said.

Adam reluctantly took the phone and stepped back. Before he could get the car in frame, Margaret jumped in the passenger seat, and leaned in with her arm around Dirk until he flushed as red as the leather seats. Adam clicked the picture.

He handed back the phone and Dirk slid out from behind the wheel. "That is an awesome car you got. Someday I'm going to buy me a Ferrari 458 Speciale. Carl said his uncle has one in Italy. Those things will fly like a bullet skimming the ground."

Margaret waved from inside the car. "See you tomorrow, Dirk!"

He grinned huge and turned to go back inside. Before Adam could close the door of the car, he ran back and bent down with his hands on his thighs to peer inside at Margaret. "Miss Parker, would you mind if I bring JT with me? I've been teaching him to work on cars."

"JT?" they both said at the same time.

Dirk looked from one to the other. "Yeah, you know. Juan Torres." He waved a hand toward the restaurant. "He's Carl's sous chief. He makes a mean tortellini, but he still needs practice with stuff like replacing ignition coils or catalytic converters."

••••

It wasn't nearly as hard as Sabrina imagined it would be to get off the island. She didn't have to eat bugs, or swim in a lagoon until she was stung by a blowfish, or snipe at the other island inhabitants until they got sick of her and voted her off. She just had to bide her time.

They spent the evening pleasantly enough, swimming, dancing and eating, just as Edoardo had promised. When the night sky darkened, the entertainment started, and they watched fire dancers spin flaming batons around their heads and bodies in perfect synchronization. It was getting late and she was getting sleepy. A little after one a.m., she turned to find her companion passed out in his chair beside her. Apparently, he'd been steadily drinking Blue Hawaiians the entire evening, with more rum than blue.

Unsure what to do, she waved over a waiter and asked for help getting Mr. Salvatore to his room. Two burly Hawaiian bellhops managed to get him in a wheelchair and roll him to the elevator. After they tucked him in his bed, she found his phone in the pocket of his suit coat and used her own phone to capture pictures of the text messages he still had not deleted. She didn't know if they would stand up in court, but they might be helpful to keep him off

Margaret's back. When she was done she emailed them all to Adam. Then she went into her room, locked the door and managed to sleep a full ten hours before she heard voices outside and the clink of dishes.

She'd showered before climbing in bed, so she just washed her face, put on a bit of makeup and slipped into one of the cute sundresses Edoardo insisted on buying her after their swim the evening before.

When she opened the door her host looked a tad unhappy. Still wearing a robe, he sat in an upholstered club chair by the bar reading a newspaper. He lifted his coffee cup, peering at her over the rim. "I must say I'm disappointed that you are already dressed for the day. Although, you look stunning as usual."

"Thank you," she said.

Room service had already brought breakfast. She could smell eggs and sausage and pancakes beneath silver warming lids on a food cart by the bar. A pot of coffee and another cup and saucer were also available. She poured a cup.

"This has been a most enlightening trip, Edoardo." She filled a plate with scrambled eggs and sausage. Looked beneath another lid and found toast. Added a slice of that to her plate. "And so refreshing. I feel like a new woman," she said.

He folded the newspaper and put it aside. Straightened in his chair. "Oahu is a special place. It always invigorates me to be here even for a short time," he said, letting his eyes travel down the length of her legs. There was no mention of the way the evening had ended, with him passed out cold at the luau. Perhaps that was his version of invigoration. "We can stay as long as you'd like, you know. I have no pressing business in San Francisco that I can't take care of right here in this room."

She fully understood what he was saying and sat on a bar stool out of his reach to eat her breakfast. "I do need to get back. I haven't spent much time with my kids and there are things to attend to in Minnesota as well."

"That's too bad. We haven't really gotten to know one another as well as I would like," he said. He got up and came to lean over her shoulder at the bar, his breath hot on the side of her neck, his voice low and seductive in her ear, "Perhaps we should spend what's left of our stay making up for that oversight." He lifted a lock of her hair and kissed her neck.

What would have sent a tingle down her spine a day ago, now left her cold inside. The man was repulsive and she couldn't wait to be out of his company. But she couldn't let him know that. Not yet. She was beholden to him for the ride home and hoped to keep it civil.

She stuffed a mouthful of eggs in and turned to smile up at him.

He straightened, a frown of annoyance turning his lips down. Perhaps no one had ever chose eggs over him before. "I'll let you finish your breakfast first," he said generously and went back to his chair.

Sabrina ate slowly to make her reprieve last as long as possible. She glanced back when she heard a text come in on his phone and watched him pick it up from the small lamp table beside him. His face went red with anger and he bit out the words, "*Lo demonizzano tutti all'inferno!*" She had no idea what he said but it sounded bad.

"Is everything all right?" she asked.

"No, everything is not all right." He jumped up and strode toward his room, his open robe flapping against his legs. "Be ready to leave in twenty minutes!" he bellowed before slamming the bedroom door behind him.

"I'll be ready in ten," she said, placed a sausage patty on a slice of toast, scooped some eggs on top, folded it over and took a big unsexy bite.

••••

Margaret, Adam, and Carl sat around the intimate dining table, a bottle of wine and plate of bruschetta before them, but no one felt like eating. After Dirk told them who JT was, they confronted him in the kitchen and he lit out of the restaurant like a dozen ICE agents were on his tail. Adam ran after him, tackled him in the strip of grass between parking lots and hauled his butt back to the kitchen. Margaret had already called the police.

Carl had not taken the news well. Finding himself in the middle between his uncle and a close friend, he looked like he might cry. But when he confronted Juan, his face turned hard and angry. He learned that his uncle had paid his Sou Chef five thousand dollars to set Margaret's shed on fire, drive over her vines, and mess with her pickup. He fired him on the spot, and yanked the white chef's coat off him before the police showed up and took him away.

Margaret looked across at her brother's best friend, afraid that family ties may have forever destroyed their close friendship. She sighed, letting her finger follow the rim of her wine glass around and around.

"I'm sorry it's come to this," she said, her voice soft. "Handel and I have always treasured your friendship. We would never want anything to come between us, but I can't let your uncle get away with this. He tried to physically harm me and my son."

"He would never harm Davy," Carl argued weakly. "I know he is a desperate man to have gone so far, but he has suffered since Agosto's death." He spread his hands on the tablecloth. "He tries to hide it, but he is a broken man. My mother tells me that he drinks more than he eats and rarely ends a day without passing out. His business partners have begged him to retire, but he doesn't know how to *not* work."

"Well, that's that then," Adam said. "We certainly wouldn't want to give him more pain. Even if he did pay one of your employees an exorbitant amount of money to sabotage Meg's pickup and send her careening off the road to her death."

Margaret put a calming hand on his arm. "Adam," she said, a soft reprimand. "It's not Carl's fault. He would never have allowed any of this to happen if he'd known."

"Of course not!" Carl shoved his chair back and stood up, shaking his head. "I'm so sorry for everything. I swear my uncle will return to Italia and never bother you again. You have my word."

Margaret had already sent a message to Edoardo earlier telling him exactly that. *Go home and never bother us again.* She informed him about their chat with JT and said if he didn't want to spend an extended amount of time in an American jail, he should bring Sabrina home and leave the country. There was no response from him, but an hour later

Sabrina texted Adam to say they were leaving Oahu and would be home within hours.

"I believe you, Carl. And I don't think your uncle wants any publicity so I'm sure he'll capitulate without too much trouble."

"Does Handel know?" he asked, his dark brows drawn tight across the bridge of his nose.

"Not yet." She smiled up at him. "I know Handel. He's not going to blame you for any of this. You two have always been like brothers. There's no reason that has to change," she said, hoping that were true.

"I should never have listened to my uncle. He tried to turn me against..." he stopped and closed his eyes, shook his head. "He is a sick man. I understand that. But I will inform my family in Italia of what he has done and there will be repercussions for him. Believe me."

••••

Billie spotted Ernesto and Javier crouched down in a row of Riesling, examining some low hanging clusters. Ernesto was instructing the young man, speaking Spanish so quickly she had no idea what he was saying. They obviously didn't hear her approach because they both jumped up, startled.

"I'm been looking for you two," she said, trying to appear non-confrontational even though that's exactly what she planned, to confront Javier about the fire – and other things. "Could you guys come to the conference room with me? I ordered a pizza for lunch. It should be there by now." She pooched out her bottom lip and blew a stream of air up through her bangs. "This heat is killing me."

Ernesto put a hand on Javier's shoulder as

though he sensed the kid was thinking about running. "Sí. We're hungry and we have some things to speak with you about too, Miss Fredrickson."

Javier's scowl was not as pronounced today, but he still didn't look as though he wished to discuss anything with the woman who had thrown him out of his free digs and got him in trouble with Ernesto.

They walked back together, Billie keeping up a constant patter of small talk to set them at ease, but it seemed to be having the opposite effect on all of them. When they trooped past Sally's desk toward the conference room, her brows rose in surprise.

"Has the pizza come yet?" Billie asked.

Sally shook her head, craning her neck to see into the room where Javier and Ernesto were already seated at the table, waiting.

"When it gets here, let me know. We're having a vineyard management meeting," she clarified, so Sally wouldn't invite the rest of the employees to free lunch.

She entered the conference room and shut the door. Ernesto was leaning over whispering something to Javier, but he straightened up immediately and pulled the cap from his head.

She smiled. "No need for formality," she said, sitting across the table from the two men. "I asked you here to discuss recent events at the winery." She held Ernesto's fearful gaze. "I owe you an apology. I'm truly sorry for accusing you of having anything whatsoever to do with the fire. I know you were only trying to help your cousin's son. Family ties are important and we all need them."

He seemed embarrassed at her apology and tried to wave it off. "You were worried about the vines."

"I think you were more worried about the vines," she said, "and I thank you."

She looked at Javier. He tried to avoid her gaze by staring hard at something just above her left shoulder. "I do hold you accountable, though. Ernesto offered you help and you turned around and tried to destroy the respect he's built with us here."

"I never did anything to hurt Ernesto," he spit out, glaring daggers at her now. "I wanted to be left alone, to start a new life, but they wouldn't let me."

Ernesto intervened, twisting his sweat-stained cap in his hands. "The gang is blackmailing Javier to do these things. He is a good boy. He didn't want to hurt anyone," he said, his gaze pleading.

Why would the gang blackmail him? That made no sense. If the gang didn't want him to leave, they would force him back or kill him. Adam's theory seemed closer to the truth. She looked at Javier. He sat stoically, arms crossed, staring at the tabletop. "What's your last name?" she asked.

He seemed surprised by her question but just smirked.

"Javier Tabares Hernandez," Ernesto said, filling the silence.

She knew that the first surname would be from the father and the second from the mother, so he could very well be the JT in Salvatore's text messages. "Why don't you tell us both the truth this time, JT."

Ernesto looked confused. "Javier? You lied to me?"

He looked up at her. "I didn't want to do any of it. He said to scare you. Make you think someone wanted you dead. If I didn't do it he would let the

Maras know where I was and tell them I was double-crossing them with Las Boyz. That is a death sentence in my world."

"I don't want to get you killed," she said. "I only want the truth. Did Edoardo Salvatore pay you to do these things?"

The confusion in his face should have been answer enough but he shook his head. "Who?"

••••

When Ernesto and Javier left the conference room, Billie sat back in her chair and shook her head. She had hoped to get proof against Edoardo Salvatore that would keep him away from Margaret and Davy permanently, but instead she'd just solved Handel's murder case.

She slipped her cell phone out of her pocket and dialed.

"Hey, babe. What's up?" Handel asked. He sounded distracted.

"Remember how you said you believe in gut feelings?"

"Yeah."

"I talked to Javier and my gut feeling is that the same person who hired him to shoot at me and burn my shed, also killed Jimena."

"He gave you a name?"

"And much more."

••••

Billie was relieved when she looked up from replanting the flowerbeds outside the winery and saw her BMW pull up to the house and stop outside the garage. She stood and dusted her hands on the legs of her navy shorts. Sabrina stepped out of the car looking just as vibrant and put-together as she always did. She wore a pretty new blue and white sundress that Billie didn't recognize.

She waved. "Hey, Mom!"

Sabrina turned her way and smiled. "Hey yourself," she said.

Billie hurried over and gave her a hug. "How many times do I have to tell you not to get into a private jet with a perfect stranger?"

Her mother hugged back a little tighter than usual before releasing her. "Once is all it takes for this old girl," she said, swinging her purse to her shoulder. "Although I have to say, the reclining seats were heavenly."

They went inside and Sabrina gave Handel and Billie a recap of her Honolulu adventure, ending with a heartfelt apology to Billie for not trusting her opinion. "Admittedly, I was hearing his accent more than his actual words," she said, with a slight flush of embarrassment. She crossed her legs and leaned her head back on the couch.

"Did he take it out on you on the flight home?" Billie asked, fearful her mother may have paid a little too dearly for the truth.

Sabrina stifled a yawn and shook her head. "He was too busy drinking all the liquor on board. Once we took off he was ensconced in his private sleeping quarters with the flight attendant to serve him... whatever," she said with a flutter of French manicured nails.

"That must have been awful," Billie commiserated.

"Actually, it was bliss. I was able to travel in style and didn't have to continually think up new ways to keep him at bay."

Handel chuckled. "Sabrina, you never cease to amaze me. If it wasn't for your finding those texts Margaret could have been in a serious accident."

"I guess God was looking out for us this round," Billie said.

"Honey, God is always looking out for us. Sometimes we just have our eyes shut so tight we don't see it."

"One bad guy down, another to go," Handel got up from his easy chair, bent to kiss Sabrina's cheek, then pulled Billie to her feet and kissed her firmly on the lips. "Wish me luck," he said, moving toward his office. "Tomorrow's the big day. Court is in session and the Honorable Veronica Matthews is expecting wonderful things from me after this long continuance."

"We're all expecting wonderful things, Handy!" Billie called after him.

Sabrina stretched out on the couch and sighed. "I'm so glad I picked that man for you. He's as perfect as a sunny day in May."

Billie just smiled.

CHAPTER SIXTEEN

Handel got off the phone with Frank and leaned back in his desk chair, hands laced behind his head. Lucky for him his new friend had a nephew who was a detective in the Mission district. The police had been close mouthed with him about the evidence they'd found in Hosea's house, not allowing him access to any information that might help him in his own case. They kept saying it was an ongoing investigation, blah, blah, blah. He knew the spiel. He'd used similar tactics in his own office. Sometimes it took a brother in blue to oil the wheels.

His phone rang again. He picked up. "Hey, Manny. What do you have for me?"

"I heard Hosea Garcia was shot," he said, shock softening his voice.

"Yeah, I heard." He waited.

"I never told you, but my sister was planning to run away with him before she was killed. I talked her out of it of course. That would be crazy, right? To run off with a drug addict when you have a perfect life already. Sometimes I think she was uncomfortable being rich. We grew up with so little and then she meets this man who never runs out of roses."

Handel thought that was a strange way to describe her marriage to Sloane. But maybe that's what Jimena told him. He didn't say anything, waiting for Manny to finish.

"I don't know how Jimena hooked up with him. She hadn't seen him since we were kids. I kept her away from that life. Sheltered her and Momma." He sounded angry at the circumstances and Handel didn't blame him. A man was born to protect his family.

"You can't stop people from making unwise decisions. You can only be there for them when they fall," Handel said, staring at the row of books on his shelf. He got up and straightened them as he talked. "Maybe your sister was trying to be there for Hosea but it turned out all wrong."

"Yeah, you could be right. He was a dangerous man. He could have lost it when she told him it was over." He sniffed loudly. "I should have been there to stop him."

It wasn't exactly what Handel meant, but Manny had taken the conversation to an interesting place. Only two people knew what really happened that night and Hosea wasn't talking.

"Maybe it wasn't Hosea," Handel said. "What if Kawasaki did kill your sister because he found out about the affair?"

His response was sharp and immediate. "I know Sloane. He would never hurt my sister, no matter what. Did Hosea tell you that?"

"No, I was just speculating. You're her brother.

Don't you want the truth to come out, no matter who is responsible? Your sister deserves justice, doesn't she?" He narrowed his eyes, squinting down the line of books to see if the spines were all evenly lined up.

"I thought you were defending Sloane because you believed him. What's changed your mind?"

"Hosea called me again before he was shot."

No response. Just traffic noise in the background. Where was Manny going?

"He said he had something for me. Some piece of evidence that would point directly to the killer," he lied. "I was going to pick it up, but the police locked the crime scene down and now I can't get to it."

"In his house?"

"Outside in an old van. It looked like a junker. I doubt it even runs. He said he put it in the glove box so I could retrieve it after he left town."

"He was probably lying," Manny said. "Just pulling your chain."

"Yeah, well I guess we may never know. The police are assuming this was a gang hit. By the time I get them to issue a warrant to look there, who knows what will happen. Someone will probably have it towed away."

Thumping music filled the background for a couple seconds. "I better go. Traffic's really bad. Don't want to get in an accident like you, huh?"

"I don't blame you. Drive safe now."

A car horn blared. "See you in court."

Handel set his phone down and pushed his hands in the front pockets of his jeans. "Truth, justice, and the American way," he said and felt a little bit like Superman.

••••

An hour later, the police picked Manny up going through the van. He told them he was working for Handel. They took him downtown and put him in a cell while they served warrants on his apartment, office, and vehicle. Tucked away in his office safe, they found over fifty thousand dollars, his mother's rosary beads and a lock of hair covered in dried blood kept safely contained in a Ziploc bag. He obviously had guilt issues.

Frank called Handel to report the news. His nephew had been one of the detectives on the case and after getting credit for solving two murders, was feeling overly generous at the moment. He told Frank to give Handel the news and a big kiss. Frank chose to call instead of coming in person.

"So when they presented him with the evidence they had on him for Garcia's murder, he fell apart and confessed to his sister's as well."

"No kidding," Handel said, shaking his head. It was more than he'd hoped for. As soon as the courthouse opened in the morning he would be filing papers for a dismissal in the case against Sloane Kawasaki. That ought to give the media something to talk about for a while. "What evidence did they have? Do you know?"

Frank hesitated. "Well, I really shouldn't say, but since I know you'll keep it under your hat... Your friend Hosea Garcia was more than a little paranoid. He taped all of his phone calls and hid them under a floorboard in his bedroom. When the forensics team found that, they found the mother lode. Seems the police may be able to close a few other cases thanks to Mr. Garcia."

Handel laughed. "That's awesome," he said.

Curiosity made him ask, "Did Manny say why he killed his sister?" He was still trying to get his head around that. Guilt-ridden, Manny had left the gang after his mother died and worked to get his sister through community college. He felt responsible for Jimena even after she was married to Sloane. Why would he turn on the one person he cared about most?

Frank cleared his throat. "Remember that hypothetical phone tape you were talking about?"

"Yes."

"Well, Mr. Alvarez happened to mention something about aqua. Seems he couldn't stay completely out of the game. He was using one of Salvatore's warehouses down near the dock for a meth factory. They were cranking that stuff out faster than you can say holy crap. Problem was, he wasn't letting the Maras in on the deal."

"He was working with the enemy?"

"Yep, Las Boyz." Frank gave a short laugh. "It all would've worked out fine too except for our Mr. Garcia's paranoid tendencies. He followed Manny one night and decided to get in on the action. He was blackmailing your very upstanding private eye."

Handel ran a hand through his hair and sighed. "That's what he meant when he said he just wanted the money so he could take Jimena to Mexico."

"Seems about right. But when he came to the house to pick her up, Manny was there too. They got in a big argument and Garcia decided to spill the beans. He told Jimena that her brother was a drug dealer and she went berserk. Manny said she started screaming and throwing things at him until he couldn't take anymore. He hit her to shut her up, but she fell against the corner of the glass coffee table and split her head open."

Handel grimaced at the thought. He'd seen the crime photos. It wasn't pretty.

Frank continued. "When he realized she was dead he went a little berserk too. He knocked Garcia out with one punch. Then overcome with grief, he cut a chunk of her hair and took it with him. For remembrance or some shit. What a nutball," he said, with caustic humor.

"He left Garcia to take the fall," Handel said, thinking out loud, "but Garcia didn't stay unconscious long enough for the police to get there."

"So it seems. And Manny didn't know about the earlier domestic disturbance call his sister made two days prior because she didn't tell him that her husband was abusive. So instead of Garcia taking the blame, Kawasaki became the number one suspect."

Handel pulled the blinds open on the window and looked out into the dark vineyards beyond. He knew all about protecting loved ones from unsavory secrets. It was hard to believe that he'd been defending a man with the same violent tendencies he abhorred. Sure, he had been defending him against false murder charges, but it still felt wrong that the man had an advocate and Jimena Kawasaki-Alvarez was in an early grave.

He heard the door open softly and he turned to see Billie coming in with a cup of coffee. She smiled and set it on the desk for him. He put up a finger for her to wait. "Thanks for letting me know. I really appreciate it. Tell your nephew I owe him one," he said.

"You owe me a double Espresso Macchiato

and a plate of those caramel rolls your friend Charley makes."

"Will do. Let me know when you're hungry," he said and put the phone down.

"Was that Frank?" she asked, leaning on the corner of the desk.

He nodded and gave her a crooked grin. "Guess what? We may be able to get away for that vacation a lot sooner than expected."

Her face lit up and she threw her arms around him. "That's wonderful. I can't wait to see you in that bikini," she murmured against his ear.

••••

They had a family picnic the following Saturday evening to celebrate Handel's closed case and to give Sabrina a fond farewell since she was flying home on Monday. Two picnic tables were lined up out under the oak trees, covered in checkered cloths that fluttered lightly in the breeze. Billie had made potato salad because she said the West coast folks just didn't know how to make proper salads. Margaret and Davy brought sliced watermelon, chips, and a bottle of her special wine. Sabrina upstaged them all with homemade chocolate raspberry cheesecake that looked to die for.

"Where's Adam?" Billie asked when Margaret and Davy showed up without him. "I thought he was picking you up."

Margaret sighed and set the watermelon on the table. "He called a while ago and said he might be late."

"Well, we're not waiting for him." She nodded toward Handel already busy working his magic at the grill. "The steaks will be ruined if he doesn't get here soon."

Sabrina held out a gift bag and Davy's face lit up. "Cool! My jersey." He yanked the shirt out along with crinkly tissue paper. "Look Mom," he said, holding it up to his chest, "now I can play hockey!"

"Not on your life," she said, hands on her hips. "I'm not going to have a toothless son."

"They got mouth guards, ya know," he informed her as though she were completely clueless.

She sat down at the table across from Billie. "Boys. Can't live with'em, can't live without'em."

Billie pushed a plate of raw vegetables and dip toward her. "Want some?"

"I thought you didn't like carrots and celery," Margaret said, giving her a strange look.

"I'm trying to eat healthier." Billie eyed her mom's cheesecake. "At least for now."

Sabrina had already opened the wine. She poured Margaret and Billie each a glass and held them out, but Billie shook her head. "None for me, thanks. I'll just have water."

"All right. More for me."

Handel waved her over to the grill. "I got two medium rare, one well-done, and four hotdogs. What's your pleasure?" He scooped the meat onto the platter and handed it to her.

Adam's Corvette crunched down the gravel drive and he parked in the shade in front of the winery. He stepped out of the car and waved, then went around to the passenger side and opened the door.

"What's he doing? I didn't ask him to bring anything," Billie said, impatient for everyone to be seated and begin. The food was getting cold.

Margaret stepped up behind her and put a cloth napkin over her eyes, tying it behind her head. "No peeking," she said. "It's a surprise for your birthday."

Billie felt Davy take her hand and pull her forward. She stepped gingerly, unsure where they were taking her and not sure she wanted to go. "It's not my birthday," she argued half-heartedly, "until tomorrow." She'd actually been expecting something, other than the red satin sex kitten outfit her mom had bought her, but up till now no one had mentioned the date.

"Okay, pull off the blindfold!" Adam said, his voice filled with laughter and maybe a little bit of reticence as though he wasn't sure if she would be happy about this surprise.

She slowly lifted the cloth and pulled it off her head. Adam stood in front of her holding a squirming ball of fur. The tri-color puppy looked at her with sad brown eyes and she felt a sharp tug of her heart. Her brother put it in her arms and stepped back.

"Your first baby," he announced solemnly. "I hope you take better care of it then you did that parakeet you had when we were kids."

She glared at him, but couldn't help a smile sneaking out. "You're the one who released the bird into the wild. Parakeets aren't meant to live outside of cages in Minnesota." They'd found the poor thing two days later frozen stiff in the back yard.

Handel stepped close, his eyes seeking hers, "So, do you like her?"

"She's from you?" she said, completely taken aback. "I thought you didn't want a dog right now. You said they take a lot of time and attention. Like children." She pressed her face into soft puppy fur and smiled. "Does this mean you've changed your mind?"

He cupped her cheek and gently bumped his forehead to hers. "Why wouldn't I want something that makes you this happy?" he murmured. He put his arm around her and they walked back toward the table. Davy stayed close and made sure he sat beside her so he could pet the new puppy between bites of hotdog.

"So, what is it?" she asked, holding the fur ball away from the food on her plate. The puppy kept trying to scramble up and out of her arms, smelling steak and thinking it was all for her. She had a brown and black face with a white chest and paws and was about the cutest thing Billie had ever seen.

Davy looked at her strangely and forked a piece of watermelon. He stated the obvious. "It's a girl," he said, as though he thought taking the blindfold off had not helped her eyesight one bit.

She laughed. "I know that, silly. What kind of puppy? I haven't really studied up on dog breeds lately," she said, slanting Handel a glance.

"A collie, of course," he said with a teasing grin. "A true Hollywood dog. Are you going to name her Lassie?"

"That's a little too cliché, don't you think?" She looked down at the pup and those liquid brown eyes and smiled. "How about Jimena?"

Handel squeezed her hand. "I think that's perfect," he said, his voice a little huskier than usual. "Jimena it is."

Davy had already wolfed down his hotdog and plate of watermelon, so he took Jimena to play in the grass while the rest of them finished eating. Sabrina was watching Billie intently.

"What?" she said, unobtrusively wiping at her eyes.

"You look different. You seem different," she said, sounding as though she was trying to figure out a puzzle. Then she gasped. "Aww. Now I know." Her smile stretched so wide Billie was sure she could see molars in the corners. "You're going to have..."

"Don't say it!" Billie put a hand up to stop her mother's announcement.

"...a sister!"

"What?" she looked at Handel. But he just shrugged.

"How did you know?" Adam asked, putting his arm around Margaret, hardly able to keep the silly grin from his face. "We didn't want to announce our engagement and take over the celebration. Today is about Billie's birthday, and Handel's successful case, and Mom's bon voyage party."

"I can see why you'd wait to announce," Handel said wryly, "there's only so much celebration energy in a hotdog."

Everyone laughed and Margaret flushed a bit pink in the cheeks. She explained that she'd left her new engagement ring at home, but would show them all later.

Billie was just beginning to breath a sigh of relief that the attention had turned to her brother and his fiancé when her mother reached out and clasped her hand. She looked up into Sabrina's eyes and felt the mother/child connection she was always hearing about, the connection that didn't end with the severing of an umbilical cord. What Sabrina called her ESP.

Her mom's eyes were filling up fast and Billie blinked back tears of her own, refusing to let go and give in to the tug of the undertow. Handel leaned in and spoke softly in her ear, "Are you all right?"

She shook her head. "I need to talk to you," she said, and got up, pulling him after her. Sabrina had tears rolling down her face by this time, but she was still smiling. Adam and Margaret were over playing with Davy and the puppy and didn't seem to notice their quick escape.

Billie kept walking straight into the vineyard, moving so fast that Handel finally tugged on her arm. "Slow up, babe. What's going on?" he asked, clearly worried now.

They were out of sight and out of hearing range of the rest of their party, so she let him pull her to a stop and turned to face him. She licked her lips nervously and looked into his eyes, as blue as the sky they reflected. "I don't know how to tell you," she began.

He held her at arms length, now obviously anxious with worry. "Just tell me. What's wrong? You never cry. You're not upset about their engagement?" he asked, trying to understand.

"No," she blew out a laugh. "Of course not. It's nothing like that."

"Then what is it like?"

Billie ran her fingers through his blonde hair, pushing it back from his forehead. She moved in close, her lips just grazing his ear and whispered, "There's going to be a new addition to the Fredrickson Parker clan. Do you want to name it Lassie?"

Their neighbors, Herbie and Hazel, probably

heard his whoop of joy. It was definitely heard by Sabrina, Margaret, Adam, Davy and Jimena. They all came running into the vineyard, wondering what was going on. At least most of them were wondering. Sabrina fairly glowed with the knowledge.

They laughed, and danced, and celebrated together between rows of vines thick with leaves and heavy with fruit. After all, it was the perfect place for a celebration of life.

Handy kissed Billie beneath the California sun and tasted the sweet new life that stretched before them, heady and as intoxicating as bottled wine.

ABOUT THE AUTHOR

Barbara Ellen Brink lives in the great state of Minnesota with her husband, their two dogs, Rugby and Willow, and their two adult children living nearby. She spends much time writing, reading, motorcycling, running, and enjoying life with the family and friends that God has given her.

CPSIA information can be obtained at www.ICGtesting.com
Printed in the USA
LVOW06s1753070114

368463LV00007B/821/P